The Pha

# The Phantom

1

Jack Murray

# The Phantom

LORD KIT ASTON BOOK 3

## Jack Murray

# Jack Murray

Books by Jack Murray

*Kit Aston Series*
The Affair of the Christmas Card Killer
The Chess Board Murders
The Phantom
The Frisco Falcon
The Medium Murders
The Bluebeard Club
The Tangier Tajine
The Empire Theatre Murders
The French Diplomat Affair (novella)
Haymaker's Last Fight (novelette)

*Agatha Aston Series*
Black-Eyed Nick
The Witchfinder General Murders
The Christmas Murder Mystery

*DI Jellicoe Series*
A Time to Kill
The Bus Stop
Trio
Dolce Vita Murders

*Danny Shaw / Manfred Brehme WW2 Series*
The Shadow of War
Crusader
El Alamein

# The Phantom

**ISBN:** 9798511030371
**Imprint:** Independently published

Jack Murray

For Monica, Lavinia, Anne and our angel baby, Edward...

# The Phantom

## Prologue

*February 9<sup>th</sup>, 1920: London*

*The policeman ambled along the street with the unhurried gait of a man who had no particular place to go nor any reason to rush there. The only noise he could hear was the sound of his own breathing. It was robber-dark. The stars were hidden behind a thick black cloud. Light was provided by the lamp posts rising from the pavement every thirty yards. The policeman took pride in the fact that all the lights were in full working order. None had been vandalised. Of course, this wasn't really the area for such misbehaviour unless some young 'nob, aided and abetted by a skinful of gin, had been unable to resist a primeval temptation to test the strength and accuracy of his spear-thowing arm.*

*Such incidents were rare, although not wholly without precedent. They were also, paradoxically, both a welcome break from the blissful monotony of patrolling such a wealthy area as well as an opportunity to supplement his calamitously low wage by dealing with these young offenders with a profitable leniency. That he might be transgressing in spirit the law he had sworn to uphold never clouded his conscience.*

*It would be another couple of hours before the sun came up and he could finally get to bed. His feet ached. His back was hurting, and the cold had invaded his bones and taken up residence for the winter. Perhaps he could risk a call to Miss Diana's house before returning home. There was always a welcome for a man there.*

*Tonight, the policeman was a lot nearer a serious crime scene than his career had, thus far, blessed him with. From inside the large mansion, the policeman was being watched. The thief looked at the constable walk towards and then away from the house until he was like a distant silhouette in an Atkinson Grimshaw painting. The watcher resumed the search using a small desk light.*

*The walls were covered with the extraordinary art collection of the mansion owner. The thief examined each expensive painting on the wall not for its beauty nor for the name of the artist but for what it may be shielding.*

*A rather slap dash Renoir proved to be the one. The thief looked at the painting with something bordering on incredulity. The brush strokes seemed lazy, the draughtsmanship non-existent and the model's face betrayed either boredom or the unhappy realisation that her state of undress would provoke the old dog into seeking an amorous conclusion to their work session. More likely still, the model suspected the artist would end up making her look positively bovine. If the latter had been the objective, thought the thief, then take a bow, Auguste Renoir. The painting was placed carefully on the table as thief looked at the previously concealed safe.*

*Opening a small black bag, the thief withdrew an instrument while offering a silent acknowledgement to René Laennec, the inventor of the stethoscope. Although a closer reading of the history of auscultation would have given the*

2

# The Phantom

*thief more chance to recognise the contribution of Irish physician Arthur Leared who developed the first binaural stethoscope. The thief duly placed a receiver in each ear and slowly began to twist the dial on the safe.*

*Within a few minutes the safe snapped open. The thief reached inside and removed a black velvet bag. A quick check inside the bag confirmed its contents.*

*Moments later the bag was placed back into the safe and the mediocre Renoir returned to its place on the wall. The thief placed an additional item inside. It was a small calling card. There were no words, only an image. It showed the silhouette of man with a fedora. The face and the hat were black save for two white eyes staring with undisguised evil intent.*

*A quick check at the window showed the constable was out of sight. The thief opened the window and stepped outside. Carefully, the thief closed the window and leapt from the sill, over the rail fence onto the pavement, landing like a prima ballerina on the stage at Covent Garden. In the blink of an eye, the thief had vanished into the cold night air.*

# Jack Murray

## Chapter 1

*February 11th, 1920: Grosvenor Square, London*

Night crept into London's Grosvenor Square like a street urchin picking a rich man's pocket - stealthily at first and then all at once. The square was comprised of grand houses surrounding a large garden. The very richest in the land chose to live in this location rather as a fish should choose to live in the sea. It was their natural habitat and always had been.

Building work began in Grosvenor Square around 1721 soon after the South Sea Bubble burst to spectacularly impoverishing effect on its numerous British investors. The square took to heart the idea that an Englishman's home is his castle and made a jolly decent attempt at bringing this concept to reality. Perhaps an unintended after-effect, made manifest in Grosvenor Square, was the idea that investing in London property was rarely a bad idea.

On this night, young Ezra Mullins was, as his mum might have said, in a right state and no mistake. He was dressed in livery only marginally less stiff than cardboard, sporting a top hat that was one or possibly two sizes too big. The sight presented by the estimable young Mullins would almost certainly have induced paroxysms of pride in his mother and

# The Phantom

mirth in his father; such is the uncommon nature of women and the immaturity of men.

Ezra had recently been recruited as a doorman for an industrial magnate, one of the few men in England able to afford a mansion in one of the least affordable locations in London. Tonight, he was witnessing and bowing to a parade of the flushest and most powerful individuals, not just from Britain but from around the world.

A Rolls Royce Phantom attracted his attention as it drew up to the magnificent mansion. The chauffeur, another young man, stepped out from the front and opened the door. From the car emerged easily the most beautiful girl Ezra had seen all evening, if not ever. The lucky fellow with her, conceded young Ezra, was also a fine-looking gentleman. He couldn't help but notice the man's limp. It wasn't difficult to guess the reason why.

As the couple walked up the steps, the young woman glanced at Ezra. His attempts to disguise his admiration were sadly undone by a mouth that had dropped open and an inability to tear his eyes away from her face. She looked back at him; her blue eyes narrowed faintly, then she smiled. Moments later she was away and moving into the hallway of the mansion.

Dominating the hallway was an enormous malachite staircase which led from a black and white marble floor to a second-floor landing which housed an enormous Van Dyck portrait of a Dutch woman overlooking the whole scene with all the patience, bonhomie and good spiritedness of a wife awaiting her lord and master's return home from the pub.

The staircase was lined with footmen who smiled as the young couple walked up towards the drawing room. Inside there was already a large crowd of men in white tie. There were relatively few women, observed the young man. The raised eyebrow of his beautiful young partner told him she was thinking along similar lines.

Mary Cavendish surveyed the room for a few moments. She noted, without caring too much, that many of the men aware of her arrival were surveying her also. She looked up at the man who was accompanying her and said with a smile, 'Two Prime Ministers, a former Prime Minister and a couple of cabinet ministers. Not bad. You do take me to all the best places, Lord Aston.' Kit glanced down at Mary and returned her smile. 'Lead on, Macduff,' ordered Mary sweetly. Up ahead she noticed a distinguished man absenting himself from the company of Prime Minister Lloyd George to have a word with a servant.

'He's rather good looking for an older man,' observed Mary.

Kit raised his eyebrow and replied, 'I happen to agree with you. That is our host.'

Mary put her arm through Kit's, looked straight ahead and said, 'Introduce us, please.'

Across the room was Lord Peter Wolf, the joint owner of Lewis & Wolf, a large industrial conglomerate. They were inside the drawing room of Wolf's mansion in Grosvenor Square. The room seemed to be the size of a small county. Overhead were two crystal chandeliers which competed unsuccessfully for attention against the *objets d'art* which included Renaissance paintings on the walls and a Canova bust situated at the end of the room.

Kit and Mary walked towards Wolf. 'How rich is he?' asked Mary nodding towards the wall housing the Titian.

# The Phantom

'Clearly not in penury,' said Kit under his breath.

Wolf turned around just as the couple moved towards him. He was a tall man, around sixty, tanned with hair turning from dark to silver. His blue eyes crinkled into a smile as he saw Kit with Mary.

'I'm sorry, I didn't see you arrive. We've dispensed with announcing arrivals.'

'I'm glad,' replied Kit, 'It would seem like a relic from the last century.'

'I agree. After Flanders, I'm not sure it feels appropriate either,' said Wolf. Turning to Mary, 'Is this the extraordinary Mary Cavendish?'

'I wouldn't quite go that far, Lord Wolf,' said Mary modestly.

'I would. Your story caused quite a stir in our household,' replied Wolf taking Mary's hand and shaking it. 'What you did in going to nurse the men at the front was very much to your credit so you may count me amongst your many devotees. Although if the rumours are true, it seems you have one particular admirer.'

Kit laughed and admitted the rumours were true. Wolf looked at them, and his smile grew wider. They made a beautiful couple. Noble without superiority, intelligent without conceit and approachable without being over-familiar.

'My wife and I weren't fortunate enough to have children but, if I may say, I'd have been immensely proud if they'd been like you, my dear. Congratulations, Kit,' and Wolf took Kit's hand and shook it vigorously. The sincerity of Wolf's sentiments was clear.

'Thank you, sir, and thank you for the invitation to your...,' he searched for the right word to convey the fact that they were amongst many of Europe's leaders on the eve of a major peace conference in London. He settled on, 'soiree.'

This made Wolf smile and he said, 'I thought it appropriate you come given your escapade in Paris last year.'

Mary looked up at Kit proudly, 'Yes he's been somewhat reluctant to tell me exactly what he did.'

'There's a man coming towards us who should be able to elaborate,' replied Wolf.

'Lord Aston, Miss Mary,' boomed a voice rich enough in timbre to suggest a long and successful career on the boards. In fact, this was not so very far from the truth as the man was playing a role. The role was as fictitious as his playing of it was true.

Both turned around to be greeted by the sight of Percy Pendlebury, gossip columnist and, as of last year's unintentional involvement in 'The French Diplomat Affair', mysterious man of, well, mystery. Wolf rolled his eyes and made good his escape.

'Percy,' said Kit shaking the journalist's hand, 'How are you? Glad to see you're fully recovered.'

'Oh, completely, Kit, but enough about me. Now, Mary, I don't believe we've met but I have met Lady Esther,' said Pendlebury fixing Mary with his full attention.

'Yes, I read the piece you wrote about her. You were very kind.'

'I should love to have included you also, my dear. My readers were bewitched by my series on what people such as yourself were doing during the War.'

Mary had nursed at the Front under a pseudonym for the last year of the War.

'I'm sorry. I didn't want to talk about my time there.'

# The Phantom

Just for a moment Mary found it hard to breathe. Unhappy images of the appalling injuries inflicted on the soldiers in her care swam in front of her eyes. Kit was aware of Mary's grip growing stronger. He looked at her face and saw a change, almost imperceptible, but clear. He fell in love with her again for what seemed like the hundredth time that day.

Pendlebury, whose own intuition was as highly tuned as Kit's, also saw the change. He took her hand and smiled sympathetically.

'Please forgive me. I quite understand your desire not to discuss those heart-breaking days.'

He did. Unusually for a newsman whose prior career had principally involved the reporting of rich people being and acting as rich people do, he had travelled to the front to see for himself and report on the lives of the men and women serving.

'But am I to assume that you two wonderful young people, have some news to share with me and all my readers?'

Mary blushed slightly and glanced at Kit who returned her look.

'Yes, Percy. I rather think you can.'

'Is this official?'

'It will be when you break it,' pointed out Kit.

Pendlebury offered hearty congratulations before nodding to two older men standing in a corner, 'Well, Kit, I must thank you for this scoop, although I think we'll both agree you did owe me one. Ah, you'll have to excuse me on that happy note. I've just seen two Prime Ministers talking to one another. I shall see if I can hear what they're saying.'

The two Prime Ministers in question were Lloyd George and Francesco Nitti of Italy. Both were due to host the Conference of London the next day.

Mary looked up at Kit suspiciously.

'What did he mean by that, I wonder?' asked Mary. 'Is this another thing you've neglected to tell me milord?'

'I'm afraid it is rather a failing of our gender that we sometimes omit details in our desire to avoid boring to death the audience.'

'Or,' pointed out Mary, 'when said detail may not reflect well on you?'

'Especially that.'

Wolf returned and taking Mary's arm said, 'If I may, Kit, I'd like to take the most beautiful lady in the room to meet her many admirers.'

'That didn't take long,' laughed Kit relinquishing Mary's arm.

As he did so he became aware of a man ambling up beside him. He turned around and found himself looking at Gerald Geddes, a man he'd encountered last in Paris around the time of the Peace Conference.

'Hello, Aston,' said Geddes.

Kit nodded at Geddes, 'Hello, Geddes.' He tried not to look surprised at seeing a spy at the soiree. But, then again, it made sense. There were a lot of senior politicians and businessmen here this evening. There were bound to be indiscretions and when alcohol was involved.

'Working?' asked Kit amiably.

'Yes. You?'

'No, purely social. I'm with my fiancé,' replied Kit.

# The Phantom

'Congratulations,' said Geddes before nodding a goodbye. This coincided with the arrival of a man Kit knew well.

'So, gather congratulations are in order,' said the man, who was at least as tall as Kit.

'Yes, Lord President,' replied Kit to former Prime Minister Arthur Balfour.

Balfour nodded, and both men regarded Mary appreciatively. Then he turned back to Kit and said, 'I knew her grandmother slightly. She was also very beautiful. You must introduce us later. How are you anyway? You've had a busy few weeks if what I hear is true.'

Kit laughed. In the last few weeks, he'd solved the murder of Lord Arthur Cavendish, and solved a crime involving several murders connected to a conspiracy to assassinate the King and the Queen Consort.

'Yes, it's been somewhat hectic,' agreed Kit.

'You met my successor, Curzon, I gather.'

'Indeed,' said Kit looking at Balfour with a half-smile.

'Indeed,' responded Balfour in an equally neutral tone. Glancing ahead he saw Mary ensconced with Lloyd George and Nitti.

'Your intended may need rescuing. One Welsh goat and an Italian seem to be wooing her. If she's in any way attracted by power, you could be in trouble. If, instead, she values men of a more philosophical bent, I may throw a hat into the ring myself.' Both observed the Italian Prime Minister put a protective arm around Mary before noting his hand dropping further down.

'Normally I would say she can hold her own but perhaps, on this occasion, she's outgunned.'

# Jack Murray

The two men walked forward to rescue Mary, who glanced archly at Kit as he arrived. Turning momentarily to Lloyd George before looking again at Kit, she said, 'The Prime Minister was just telling me how you probably saved his life last year in Paris. I must say I'm looking forward to getting to know my future husband, Prime Minister. He tells me nothing.'

'And the King's life this year,' added Balfour. 'By the way Mary, I'm Arthur, as none of these gentlemen seem in a rush to introduce me.'

'Lord President,' said Mary smiling up to Balfour, 'I've been an admirer of yours for many years.'

'And I of you for many minutes,' replied Balfour nobly.

-

Around midnight, the main dignitaries had retired for the evening. Wolf suggested they withdraw to the library for a nightcap. The library, if not as large as the drawing room, was as impressive. Books lined the walls from floor to ceiling. Some wall space was occupied by paintings from the French Impressionists who were gaining in popularity and value by the year in England.

The room was lit by an enormous crystal chandelier which had, as Wolf demonstrated, several dimmer switches around the room. Mary had been subject to vigorous displays of what she and Kit later agreed was behaviour only marginally differentiated from a Gorilla beating its chest and a lot less impressive. All of which amused Kit and provided no end of entertainment to Mary as well as to her newfound friend, Arthur Balfour.

With the politicians gone, bar the indefatigable Balfour, the conversation moved on to the recent spate of robberies in the

12

city. This brought back memories for some of the thief known as 'The Phantom.'

'You're not going to claim credit for that one also, Kit?' asked Balfour, with one eyebrow raised.

Kit laughed, 'No, I was just getting ready to go to the War when the Phantom was captured. I do know the chap who caught him: Chief Inspector Jellicoe. Good man.'

'I must say, I was relieved when they caught him,' admitted Wolf. Upon saying that, he went over to a painting on the wall and moved it to one side. Behind it was a safe. Given that he was with men and women of unimpeachable background, Wolf felt completely at ease in what he was doing.

He opened the safe and removed a small black velvet pouch. From the pouch he extracted a diamond necklace. Mary gasped involuntarily. She wasn't the only one. There were over a dozen sizeable diamonds on the chain. It was beautiful and unquestionably worth a small fortune. Everyone in the room inched forward to get a better look at the necklace Wolf had placed on the table.

Just as Wolf stepped back, the lights went out leaving the room in complete darkness. Two of the women screamed and there were shouts from a couple of the men. The lights came on again after a few moments. When everyone looked down at the table, the diamonds were gone.

Wolf looked at everyone in the room, and said, 'Is this some sort of joke? If I may say, it's in very poor taste.'

Mary looked up at Kit and whispered, 'Do something.'

'Me?'

'Yes, you.'

Everyone turned to Kit.

13

'Oh,' said Kit, unsure of what was expected from him, 'Perhaps we should lock the doors.' Behind him the footmen in the room did as they were bid. Kit looked at Wolf. The room was silent as they waited for Kit's next words. And then Mary spoke.

'Well, clearly they're hidden up above. Who's going to look?'

Everyone looked up at the chandelier.

'Good thinking,' said Balfour smiling.

A young man volunteered, and space was cleared for him to stand on a chair and to root around the chandelier with his outstretched hand. All this time Kit kept his eyes on Wolf.

'I can't find anything,' admitted the young man.

'Oh,' said Mary, clearly disappointed that her first stab at detection had, on this occasion, been a failure. She felt a comforting hand on her elbow from Kit. She looked up and made a face. Kit had a faint smile. Mary frowned. She sensed what was coming.

'What are you thinking, Kit?' asked Wolf.

'A greater and, frankly, more credible detective than I once said that if you can eliminate the impossible then whatever remains, no matter how improbable, must be the truth.'

'Go on Sherlock.' said Mary, who made having a grin and frown at the same moment not only physically possible but very enticing.

'Well, with that in mind,' said Kit walking forward to the safe and looking inside, 'I would suggest that the necklace is back in the safe where Lord Wolf placed it when the lights went out.'

The safe was empty.

14

# The Phantom

Wolf's face was non-committal. Kit turned to face the room. No one had moved except to look either at Kit or the empty safe.

'As you can see the safe is empty,' said Kit. He caught Arthur Balfour's eye. The glint suggested the former Prime Minister was enjoying this as much as he was fascinated by what the solution to the mystery might be. Mary was beside him. Her face now betrayed a degree of nervousness. With the safe empty, she was worried he was going to make a fool of himself. So was Kit.

'However, if I do this,' said Kit, pressing down on the base of the safe and extracting from the compartment underneath, a diamond necklace which he held up for all to view, 'then the diamonds reappear, as if by magic'.

Everyone broke out into spontaneous applause, none more so than Lord Wolf who was laughing in delight. Shouts of 'Bravo' filled the air. As the ovation died down one voice broke the silence.

'Of course, you're now in trouble,' said Arthur Balfour.

'Indeed, that thought has also just occurred to me,' admitted Kit.

Wolf and the others in the assembly turned to Balfour for an explanation, who duly provided it.

'Well Kit has, rather publicly, been proved right. I fear his delightful fiancée will, indeed must, make Kit spend a lifetime reflecting on how he chose to deploy his unquestioned intellect ahead of a piece of wisdom that has existed at least as long as humanity.'

'Which is?' prompted Mary, with something approaching relish.

'That women are always right,' finished Kit, shamefacedly.

15

Mary stepped forward and kissed Kit gently on the cheek. This brought a second round of applause. Kit glanced and saw Gerald Geddes.

'Any other party tricks?' asked Geddes. He was smiling but there seemed to be little humour in his tone. Kit was distracted by Lord Wolf coming up alongside him clutching the diamond necklace.

'I wouldn't want to be in your shoes when you go home, Kit,' said Wolf with a grin. The smile on Wolf's face changed in a moment to confusion. He stared at the diamond necklace and then looked back up at Kit.

'What's wrong, Peter?' asked Kit, looking also at the necklace. He looked back at the ashen face of Lord Wolf.

'It's fake. The necklace is a fake.'

Wolf went over immediately to the safe. He placed his hand down on the base which tipped down to into the hidden compartment found by Kit during the practical joke.

He turned to face the assembly. Incredulity was written on his face. Kit picked up the black velvet pouch and turned it inside out. As he did so, a small card fell onto the table. Kit lifted the card and showed it to Lord Wolf.

On the card was the face of a phantom.

# Chapter 2

There was at a gasp as Kit showed the card to the assembly. Wolf sat down in shock.

A voice from the back of the group asked, 'But how? He's in prison.'

Kit looked around at the group. Every person was someone of rank either through inheritance, patronage, or wealth. It was inconceivable to Kit that one was a thief.

'I believe the best course of action, Peter, is to call Scotland Yard immediately. We need Jellicoe. I also think it best if your guests retire for the evening. You'll all probably be asked to give a statement tomorrow. My feeling is that the diamond necklace was stolen before tonight. The security I saw this evening would be something no sane thief would look to take on.'

Wolf looked up at Kit and nodded gratefully. Kit turned around to search out Mary, but she was already at the door instructing a footman to call the police. In fact, she had moved before Kit had addressed the group, clearly anticipating the need. Kit felt a glow of pride as she returned.

'Police?' asked Kit.

'Police,' responded Mary.

'I would get used to this if I were you. They're always one step ahead of us,' pointed out Balfour. This lightened the mood in the room and even seemed to raise the spirit of Lord Wolf.

'Did you ask the footman to insist on Jellicoe?'

'Of course,' said Mary, 'I do listen to you, you know.'

'Enjoy that while it lasts, Kit,' added Balfour glancing archly at Mary.

-

Half an hour later the only remaining people in the room were Kit, Mary, and Lord Wolf. A maid brought some tea as they discussed what would happen next. Wolf, by now, had regained his composure following the initial shock. However, he remained bewildered at how a thief could have entered the house never mind located and stolen the diamonds.

'By the way, Kit, you know that you don't have to stay,' pointed out Wolf.

'I'd like to, Peter,' replied Kit before adding, 'besides which, I know Jellicoe.'

'I understand, Kit, and thank you. But you, Mary?' asked Wolf.

Kit glanced at Mary one eyebrow raised.

'I should like to stay also, Lord Wolf, if I may. The alternative is to return to Kit's aunt or stay with Kit and yourself. Not such a difficult choice when you think of it.'

Wolf smiled and bowed his head.

'Your aunt, Kit?' asked Wolf turning to Kit.

'Yes, Mary and her sister have moved into the house of my aunt now that she's back from the Riviera. You may know her, Lady Agatha Frost?'

The look on Wolf's face suggested a delicate mixture of surprise, amusement, and fear, rather in the manner of meeting a baby shark and then its mother.

# The Phantom

'Well,' smiled Wolf, 'I do know the lady in question. Quite formidable if I remember correctly.'

'Your memory does not betray you, sir,' smiled Mary, 'Formidable is one way of putting it. Terrifying would have worked also. Thankfully I, too, have an aunt who provided rigorous training in dealing with, well aunts, Lady Emily Cavendish. Their meeting a week ago was really quite something.'

-

## Two weeks earlier:

*Kit looked at the two sisters as the hugged one another at the railway station. So different in temperament yet so alike in their beauty. The bond between them was palpable. The very difference in their nature, the electrical vibrancy of Mary and the serene, inner harmony of Esther, it seemed to Kit, strengthened their attachment at an atomic level.*

*Harry Miller appeared on the platform to help with the bags.*

*'Hello, Harry,' said Mary somewhat shyly. She had not seen him since Kit had unmasked Eric Strangerson as a murderer and, in doing so, saved Miller who had been the chief suspect thanks to Mary and Esther's early attempts at detective work.*

*Miller smiled at Mary and said, 'Great to see you again under happier circumstances.'*

*'Thank you, Harry,' said Mary, fighting to control her tears. Seeing Harry had caused a wave of guilt to engulf*

*her as she remembered the period when he'd been taken away by the police. She looked at Harry and said, 'I'm so sorry about what happened. I hope you'll forgive me.'*

*'Nothing to forgive. I'm just glad we're on the same side now,' said Harry with a wink. Mary laughed and then nodded in gratitude to the small Londoner.*

*'Thanks,' she whispered. They moved towards the car and soon were on their way back to Kit's apartment in Belgravia.*

*Much to Mary's delight, or so she made it seem, there to greet her was her aunt, Emily, and her cousin, Henry, who had become the new Lord Cavendish, following the death of her grandfather Arthur over Christmas.*

*'Well, you're certainly looking much improved since the last time I saw you,' announced Lady Emily. 'Scotland must have done you some good. Anyway, I don't understand why you're not returning to Cavendish Hall.'*

*'We've been through this, Aunt Emily,' replied Esther sternly. 'I want to be close to Richard and Mary.'*

*'Well,' replied Emily stiffly, 'I find the situation distinctly odd. Your hasty engagement to a man you've just met. Then high tailing it down to London to stay near him. You read about this sort of thing, of course, in the News of the World. I never thought for a moment my own niece would indulge in such behaviour.'*

# The Phantom

*'It certainly conjures up an interesting image of you reading the News of the World, mama,' said Henry, giving voice to everyone's thought at that moment*

*Emily turned to Henry who was smiling. All at once a few thoughts went through her mind: horror at being mocked by her son, shock at the public nature of the jest and, even more surprisingly, pride. More and more these last few weeks, she was beginning to see the things in Henry's character that she had longed to see for many years. That this would necessitate occasional opposition to her wishes, she was growing to accept.*

*Slowly.*

*Humour had become a new weapon in his armoury. In this, he was becoming more like his father, Robert. His comment had produced smiles in the group around her which confirmed where their sympathies lay. A natural military tactician, Emily withdrew from what was a weak position to one where she felt she could regain the high ground.*

*'Well, you're young and it's your life, Esther, it's not for me to undermine your wishes by dint of such minor considerations as wisdom and experience.'*

*This signalled an end to the initial conflict. However, as Kit was acutely aware, the second was imminent. Kit felt it best to prepare the ground for the looming encounter.*

*'So, Lady Emily, my aunt is coming to visit this afternoon. She may have a solution to our problem.'*

'Your aunt?' said Esther, Mary, and Emily in unison.

Kit smiled, grimly and said, 'Yes.'

'And remind me of your aunt's name, Lord Aston,' asked Emily.

'Lady Agatha Frost,' offered Kit.

This prompted an unexpected reaction from Emily. She burst out into uncontrollable laughter. Esther looked mystified. Then Kit looked at Mary. He tried to smile. A mistake, he realised afterwards. Her eyes narrowed. This wasn't good. In fact, this was the opposite of good.

Emily sat down as she sought to regain control of herself. In fact, it took longer than expected as one glance at Esther and Mary caused a further relapse.

'Is this as bad as it seems, Kit?' asked Mary in a dangerously slow and even tone.

A further burst of laughter from Emily made any answer from Kit academic.

'You can always say 'no', Mary,' offered Kit. Rather feebly, it must be said.

'Do you know, Lord Aston, you've just made my day,' said Emily finally recovering composure. This prompted another look from Mary that had Kit squirming inside. Thankfully Esther, the angelic, beautiful Esther, offered an olive branch of hope.

'I look forward to meeting your aunt, Kit. She has a residence in London?'

'Yes, Grosvenor Square.'

-

# The Phantom

Lord Wolf looked at Kit and Mary with a smile, the undercurrent regarding Lady Agatha was plainly visible although he sensed something else which he couldn't quite divine. If pressed he would have described it, unfathomably, as amusement on Mary's part.

A footman appeared in the room to announce the arrival of Chief Inspector Jellicoe. Moments later James Jellicoe entered Wolf's library accompanied by a young detective. The arrival of Jellicoe caused Wolf to do a double take such was the policeman's resemblance to the reigning monarch, George V. His beard and moustache were a case study in different evolutionary periods. His beard flecked, as it was, with large patches of grey seemed positively pre-Cambrian compared to the more Cenozoic moustache that, so far, seemed to be a relatively recent development. The overall effect was to give Jellicoe a mournful appearance which his naturally sober personality did little to mitigate. He was a serious man doing a serious job.

If Wolf had done a double take at the royal resemblance, it was matched by Jellicoe's surprise at seeing Kit again.

'Lord Aston,' he exclaimed, unable to add much to this initial thought.

'Chief Inspector. I hadn't anticipated meeting you again so soon after, shall we say, our last case. May I present Lord Wolf.'

Lord Wolf walked forward and shook the hands with Jellicoe and the young officer. 'I'm sorry we should meet in these circumstances, Chief Inspector. My young friend here speaks very highly of your capabilities.'

Jellicoe looked at Kit. 'I have a very high regard for his ability also, Lord Wolf. If I may, this is Detective Sergeant

Ryan,' said Jellicoe turning to the young officer beside him. Kit looked up at Ryan, for he was at least as tall, if not taller than Kit. Ryan was, in Kit's estimation, in his mid-twenties, well made and quite handsome.

Once the introductions had been made, Jellicoe became aware of Mary's presence. She had remained sitting down as the police had arrived. Kit saw the direction of Jellicoe's gaze and smiled, 'And, this Chief Inspector, is my fiancée, Mary Cavendish.'

Jellicoe glanced at Kit, who nodded.

'Miss Mary, I'm happy to see you recovered. When I met Lord Aston, you were still,' Jellicoe paused for a moment to find the right word.

'Out for the count, Chief Inspector?' suggested Mary with a grin.

Jellicoe's face broke into what, for him, constituted a grin.

'Indeed, Ma'am.' He turned to Ryan, who was clearly entranced by the vision of Mary, 'Wake up sunshine. Work to do.'

Jellicoe asked some questions to understand what had taken place in the evening, occasionally allowing Ryan to speak. It was clear to Kit that Ryan was a highflyer. He was relatively young to be in the position of supporting a man such as Jellicoe. His few questions were probing, spoken in a London accent that suggested he had not arrived at his position through contacts or preferential treatment based on class.

Kit glanced at Jellicoe. He seemed amused at Kit's assessing of his young protégé. This made Kit smile and he nodded an acknowledgement to Jellicoe to congratulate him on his choice of assistant.

# The Phantom

After the initial scene-setting questions from the two policemen and sensing that Kit would have a better idea of how to communicate with Jellicoe, Wolf requested that he provide a summary of the events of the evening.

Wolf was impressed by Kit's lucidity as he recounted concisely every aspect of the evening that might be of interest to the Chief Inspector. Perhaps more impressive than his memory for detail was his observation of anomaly. He noticed several occasions when the behaviour of the servants, many of whom were agency staff brought in for the evening, was strange

When Kit had finished, Jellicoe congratulated him on the comprehensiveness of his report. Ryan had taken several pages of notes. Then Mary interjected.

'I think Lord Aston also meant to mention one other thing.'

Kit turned to Mary barely able to disguise his surprise, 'Of course, silly me, perhaps, Mary, you should mention it.' It was clear Kit had no idea what was coming much to Jellicoe's amusement and Ryan's bemusement.

'The red blemish on the fake diamonds,' said Mary.

Kit reached over and scrutinised the necklace closely until he found the mark. He showed it to Wolf and Jellicoe.

'Good spot, Mary,' murmured Kit.

'Any thoughts on what the mark might be, milady?' asked Jellicoe.

'I can't be sure, of course,' acknowledged Mary, 'but my guess would be a women's nail lacquer.'

## Chapter 3

Kit and Mary walked across Grosvenor Square. It was after three in the morning. Both were tired and keen to return to the warmth of Agatha's house. However, there was a brightness in Mary's eye that Kit suspected owed as much to the events of the evening as the strength of her ardour. There was also the possibility it spelled trouble.

'Whenever we have a spare minute, or lifetime for that matter, Lord Aston, I think you need to fill in one or two of the several hundred gaps in your past.'

'Do you know, Mary?' replied Kit, 'when you call me Lord Aston, I feel as if I'm about to visit the head of form to be punished.'

'Good analogy and highly accurate,' responded Mary with a grin.

'I fear you may soon be feeling the same when my Aunt Agatha realises what time you've stayed out until,' pointed out Kit.

'Even more apposite,' said Mary, as it dawned on her that dawn would soon be dawning. She thought for a moment before asking, 'Do you think climbing in through the window might help me avoid capture by the armed patrols outside my bedroom?'

'What floor are you on, again?' inquired Kit.

# The Phantom

'Third.'

'Hard lines.'

Mary looked up at Kit wryly, 'Speaking of lines, I think you'll be in the firing line as much as myself. I mean, leading a poor, innocent girl, all alone in the world astray, in this manner. It's a bit ungentlemanly.'

This caused Kit to laugh, 'You're certainly not poor and as to how innocent you are, that remains to be seen.'

'Sadly, that bit may be true. Perhaps you should whisk me off to a hotel. We may as well commit the crime for which we are about to be condemned.'

Kit glanced down at the grinning Mary and just for a moment the thought caressed his mind. Mary had no difficulty reading his mind and shrugged, 'Last chance, Lord Aston. We're nearly there.'

They arrived at the door of Aunt Agatha's townhouse. With a heavy heart Kit fished out the front door key and inserted it in the lock. Mary made a glum face.

'I'll come in with you,' said Kit, 'You shouldn't have to face this alone.'

'Do you really think she'll be up at this hour?'

One look from Kit confirmed her question was both unnecessary and naïve. Mary smiled. As she made ready to go through the front door, her fate to be determined by the woman who took over where the gorgon had left off, Mary cast her mind back, once again, to the first meeting between herself, Agatha Frost and Lady Emily. A meeting so seismic, it made the movement of tectonic plates under the earth seem like a kitten's paw stroking its mother's nose.

-

Jack Murray

*The rap at the door had been forceful to say the least. Harry Miller rushed down the stairs at the sound of the increasingly impatient knock. He opened the door to find a lady of around seventy, of imperious aspect, around five feet tall, stoutly made and wearing a hat that might once have been an aviary.*

*'Lady Agatha,' exclaimed Miller with a delight he surely did not feel.*

*'Well don't just stand there, young man, let me in,' came the brusque reply.*

*'This way, my lady,' said Miller.*

*'I know the way, young man. Out of my way,' said Aunt Agatha, brushing Miller aside with her samurai umbrella before marching up the stairs like a Grenadier guard going to battle.*

*Miller watched the diminutive Medusa ascend the stairs with something approaching relish. This would be a fascinating contest between the two ladies. The relative youth of Lady Emily against the old war elephant herself. Lady Emily may have built up a winning record against lower ranked opponents in the country, but today she was testing her mettle against an undefeated legend.*

*Aunt Agatha burst through Kit's doors like a storm gathering strength. She first came face to face with Lady Emily.*

*Silence.*

*A little bit more silence broken only by the sound of Sam, Kit's Jack Russell, escaping out of the room. Mary glanced down at the little terrier's exit stage left and then shifted her gaze to Kit, who merely raised one eyebrow and suppressed a smile.*

# The Phantom

*Esther realised she was holding her breath. She glanced at Mary who, sensibly it seemed, had taken the precaution of inhaling deeply as the infamous aunt's footsteps grew louder.*

*'I presume I have the pleasure of addressing Miss Mary?'*

*Lady Emily nodded. Whatever her faults, and they were numerous, she was not easily cowed and replied, 'Three Ladies Cavendish, in fact.'*

*Mary couldn't bring herself to look at Esther otherwise the game would've been up. But she did feel a swell of pride for her aunt's opening salvo. Before Aunt Agatha could respond, Emily pressed home her early advantage.*

*'I am Lady Emily Cavendish. My late husband was Robert Cavendish. Esther and Mary are the daughters of the late John Cavendish. Perhaps you had the pleasure of meeting their grandfather, Viscount Cavendish.*

*This early engagement was, as the girls and Kit acknowledged afterwards, brilliantly executed by Emily. It spiked Aunt Agatha's guns right from the off, putting her firmly on the back foot. Kit's aunt nodded to Emily recognising, perhaps with something approaching pleasure, a worthy opponent. True champions seek not to build a career on walkovers. Instead, their desire is to test themselves against the very best: to defy, to overcome and, ultimately, to triumph.*

*Henry walked into the room just as his mother had finished. All eyes turned to Henry, which he seemed to find amusing.*

*'Have I missed anything?' he asked lazily, completely unaware of the tension crackling in the room.*

*Aunt Agatha raised one eyebrow and turned to Emily for an explanation.*

*'My son, Henry, Lord Cavendish.'*

*'I see,' replied Aunt Agatha. 'I am pleased to meet you all. I'm afraid I never had the pleasure of meeting your Grandfather. My late husband, Eustace, and he were acquainted I gather; he spoke highly of him, if my memory serves.'*

*Emily found herself fighting a groundswell of guilt. The wasted years. How she regretted that time. The regret made more painful by the sense that Arthur, too, shared that regret and had patently been making efforts to build bridges in the days leading up to his death. For Esther and Mary, also, the reminder of their loss was almost unbearable. The memory of Arthur Cavendish hung in the air, dispelling some of the tension brought on by the arrival of Kit's aunt.*

*Finally, after a few moments, Agatha turned to the two girls, 'And which of you is to marry my nephew?'*

*Mary wiped her eye and then said, 'I will be marrying Kit.'*

*Aunt Agatha looked at Mary and then walked up to her, ignoring Kit who, like Henry, wore a smile of relaxed forbearance. The two women eyed one another like two gunfighters in a Hoot Gibson western.*

*'You're certainly a very pretty young lady, I'll give you that,' pronounced Aunt Agatha.*

*'Thank you.'*

*The direction of Aunt Agatha's gaze turned to Mary's hair which was fashionably short. No comment was made but the silence and barely perceptible raising of one eyebrow spoke more eloquently to the elderly aunt's views about short hair than any tirade would have achieved. She glanced up at Esther, whose serenity and beauty were almost tangible. Both girls seemed to meet her approval.*

30

# The Phantom

*Aunt Agatha abruptly turned around and looked at Emily, 'I think it makes sense for these young ladies to stay at my residence in Grosvenor Square. I shall instruct my staff to make ready. Christopher,' said Agatha, turning to Kit, 'please arrange for their things to be sent immediately. Good day.'*

*Lady Emily watched askance as Aunt Agatha cruised regally out of the apartment. By the time she regained her senses, the ship had sailed. The horse had bolted. The off stump was bowled. Silence reigned save for the sound of the clock ticking on the mantlepiece. Finally, Kit decided a decent enough amount of time had elapsed before breaking the hush, if not the calm.*

*'So, that was my Aunt Agatha. You know she's really quite likeable once you get to know her.'*

*Three ladies Cavendish turned around to Kit at that moment with looks on their faces that caused a hero of the Great War, the rescuer of Kerensky and hero of countless other perilous missions to wish he could shrink into the wall. Such is the implicit power wielded by the distaff side of humanity.*

-

Kit spent a few seconds wiggling the key in the lock. Beside him Mary stamped her feet to keep the circulation going against the biting cold.

'Hurry, sir, before your future bride freezes to a block of ice.'

Finally, Kit opened the door. They stepped into an expansive hallway, no less impressive than Lord Wolf's, with many paintings from the Dutch school decorating the walls and a knight in shining armour at the base of the stairs standing beside a latter-day maiden of an elderly vintage

31

wearing a frown that would have frozen the heart of any knight errant at twenty paces.

Mary looked at Aunt Agatha's face and then turned to Kit.

'What on earth is the meaning of this outrage, young man? Have you no regard for the reputation of this young lady?'

'On the contrary, Aunt Agatha,' said Kit more casually than Mary thought wise, 'Nothing is more important to me than the unblemished nature of Mary's character.'

Aunt Agatha looked as if she were about to erupt like a South Seas volcano. Her face went red and she inhaled deeply to get good purchase on the string of verbal abuse about to be launched in a Kit-ward direction.

'Before you get angry, Aunt Agatha,' continued Kit, 'A crime was committed at Lord Wolf's house. We have a case.'

'A case you say?' asked Agatha, her tone changed to a quite remarkable degree. So did her posture. Where previously she had been tensed like a samurai warrior about to strike, she relaxed and leaned forward.

'Yes,' said Kit, moving towards the door, 'And I shall let Mary tell you all about it. Cheerio.' With that, Kit gave a rather stunned Mary a peck on the cheek and left via the front door.

Agatha looked expectantly at Mary.

'Well,' said Mary.

'Well, don't just stand there, young lady,' replied Agatha, 'Give me the skinny.'

Mary walked up to Agatha. Her eyes narrowed slightly as she looked down at the elderly woman. She was at least three inches taller than her host.

'Kitchen?'

'Kitchen,' agreed Agatha. 'I'll make us some hot milk.'

# The Phantom

Chapter 4

*February 11<sup>th</sup>, 1920: London*

The young man pulled his coat tightly around him in a futile attempt to avoid the chill. The night air seemed to freeze on his cheeks and the breeze stung his eyes. A cloth cap provided some shield against the freezing air circulating around his head. But his ears stuck out and bore the full brunt of the wintry evening.

He hurried forward. There was still another mile to walk. The noise grew louder as he approached the pub on the corner. Raucous laughter came from within and even more raucous singing. An elderly gent came stumbling out of the pub, completely pickled, bumping into the young man.

'Get out of it,' snarled the drunk, pushing the young man out of his way.

The young man was several inches taller than the old man and could probably have ended his night there and then. Instead, he ignored him and pushed on wearily in the direction of his home.

Crossing the road, he ducked up a side street. A young woman was coming the opposite direction. Their eyes met momentarily and then she looked away a little fearfully. The young man kept walking, berating himself for glancing at the woman, for making her feel afraid.

His journey took him through a series of winding streets, many of cobblestones, which he found difficult to walk on. Street after street of terraced houses. It was after eight o'clock, but the streets were still relatively crowded. Beggars confronted him on every corner, many missing limbs, their eyesight, their mind. Hand scrawled messages proclaimed a similar story of why they were begging. A land fit for heroes, thought the young man. He laughed sardonically to himself. Home was just up ahead.

In front, though, was a policeman kneeling beside a street dweller. The smell near the beggar was appalling. The young man recognised the tell-tale sign of gangrene. He kept on. The man was a goner. Nothing to be done. How many times had he thought that thought? How many times had he kept his eyes ahead? Nothing to be done. Nothing.

The young man was twenty-eight years old. He looked older. A lot older. His body, his mind and his spirit all ached with the effort of surviving each day. This daily battle had not ended when they'd handed him his Z11.He'd walked away from His Majesty's Armed Forces. Many had not.

A noise behind. He spun around. A dog had knocked over a bin. He breathed again. Loud noises. He hated loud, sharp noises. His step quickened until he was finally at his front door. The house was like a hundred other houses on the street.

Inside he was greeted by a young woman holding a year-old toddler. Another child, perhaps four or five years old, jumped up from a chair and ran over to him.

'Daddy, daddy,' she said delightedly.

# Jack Murray

The young man looked at his wife. The other child seemed quiet, asleep. Then the coughing started. Then the gulps of air. Then the tightness in his lungs. Again, and again. It never seemed to end. The cheeks of the young woman damp with tears. She shook her head. He took the child from the arms of the young woman. He fought to keep the tears from his eyes

'There, there Ben. Don't worry, daddy's here.' He gently kissed his wife and knelt to greet the young girl.

'Alice, my love,' said the young man as the little girl enfolded his neck with her arms. "Watch young Ben,' he laughed. The little girl took the cloth cap from his head and put it on her own head. She was beautiful, sweet, funny, and sad all at the same time. Just like Chaplin. One day he'd take her to the picture house to see him. One day.

'A bit big for you my love,' he said, smiling.

-

An hour later, the young man and woman looked down at their children, asleep on the bed. They looked so peaceful. He put his arm around his wife. She looked up at him.

'How was it today?'

A dozen images passed through the young man's mind. Twelve hours in the varnish factory. His lungs and his throat were burning.

'Just the usual,' he replied unenthusiastically. He would never tell her the full truth. It would break her heart. Well, break it even more. She had enough to cope with. She didn't know the hatred he felt for the workplace. The bosses. The union leaders. The smell.

God almighty, the smell. He knew the factory would do for him. Where the German mustard gas had failed, the factory would surely succeed. He looked at his wife and tried to smile.

# The Phantom

'Come on, I'm hungry. I could eat a horse.'

She looked into his eyes and knew there was pain. Standing on tip toes she kissed him. Grateful for his stoicism, grateful for his wage, grateful for the life he was trying to provide for his family. He was a good man. She felt blessed.

-

The young woman watched him devour his supper. His hand was a blur as it scooped food onto his fork. Every scrap was accounted for. He drained his tea and sat back with a look of satisfaction.

'You're not just beautiful.'

She stood up and collected the plate and brought it over to the sink. Neither said anything for a few moments. The subject of their boy, Ben, hung heavily in the air, as it did every evening.

There was a knock at the door.

The young man stood up and went to see who it was. He turned to his wife and said with a smile, 'I hope you've some of the stew left.'

He opened the door. Another young man wearing a suit and a fedora was stood outside. He took the hat off and walked in without saying anything.

'Evening, Sally,' said the other young man. He looked like a younger, taller version of her husband.

Sally went over and gave the man a hug, 'Hello, Ben. If you've come to see your niece and nephew, they're in bed this last hour.'

'Can I?' asked Ben.

'Go on,' said his brother.

Ben moved to the doorway of the bedroom and looked in. The only sound was the rumble of one child's breathing. He

# Jack Murray

inched forward quietly to get a better look at the two children. Behind him, the young couple looked on. Finally, he turned and silently retraced his footsteps back into the living room.

'Something smells good,' said Ben with a grin.

'Here we go,' replied his brother rolling his eyes, 'What did I tell you, Sal?'

Moments later Ben was tucking into the remainder of the stew and half a glass of beer. The three of them chatted happily until the coughing started. Sally rose to her feet as young Ben began to cry. The two men watched Sally go to the bedroom and then Ben grew more serious.

'He needs to be in a hospital,' said Ben, as much to himself as his brother. They both knew this.

'I know but I can't cover that and all of this. Even with Sally's stitching, it's barely enough. I'm not smart like you, Ben. I've never had a head for numbers or words. I can't do what you do.'

Ben didn't try to argue with his brother; there was no point. The sound of coughing continued to stab the air. Tears glistened in the eyes of the elder brother. The younger one too. He hated to see his brother so sad.

'I'm letting him down.'

'Don't say that, Joe,' replied Ben getting up. He took out his wallet and put a pound note on the table.

'Ben, you can't keep doing this,' said Joe, hurt but the gratitude in his eyes was unmistakeable.

'Can and will, Joe. I feel like they're mine. Anyway, can't stay here talking rot with you, I must return. I'm on duty again tonight.'

38

# The Phantom

The two men walked out of the kitchen. Ben turned to go to the bedroom, but Joe shook his head, 'You'll excite him if he sees you here. Best to go.'

Ben nodded. It made sense. He went to the door and opened it. As he did so, he turned to his brother, 'Anything you need Joe. I'll do anything. remember that. Family first. That's what ma used to say. Family first.'

Joe nodded but couldn't speak. He watched his brother leave then walked slowly into the bedroom. Family first. Always.

Chapter 5

*February 12th, 1920: New Scotland Yard, London*

New Scotland Yard, the red brick building, home of the nation's police force, rose unimposingly over the Thames embankment. Kit, who had visited the building on a few occasions, had never failed to be impressed by its resemblance to a block of apartments for the rising mercantile class in the city. It seemed just a little bit too cozy to be a centre for fighting crime in the city and beyond.

'I'll pull over here, sir,' said Miller, 'I'm not sure there's anywhere to park.'

'London's getting worse,' said Kit in response.

Kit stepped out of the car. Up ahead he saw an equally impressive Rolls Royce from which debouched Lord Wolf. The two men acknowledged one another with a nod and walked up the steps together.

'This is a bad business, Kit,' said Wolf as they were led towards an office on the second floor.

'Strange business, also. Hopefully Chief Inspector Jellicoe can be more forthcoming than he was last night.'

The two men entered the large office housing the Chief Inspector. There was a magnificent view of the Thames below, but Jellicoe chose to sit with his back to the river. The room was spartan. There were no drawers, no stacks of paper, no in-tray. Jellicoe permitted himself the luxury of a telephone and a notebook. Kit decided that Jellicoe was either a brilliant delegator or had an extraordinary memory.

The Chief Inspector and Detective Sergeant Ryan both rose to greet the two men. Jellicoe, as ever, retained his naturally lugubrious expression but Ryan smiled at the new arrivals. Once the almost-ceremonial handshakes and greetings had been dispensed with, the real business of the meeting began. Jellicoe started by acknowledging a few of the matters uppermost on the mind of Lord Wolf.

'I asked Lord Aston to attend. I hope you won't mind. Normally the idea of amateur sleuths would be abhorrent and the stuff of a "penny dreadful". But Lord Aston proved an able assistant to the police recently and the fact of his presence in your home when the crime was discovered seems to me to be worthy of making an exception, for the moment.'

Kit noted the end comment. This seemed reasonable to him. He could not expect to become part of a police matter even if curiosity was eating away at him. Jellicoe and the young sergeant would want to do their job with little or, better still, no interference from an amateur.

'I have great admiration for Kit, Chief Inspector, so there are no complaints from me at his presence.'

Jellicoe nodded and then continued, 'Forgive me if I was less than forthcoming last night. I sensed your desire to understand more about the meaning of the card and what the next steps in the investigation might be. I will try and deal with this at the start, and then I would like to ask you a few questions, if I may.'

'By all means,' replied Wolf.

'The card you found was identical to a number of cards that were left at the scene of crimes committed by a man the press, as is their wont, rather luridly titled "The Phantom". His real name was Raven Hadleigh. As you are aware, Hadleigh was captured just before the War and sentenced to fifteen years imprisonment.'

Jellicoe modestly neglected to mention his role in the capture of "The Phantom". Ignoring the knowing smile on Kit's face, he continued, 'So that was that, or so we thought. However, it appears a man is now impersonating Hadleigh, and committing crimes in an identical manner.'

'There have been other similar burglaries?' asked Kit.

Jellicoe's features achieved the almost impossible effect of becoming even more crestfallen than previously.

'Sadly yes. You may have seen something of them in the press already.'

'Does this mean the wrong man is in prison?' asked Wolf, giving voice to Kit's thoughts also.

'No, the evidence convicting Hadleigh was comprehensive and incontrovertible. However, there's no denying these new cases are something of a mystery. The cards being used are the same as the ones used by Hadleigh, which, at the very least, could be explained by using the same printing firm although the firm in question has ceased trading. This means, as yet, we have few leads from the other two cases.'

'Two,' exclaimed Kit. 'My goodness, I'd noticed the robberies but hadn't connected them to the same person, never mind the Phantom.'

'We have kept the details away from the press for obvious reasons,' said Jellicoe, 'I can only begin to imagine the kind of campaign they would create on Hadleigh's behalf, as well as the number of cranks who may come along wishing to claim credit.' Jellicoe shook his head as images of the motley crowd of prospective master criminals flooded his mind, and worse, Scotland Yard.

'But this is incredible,' said Wolf. 'Even if we accept that this Phantom was captured, is it possible he had an accomplice that you were unaware of?'

'It's entirely possible, of course, but there was no evidence to suggest Hadleigh was anything other than a lone agent in the commission of the early burglaries.' After saying this, Jellicoe turned to Ryan and said, 'If he may, Detective Sergeant Ryan will take a statement from you Lord Wolf. Lord Aston, can I ask you to stay on a few moments?'

Ryan and Wolf both stood up. The young man led Wolf out of the room to a nearby office.

'Can you be absolutely sure you have the right man, Chief Inspector?' asked Kit. 'There was no element of doubt?'

'None, Lord Aston' confirmed Jellicoe. 'We have the right man all right. But, no question, this is a very troubling situation. There's only so long we can keep this story away from the press. Once they get hold of it, there'll be hell to pay.'

'Yes, I can see the potential problem. He was quite a hero in the end, wasn't he?'

'Don't remind me, Lord Aston,' said Jellicoe in a voice that managed to be both weary of the folly of human nature and awestruck by it. 'You wouldn't have believed the reaction of women to his incarceration. I must admit, notwithstanding what he was doing, I never disliked him as a man. He was always the gentleman. When one looks at it this way, I suppose it wasn't difficult to see why he caught the imagination of the press, and of ladies in particular.' He shook his head as he, clearly, still found it difficult to understand.

'Yes, I must admit I followed the case with great interest. I think I did meet him once in passing because he knew some of my chums. Not sure though. They liked him immensely, I understand,' admitted Kit.

Jellicoe laughed. It was as pleasant a sound as it was unusual coming from the, otherwise, sombre detective.

'Yes, I suppose I should know him,' continued Kit with a wry smile that acknowledged the reason for the Chief Inspector's amusement. Jellicoe's eyes twinkled at this confession.

'Your Detective Sergeant is interesting. He must be quite a talent.'

Jellicoe looked at Kit shrewdly, 'May I ask why you say that?'

Kit smiled and replied, 'Well his youth for one thing and, dare I say it, he doesn't sound like you.'

'Or you, Lord Aston?'

'Or me,' laughed Kit. 'I imagine he must be useful undercover.'

'Very useful, sir. One of the best I've seen. He joined us straight from the army, but he didn't come to my attention until six months ago on another case. We needed someone to pose as a gang member. A police sergeant acquaintance of mine recommended him. Anyway, we rounded up the gang thanks to his intelligence and no little bravery. I had him promoted immediately and transferred to my office. He's going places. Remember the name, Lord Aston. Ryan, Ben Ryan.

-

# The Phantom

Lady Agatha Frost had always been an early riser. She had lived by the motto: early to bed, early to rise makes the heart grow fonder, or some such notion. She sat in her dining room polishing off a breakfast that was nothing short of hearty. Two eggs, bacon, and black pudding with a single kipper.

'Fish?' said Lady Agatha, turning to her equally elderly butler.

'Yes, milady?' replied Fish.

'Can you send young Alfred to collect Betty Simpson? I take it he's here now?'

'I haven't seen the young man yet, but I shall tell him once he arrives.'

'Thank you, Fish. That will be all.'

Meal finished, Lady Agatha rose from the table and went to the hallway. On a small table beside a Tiffany lamp sat one of these new-fangled communications devices: the telephone. Initially distrusting of the device that seemed as intrusive as it was ugly, she had grown to become quite addicted to its utility and could spend hours on it with her friends. She sat down at the table, picked up the receiver and put it to her ear. She dialled a number and waited a moment.

'Mayfair 6237. Yes, I'll hold.'

A few moments later someone answered.

'Betty, it's Agatha. We have a case. I've sent Alfred to collect you. The Phantom is back. Yes, I know. Oh, and bring the book. We have a new colleague.'

This brief, rather one-sided exchange formed the sum of the conversation with Betty. Lady Agatha replaced the phone just as Mary was passing her by.

'The book? Betty?'

'You'll see,' said Lady Agatha's excitedly, 'It's big'.

Mary smiled and walked into the dining room to see if any food remained unconsumed on the breakfast sideboard. An initial inspection suggested Agatha had been a bit hungry. Not that Mary minded. She picked a few items from the debris on the sideboard and sat down, intrigued by the latest twist in her increasingly fascinated take on Kit's aunt. Eccentric hardly seemed adequate in describing either the wonderfully unpredictable nature of the lady nor an extraordinary life force that was almost palpable.

Half an hour later as she was finishing her breakfast there was a commotion outside the door. Giving her mouth a quick dab, she rose and went to see what was happening. In the hallway there were two elderly women. One was Aunt Agatha, the other was a lady that Mary took to be Betty.

Betty Simpson was, if anything, slightly shorter than Kit's already diminutive aunt and arguably stouter. She was dressed in a tweed skirt, sensible brown brogues. Her woollen pullover was barely up to the job of containing the ample bosom of the worthy lady. Mary noted, with a smile, her hair was styled not dissimilarly to her own. This was also noticed by Aunt Agatha.

'What on earth have you done with your hair?' she exclaimed in surprise once Betty had removed her hat and tossed it towards the sideboard.

'Do you like it?' asked Betty, innocently.

'You're too old,' said Aunt Agatha tartly.

'Nonsense, my dear,' replied Betty, touching the side of her hair.

'Seventy-three, not too old?'

'Seventy-two,' responded Betty before adding, 'and a half.' It was then she noticed Mary standing at the dining room door. She turned to Agatha for an explanation.

# The Phantom

'This is Mary Cavendish. She and Christopher are going to be married.'

Betty turned with a look of delight and walked towards Mary, "Well I must congratulate that young man. You are quite a beauty young lady.'

'More than a pretty face you'll find, Betty,' pointed out Agatha, 'Now let's retire to the library. We've work to do.'

Although she didn't show it, Mary felt unaccountably delighted with the compliment as Betty embraced her in a bear hug. After a suffocating few moments, Mary felt a powerful hand grip hers and she was being led into the library.

'Alfred,' ordered Agatha, 'Can you bring Mrs Simpson's bag in and then tell Fish to organise some tea. We're not to be disturbed.'

The young chauffeur had escaped Mary's attention initially. She smiled at him on the way past. He was rather portly with dark hair and a rather feminine mouth.

'Hello, Alfred.'

'Ma'am,' replied the young man shyly, touching his hat.

Chapter 6

Detective Sergeant Ryan read through the statement given by Lord Wolf. Both Kit and Jellicoe listened intently. Every so often Kit caught Jellicoe's eye. The look was a question: what do you think? The answer returned by dint of a look also was I'm impressed. The young sergeant had clearly given the industrial magnate a comprehensive interview. He easily fielded questions from both Jellicoe and Kit as he delivered his report. When the summary was complete, Jellicoe said nothing to praise Ryan, instead he turned to Kit, and asked, 'Have you any further questions, Lord Aston?'

Kit fixed his gaze on Ryan, 'Was Lord Wolf hiding anything?'

This was an unusual question which caught both Jellicoe and Ryan by surprise. Ryan glanced at Jellicoe and then replied, 'No. He was genuinely shaken by what had happened. This is normal. The sense of invasion is the same whether you're a lord, a lady or just a normal bloke whose house has been broken into.'

'That was my sense also, Lord Aston,' added Jellicoe. 'No one ever thinks it will happen to them. When it does, when the realisation sets in that your home, your castle, even, has been breached, that you, your family, your possessions are not as safe as you first thought. It can be troubling, and it doesn't matter who you are. The reaction of Lord Wolf was entirely sincere in my view.'

Kit nodded. He thought so too.

'Why did you ask that, sir?' asked Ryan.

'I'm not sure. I suppose it was the joke he played last night, pretending that a robbery had taken place. It seemed out of character.'

Jellicoe thought for a moment then asked, 'How did you guess the safe had a secret compartment?'

Kit laughed, 'It was certainly a guess. You see, I was standing near the chandelier and didn't hear anything thrown into it or, for that matter, anyone come near me to put anything inside. Based on this, I reasoned Lord Wolf had simply put the diamonds back into the safe. It wasn't such a big jump to guess you could press down on the bottom of the safe to get to another compartment.'

'But how did you know it was a practical joke?' continued Ryan.

Jellicoe answered this one on Kit's behalf, 'That was easy, lad. The only people in the room were Lord Wolf, Lord Aston, Mary, a former Prime Minister, a few cabinet ministers and their wives.'

'A dishonest politician? Perish the thought, Chief Inspector,' added Kit with a grin. Jellicoe's eyes crinkled so Kit assumed that underneath his beard there was a smile.

'What are your plans now, Lord Aston?' asked Jellicoe. There was a look on his face that Kit suspected was meant as an invitation. He certainly hoped so. This case was intriguing, and he hated to admit to himself how much he wanted to be involved.

'I've no plans, but I'm certainly open to suggestions, Chief Inspector,' replied Kit, hoping his intuition was correct.

'How would you feel about renewing a couple of old acquaintances?'

Unsure of who the second one could be, Kit was sure of the first.

'I would be delighted, Chief Inspector.'

-

The library at Aunt Agatha's house had been one of several pleasant surprises for the Cavendish sisters, stocked as it was not only with the classics, in several languages, but also with the latest book releases, many of an eyebrow raising quality. One cabinet seemed to have been devoted to "penny bloods" and the works of Conan Doyle, R Austin Freeman, Arthur Morrison, Guy Boothby, and the like.

'Now you sit there, my dear,' suggested Betty to Mary, pointing to a seat at the head of the table. The two ladies sat either side of Mary. Betty took a large scrapbook out of a carrier bag and placed it on the table.

'The Phantom is back you say?' asked Betty.

'Looks like it. Mary, can you tell Betty what took place last night at Lord Wolf's? Listen to this, Betty.'

Mary looked at the two ladies and, suppressing a smile, began her report. Like Kit she had the ability to provide sufficient detail without it slowing the overarching narrative. Neither of the ladies said a word, listening intently. Both took notes in large, well-worn notebooks.

When Mary had finished, Betty asked, 'And you say you saw the card?' Mary nodded in response. Betty pushed her notebook in front of her and said, 'Can you draw it my dear?'

# The Phantom

'I have to say Essie is the better artist,' admitted Mary, 'But, as you know, she's in Sussex with Richard's family. I'll do my best.' Mary proceeded to draw the outline of the figure, roughly colouring in the black features but leaving the eyes white. 'Something like this,' said Mary. When she'd finished the two ladies looked at one another.

'There can be no doubt,' said Agatha.

'None,' confirmed Betty.

Mary looked them both for an explanation. Betty nodded to Mary and opened her scrapbook. A card was clipped to the inside. She handed the card to Mary.

'Is this what you saw?'

The small business card was blank save for a black silhouette wearing a fedora. The eyes were white.

'My goodness,' said Mary, fixing her gaze on the card before turning to the others. "Where on earth did you get this?'

'We weren't robbed if that's what you're thinking,' said Betty, 'Let's just say we have contacts.'

Betty took the card back, holding it with something approaching reverence before carefully replacing it inside the cover.

There was a knock on the library door and in walked Fish with a trolley containing the tea and some biscuits. Spying the scrapbook and the presence of Betty he said, 'A new case, milady?'

'We live in hope,' replied Aunt Agatha.

Once the tea had been served, Betty got down to business.

'What do you know about the Phantom, my dear?'

'It was a little before my time. I was aware of him obviously. Who wasn't? It was all over the papers. But I didn't

51

really follow the case. War was in the air and with my papa and Uncle Robert, well, our minds were elsewhere.'

'Perfectly understandable,' acknowledged Agatha, 'Perhaps, Betty, you should do the honours.'

'Good plan. Before I start, where is Christopher?' asked Betty.

Mary smiled; Kit hated his Christian name. 'Kit is with the police. He went to Scotland Yard this morning to see Chief Inspector Jellicoe.'

'Jellicoe, you say. Makes sense,' said Betty, looking knowingly at Agatha, 'Still, bit of a bad show that you weren't invited. Typical men.'

'Indeed, typical men,' agreed Mary. She had been rather put out by Kit going alone. 'If he thinks this is the way it'll be in the future, he's in for a rude awakening, I can tell you.'

'Quite right, Mary,' nodded Agatha. 'Betty?'

'Right, where are we? The Phantom. Also known as Raven Hadleigh. Born 1871 in Gloucester to the youngest brother of Lord Ronald Hadleigh. Went to a local public school before a successful career at Oxford studying geology.'

'He obviously had an interest in rocks right from the start,' pointed out Agatha. This made both ladies giggle conspiratorially, causing Mary to start also. In fact, such was the mirth at Agatha's joke it took a few minutes and another round of tea before the meeting was able to resume.

'The first recorded crime was,' continued Betty, turning the page of her scrapbook to a newspaper cutting, 'In 1907. Before then it seems, he'd spent time abroad working for a petroleum company.'

'So, it's entirely possible, his criminal career could have started long before then,' pointed out Mary.

# The Phantom

Agatha and Betty exchanged glances and nodded.

'Entirely possible, Mary. We both certainly believe so,' replied Agatha, 'I'm glad you're of a like mind.'

Mary studied the press cutting of a robbery of a small painting by Reynolds in Glasgow in which the robber had left behind a small calling card.

'Between 1907 and 1914 a further thirteen robberies were reported. In each case a calling card was left behind by the Phantom. Interestingly, the calling card was never made public.'

'I'm not surprised. I think a few other phantoms would've emerged from the woodwork. But what did he normally steal?'

'Beautiful objects mostly. In fact, beautiful things which were portable. Diamond necklaces and brooches, small but valuable paintings. He never took sculpture, probably too fragile,' said Betty.

'Or heavy,' pointed out Agatha.

'Indeed,' replied Betty. 'He was finally caught in June 1914. The printer of the cards, a man named Felix Kane, was in custody for another crime and he traded time in prison by pointing the finger at Mr Hadleigh as being the Phantom.'

'Did they recover the stolen objects?' asked Mary.

'Well, that is one of the more interesting aspects of this case,' interjected Agatha, 'Some of the objects were sent back to the owners soon after the theft. The paintings were found at the home of Hadleigh, however, and that was that.'

'The man who caught the Phantom was your friend, Chief Inspector Jellicoe, or Detective Inspector as he was then.'

'Why did he return the objects?' asked Mary.

'Good question. The belief was that he enjoyed the thrill of the crime more than the actual end product. In fact, the theory at the time was he only needed the necklaces for his wife when they were attending society events. Remember Hadleigh was a respected member of society and would have attended many balls in the city over the years,' explained Betty.

'His wife was a beauty,' added Agatha.

'Was?'

Betty took up the story, 'I believe she died relatively recently. Not sure if it was that ghastly flu or something else. There was a daughter I believe.'

'How terrible,' said Mary, 'She's effectively an orphan.'

'A very well-off orphan,' suggested Betty, 'And not a child, either. I would say she must be your age, Mary, perhaps slightly older.'

At this point there was a knock at the door.

'Yes?'

Alfred walked in, 'Sorry to disturb you, ma'am, but I was hoping I could get off now. The studio has been in touch.'

'Yes, perhaps you can take Betty on your way. Just wait there for a moment, we'll be finished soon,' said Agatha.

'She would be in her early twenties by now, Mary.'

'Really? That's interesting,' said Mary, her mind considering an extraordinary possibility. The three women looked at one another, each thinking the same thought.

'I see no reason why a woman can't do what this Phantom did,' pronounced Mary.

'I quite agree,' replied Betty, 'Especially if it's his daughter. Imagine that, a chip of the old block. The daughter of the Phantom becomes the new Phantom. How wonderful.'

'I'm not sure we should be delighting in criminal behaviour, Betty dear,' pointed out Agatha although she didn't seem completely convinced by this idea herself. Especially if the master criminal in question was a woman.

'I think we may be close to cracking this case,' announced Betty excitedly standing up and putting the scrapbook into her bag which she then handed to Alfred. Mary and Agatha walked Betty to the door. 'I'll make a start in finding out where the young lady is living now and report back to you tomorrow morning.'

'Excellent idea, Betty,' said Agatha. "but can you remember her name?"

'Caroline according to one of the cuttings. Caroline Hadleigh,' replied Betty on the doorstep. With that she turned around and followed Alfred down the steps towards a large Bentley parked on the street outside.

Agatha closed the door and looked at Mary, 'A productive morning, I think. Now, we must plan our next steps carefully. I don't think Christopher need know what we're doing, do you?'

'Certainly not,' replied Mary, 'Let's see if we can do this ourselves.'

'That's the spirit.'

'By the way, where or what is Alfred doing? He mentioned the studio,' asked Mary.

'Alfred? Oh, I believe he has a part time job in one of those moving picture studios. He wants to direct films, apparently. A bit like those chaps Griffith or de Mille. Preposterous of course, but young people will get these ideas in their heads.'

## Chapter 7

'Would you like to come in my car?' asked Kit as he descended the stairs at Scotland Yard with Jellicoe and Ryan.

'I'm sure that won't be necessary, Lord Aston,' replied Jellicoe until he spied Harry Miller pulling up in the Rolls Royce. 'On the other hand,' said Jellicoe. He didn't finish the sentence. One look at Ryan and the decision was made.

The three men walked down towards the Rolls. Harry Miller hopped out of the car to let them in. Jellicoe and Ryan looked around the interior of the car. Kit looked at the two men with a wry smile.

'How the other half live, Chief Inspector?'

Jellicoe seemed amused but made no comment of a feudal nature, confining himself to saying, 'It's certainly an improvement on our usual mode of transport. When I first started this job, sir, we were lucky to have a carriage. That was a long time ago.'

Miller turned around to Kit and asked, 'Where to, sir?'

In response, Jellicoe gave an address south of the river, which caused Kit and Miller to look at one another.

'Is this a new prison?' asked Kit, 'I can't say I'm familiar with it.'

Jellicoe replied with a twinkle in his eyes, 'Not new so much as special.' He didn't elaborate further, so Kit let the matter drop despite his curiosity.

The address of the facility was a little way out of the centre of town. Miller drove them south towards Clapham. The journey took around fifteen minutes. As they passed through the London streets, the three men chatted amiably about commonplace subjects. This was frustrating as Kit was burning to know who the second prisoner might be, but the good Chief Inspector resisted any subtle invitation of Kit's to talk further on the matter.

They finally arrived at the facility which was cunningly disguised as a small mansion with a high wall and trees around its border. The area seemed relatively well-to-do. It amused Kit to think about how residents would feel about having a prison in their midst.

As the car drew up a man, dressed in country tweeds, came to meet them at the gate. Although his attire seemed to suggest a county gent, his face told a different story. The skin was rough-hewn, with heavy eyelids that slanted downwards; his nose had been broken once too often and been given up as a bad job. Kit recognised a boxer when he saw one. Up close, as they sped in, it was clear the tweed suit was scarcely able to contain the epic dimensions of this particular squire.

The driveway was around fifty yards long and ended in a large area in front of the house set aside for vehicles. It seemed to Kit, once he was out of the car, that they were in the countryside rather than the heart of a major capital city. The doors of the large house opened and out stepped a man who greeted them on the steps. The man was in his fifties with a bearing that was unmistakably military.

'Hello, sir,' said Jellicoe, shaking the man's hand, 'Are you Major Hastings?'

The man smiled, 'No longer a Major, Chief Inspector, but thank you notwithstanding that.' He looked at the car and smiled.

'Police cars have certainly come a long way.'

Jellicoe smiled and turned to Kit, 'May I present Lord Aston and my colleague, Detective Sergeant Ryan.'

After the usual greetings, Hastings ushered the men inside. The interior was dominated by dark wood walls, flooring, and staircase. It was perhaps a little dark for Kit's taste, but this was a detail in what was otherwise the most extraordinary prison Kit had ever visited. A sense of anger began to build as he hoped that the second prisoner was not the murderer of Mary's uncle. As he thought this, he quickly scolded himself. Such a trick would be out of character for the Chief Inspector, a man he found he had increasing regard for.

-

Joe Ryan knew something was wrong as he walked towards the factory gates. Several men were walking away rather than to the factory. Some looked angry; a couple were in shock and others had the muted resignation of another defeat. He felt his skin tingle and for once he knew it wasn't the cold. The feeling in the pit of his stomach grew with each step towards the gate. He knew the feeling well. It was almost an old friend. Or enemy.

Once through the gates he made his way towards to the entrance of the factory. Inside, the noise of the machines was loud but not quite deafening. The height of the vast arched roof overhead meant that the sound was dispersed more widely making it just about bearable. A few of his mates were strolling around the factory floor. He waved to one but was not acknowledged. Not a good sign.

'Joe,' shouted someone from behind.

He turned to see Alf Fairfax motioning for him to come over. Fairfax was the local union organiser for the factory. He was a sharp featured man in his forties with a look that was, whether by design or good fortune, permanently sly. This made him an ideal interlocutor with management, who probably disliked him as much as the workers unquestionably did. Ryan tended to avoid him if he could, which made him more like the factory management than the union man would have imagined.

Ryan felt his feet begin to drag. Fairfax looked at him impatiently. Before he reached the union leader, Fairfax turned and walked through a door. It led up to the management office on the floor overlooking the factory.

Ryan followed Fairfax up the stairs. There was no conversation. There was no need. Ryan had seen this before. He knew why his workmates had not looked at him. Why should they? He would have done the same. In fact, he had done the same. What could any of them do?

Fairfax pushed open a door marked Factory Manager. Ryan followed him to the office. Inside was a young woman, Lily, the secretary to Ken Tippett, the factory manager, who was sat behind his desk. Ryan nodded to Lily, who was liked for a variety of reasons by the boys on the factory floor, although none had ever come close to courting her. She smiled sympathetically.

'This is Joe Ryan,' said Fairfax to Tippett.

'Ah, Ryan,' said Tippett, looking up uncomfortably at Ryan. Fairfax remained standing, so Ryan did likewise. Lily had stopped using the typewriting machine since Ryan's arrival in the office. 'Come forward,' ordered Tippett.

Ryan walked forward, taking off his cap. Holding it in both hands at his waist. Tippett was holding a letter. He looked from Ryan to the letter and then back to Ryan.

'I shan't beat around the bush. We're laying you off,' said Tippett. He paused for a moment to let the news sink in. It already had. Then he continued, 'We're having to do this to a number of chaps. I'm afraid it's based on last in first out. You understand, don't you?'

'Yes, the ones that didn't fight get to stay, sir.'

'Ryan,' said Fairfax sharply. 'Enough of that, lad. It can't be helped.'

Tippett looked even more uncomfortable now. He was of an age at which he could have fought in the War. He hadn't. His occupation was deemed too important for the overall War effort.

'We're aware that you served your country, Ryan, and of course we're grateful. The sad fact is we are suffering. Cheap imports are undercutting us. We must become more competitive. This is the reality of the marketplace. You understand?'

Of course, I understand, thought Ryan bitterly. I'm not an idiot. He stayed silent, leaving Tippett with the impression he was dealing with someone intellectually deficient. He decided to bring the meeting to a swift conclusion.

'This letter explains it all. The management is also being quite generous to people like yourself, and there is a not insubstantial payoff,' continued Tippett. He motioned his head and Ryan heard Lily rise from her desk and come forward. She handed Ryan an envelope that jingled. With

# The Phantom

coins. Tippett meanwhile sealed his envelope also and handed it to Ryan.

'Come on, lad,' said Fairfax moving forward and touching Ryan's arm.

Ryan turned and walked out of the office in silence. As the door closed, he heard Lily begin typing again. The two men walked down the stairs and then down a corridor to another smaller office. This belonged to Fairfax.

'I'm sorry about this, lad. A dozen blokes have been laid off, too. Do you have any other work you think you can find?'

'No,' replied Ryan. He knew a lot of men who had lost their jobs were looking around all the usual places. It seemed to be the same story everywhere. It didn't matter that you'd fought for King and country. If anything, it made things worse back in civilian life. You'd missed out in gaining work experience that others, who hadn't served, were able to have. He felt himself sinking into a dark hole. Life wasn't meant to be easy, but this?

Fairfax wrote down a name and an address. As he was doing so, he said, 'I know someone that might be able to help.'

Ryan took the piece of paper and looked at it.

'A job?'

'No guarantees. Tell him I sent you, mind. That's important. Ask to speak to him and tell him you've been sent by me. Understand?'

'Thanks,' said Ryan, feeling some relief. The room became slightly brighter. The weight crushing his stomach lightened immediately through hope and gratitude.

'Go along this morning, lad.'

61

# Jack Murray

Ryan didn't need a second invitation. Within moments he was on his feet and heading out of the office.

'Thanks, Alf,' said Ryan at the door. He meant it.

-

Major Hastings led Kit to a large office with a view over the expansive garden at the back. The office was sparsely furnished and there were no pictures on the walls bar one regimental photograph. Kit walked over to it. It was typical of the period. Very wide and containing ranks of men. Hastings was in the middle of the front row. The picture was taken in June 1914.

'Not many of us left, I'm afraid,' commented Hastings as Kit turned away from the photograph.

Kit and Hastings looked at one another. Nothing else was said. Hastings sat down and bid the men do likewise. Jellicoe began to speak, 'Thank you for allowing us to see the prisoner at such short notice, Major Hastings.'

'It's not a problem, Chief Inspector. I must confess it was rather a surprise, though. May I ask why?'

Jellicoe, it seemed to Kit, looked reluctant to reveal the reason, and Kit's hunch proved accurate.

'There have been a number of recent robberies which bear similarities to Hadleigh's imprint. We thought he might have some ideas that could help us in our enquiries.'

Hastings nodded and then looked at Kit. Jellicoe caught the direction of the Governor's gaze. 'Lord Aston is here because he was the one who uncovered that a robbery had taken place.'

'And of course, I remember now, his connection to the other prisoner.'

# The Phantom

Kit sat forward as he realised the other prisoner's name was about to be revealed; however, at that moment there was a knock at the door and a uniformed man walked in. He was short but powerfully built. He didn't so much walk forward as march, coming to a dramatic halt near the Governor's desk.

Hastings smiled and introduced the new arrival, 'Gentlemen, this is Chief Warder Brickhill. As you've probably surmised, he is, like me, ex-army. In fact, he was my sergeant major.'

The two policemen and Kit rose to greet Brickhill. His dark slicked back hair and features suggested a man who could have been aged anywhere between forty and sixty. The steel grey eyes bespoke a man you didn't mess with.

After the initial introductions, Hastings continued, 'If you would take these gentlemen down to our guest Mr Hadleigh.'

'Yes sir.' A man of few words thought Kit, unless he was barking at some poor unfortunate. The three men followed Brickhill out of the office, down a flight of stairs to a basement floor with an impressively thick oak door.

Another prison guard opened the door for the men which led to a long corridor, dimly lit. There were four cells it seemed. This made Kit even more curious as to what type of facility this was. A prison dedicated to a handful of men was highly unusual.

Brickhill gave a brief rap on the door before extracting a set of keys from his pocket. Selecting a mortice key from the band, he opened the door, and all four men walked in. When Kit saw Hadleigh's cell his mouth almost fell open.

Chapter 8

The address on the piece of paper given by Fairfax was in Southwark. Ryan decided to make his way straight there. The alternative was to go home and break the news to his wife as well as risking someone else would get there before him and nab any potential job.

Two bus rides later he was still a short walk away. The factory was one of a number in the city dedicated to the production of tobacco, cigars, cigarettes, and snuff. Ryan walked down one of the most desolate roads he had seen in London. There were no houses or shops or pubs. There were several small businesses and factories. Some of the businesses had been abandoned. Dogs roamed around the grounds, barking, and fighting.

Ryan kept on walking past one vacant unit after another. He turned a corner and saw a fairly austere red brick facility at the end of a road that even the kindest observer would have described as abandoned by the rest of society.

Outside the factory gates, there were hard-looking men smoking cigarettes. They barely glanced at Ryan as he walked towards the office at the front. Outside the office sat another group of men. They eyed Ryan as he headed in their direction. Ryan overheard one say, 'Another one.' One of the men stood up. He didn't seem that much taller once on his feet. He was powerfully built and walked aggressively towards Ryan.

Two years at the front meant that Ryan didn't shrink in the face of physical intimidation. The man's hands remained in his pockets, however, so Ryan assumed he was going so to speak to him instead. Rather than wait for the man, Ryan spoke.

'I've been told I should speak to a Johnny Mac.'

'Who told you that?' asked the man. His face, his voice and his posture still suggested Ryan's next answer could land him in a fight.

'Alf Fairfax.'

The man laughed mirthlessly.

'Hear that boys,' said the man turning to his work mates, 'Another one of Alf's lost souls.' He turned back to Ryan and said, 'Any proof of that?'

Ryan handed him the scribbled note from Fairfax. The man put it in his pocket and motioned for Ryan to follow him inside the factory. Once inside, the man led Ryan down a corridor to a small office. He knocked and opened the door. He put a hand on Ryan's chest, however, and walked inside himself.

Two minutes later he came out of the office. He gestured with his thumb and said, 'In you go.'

Ryan walked in, but the man remained outside. Inside the office was a relatively young man, perhaps Ryan's age or slightly older. He stood up as Ryan entered. The man was slender, his hair was close cropped and there was a scar running from his left eye down the side of his cheek. This alone would have had most men checking for the nearest exit.

He was also one of the tallest men Ryan had ever seen. At least six feet five.

The giant made no attempt to be welcoming. Wisely, he had long since realised that his appearance was unlikely to make a first impression anything other than uneasy for the viewer. Fortified by this certainty, he always strove to ensure the second impression confirmed the first. In spades.

He walked up to Ryan with a smile that was reminiscent of a lion coming across an antelope catching forty winks in the hot African sun. Ryan tensed himself. Whatever happened, the man would find himself in a fight all right. The years at the front had deadened much of his fear: he was no coward.

'I'm Johnny Mac.'

An Ulsterman. Ryan had met many in Flanders. He'd liked them, mostly. They'd fought with a ferocity, a mad courage and a hatred that seemed almost spiritual in its purity. Ryan had almost felt sorry for the Germans. Ulster folk were a God-fearing people who showed no mercy to the enemy.

'I'm Joe Ryan. Alf Fairfax sent me here.'

'Why?'

'I was laid off.'

'Why?'

'Last in, first out.'

'War?'

'Yes.'

This seemed to satisfy Johnny Mac for he nodded, 'Can you do nights?'

Ryan nearly jumped for joy. 'Yes, no problem.'

'You start at six, finish at four,' said Johnny Mac, not taking his eyes off Ryan. In fact, Ryan could swear the man had not blinked in all the time he'd been in the office.

The Phantom

'Thanks,' said Ryan for wont of anything else to say.

Johnny Mac looked to the door and shouted, 'Rusk.'

The man who had led Ryan here re-entered. He looked to Johnny Mac, who merely nodded.

'Go with Rusk. He'll get you details. Give him the two pounds.'

Ryan turned sharply to Johnny Mac.

'What?'

Johnny Mac glowered at Ryan, 'You want the job, it'll cost you two quid. Understand?'

Ryan felt rage and fear. He needed the job, but he wanted to kill the man in front of him. And Fairfax. The other man moved forward towards Ryan. The air seemed to leave the room. Finally, Ryan nodded to Johnny Mac. He needed the job. There were still a few shillings left over from his pay off.

'Where do I sign?'

He had a job. That was the main thing.

-

Kit stepped into the prison cell after Jellicoe, Ryan, and the Chief Warder, Brickhill. The cell, if it can be so described, was around five times the usual size. There were a couple of landscapes on the wall, a gramophone, a leather armchair with matching Chesterfield sofa. Over by the wall was a dining table with three seats and a large bookcase. On the floor was, to all appearances, an expensive Persian carpet. Only the single bed with the steel grey blanket betrayed the location. The rest of the room was more like the room of a man of independent means in London.

'Jellicoe,' said the man in surprise. He rose from the armchair to greet a man who seemed like an old friend.

'Chief Inspector, I gather now. My congratulations, albeit belatedly. What a pleasant surprise. And if I'm not mistaken, this is Lord Kit Aston.' The voice was more aristocrat than convict. Kit stepped forward and shook the outstretched hand.

'Hello, Hadleigh,' said Kit who if not nonplussed, was certainly not exactly plussed either. Looking around the cell, Kit added, 'They seem to be looking after you well.'

The convict smiled. Something in the smile made Kit start. There was a look on Hadleigh's face, something indiscernible. Without knowing why, Kit wondered about where he could have met Hadleigh, but the connection to where and when was frustratingly just out of reach. They looked at one another for a moment. He sensed Hadleigh recognised him but not for the reasons that might appear obvious. There was something in the look. Was it sympathy? Sadness? It was hard to tell and Hadleigh understood Kit's confusion. However, Kit was certain Hadleigh knew their connection. The moment passed quickly and Hadleigh's attention was drawn to the younger policeman.

Jellicoe introduced his colleague, 'And this, Mr Hadleigh, is Detective Sergeant Ryan.'

Hadleigh nodded to the young man, 'Detective Sergeant. You're a very fortunate man to have such capable mentor. I have him to thank for my present circumstances.' This was said with a smile and no hint of malice towards Jellicoe. It was clear there was not just a respect for the older policeman who had caught him, but a liking also. Kit sensed a similar regard in Jellicoe.

'Take a seat, gentlemen. Can I offer you a drink?' asked Hadleigh.

# The Phantom

Kit nearly fell off his seat as he realised Hadleigh had a drinks cabinet as well.

'A little early for me, Mr Hadleigh,' said Jellicoe before turning to Kit with one eyebrow raised archly and the trace of a smile, 'Lord Aston?'

'Thank you but a little early for me, also.'

Hadleigh was a couple of inches out of danger of being short. Some lines were apparent on the fine contours of his face. Dressed in a prison uniform that could have been cut by Saville Row, his slender frame was clearly well maintained. His hair was greying with just a hint that it was receding at the temple, but he remained, to all intents and purposes, a good looking and successful man, notwithstanding the curious environment in which he appeared to be residing rather than incarcerated.

Kit became fascinated by the hands of Hadleigh. They could have been those of a pianist. Long and perfectly manicured, they seemed to have an external life to the rest of the body. Their movement was graceful yet precise. It was as if they could reveal the character of the man, the most famous cat burglar of his day. The man who became a thief, not through need but because he could, for the thrill: it was a choice. It was perhaps on this basis the judge had sentenced him so harshly.

Brickhill appeared satisfied that all was in order and said, 'I shall leave you gentlemen to your meeting.' Hadleigh nodded to the Chief Warder as he turned to leave the cell.

Turning to his guests, Hadleigh said, 'Well, gentlemen, as much as I would like to believe this a social call, I presume we have business to conduct. Please have a seat.'

Jellicoe's eyes crinkled just enough to suggest a smile and he and Ryan sat down.

'Yes, Mr Hadleigh. We do have some questions. I hope we won't detain you long'

Hadleigh resisted the temptation to point out he was being detained for at least another five to ten years. Instead, he raised his eyebrows and smiled.

"My apologies,' continued Jellicoe as it dawned on him what he had said. Over the next few minutes, Jellicoe outlined details of the three robberies that had taken place in London over the previous few months. Kit wandered over by the bookcase and looked at his library. His tastes were eclectic, ranging from the classics to science and philosophy. Some of these tomes were in French and German.

Every so often, as Jellicoe outlined why they were here, Kit would glance at Hadleigh. He was sitting forward and listening intently, a smile never far away from his face. He nodded as the Chief Inspector spoke but did not interrupt. When Jellicoe had finished, Hadleigh sat back and exhaled.

Turning to Kit he asked, 'If I may, Lord Aston, what is your involvement in this case?'

'By all means. I was at Lord Wolf's on the night that the robbery was discovered.'

'I see. But even so, Lord Aston, that still doesn't quite explain your presence here today. If you don't mind me pointing out, you're just a witness, not a detective.'

Kit laughed, 'I certainly don't claim to be a detective.'

Jellicoe glanced at Kit, who stopped to let the policeman speak.

'Lord Aston's being somewhat disingenuous, if you don't mind me saying, sir. He was instrumental in helping resolve a recent case. I thought it would be an idea to bring him along to meet you.'

Hadleigh smiled broadly, 'And obtain his thoughts also, no doubt. Are you worried you have the wrong man, Chief Inspector? You know, each crime committed by this thief will add to the evidence in this regard. I haven't read anything in the newspapers about a new Phantom, although the first two crimes you mentioned did capture my attention.'

Jellicoe's face suggested there was a smile buried underneath his beard.

'No, Mr Hadleigh, as you've correctly guessed, we've withheld some details of the crimes not, I would add, for fear we've made a mistake in your case, but principally to avoid distractions in apprehending this thief.'

'I understand, Chief Inspector. Now, you clearly believe I can help you in some way otherwise you wouldn't be here.'

'Perhaps, Mr Hadleigh,' nodded Jellicoe. 'Is there anyone, to your knowledge who would have either your, shall we say, unique skills in this field, that we might consider speaking to?'

Hadleigh shook his head, 'I'm sorry, Chief Inspector, but as you may have gathered back then, I was never a part of the criminal underworld. What I can't understand is how this thief can imitate the Phantom so perfectly. It has to be someone who knew every detail of the Phantom's technique.'

'A gentleman player?' suggested Kit.

'Perhaps, Lord Aston. Or perhaps a member of the police,' replied Hadleigh smiling. 'Perhaps the Chief Inspector is preparing for his retirement.'

This made Jellicoe smile before he acknowledged, 'I'm a little past such a caper.'

Hadleigh turned to the young sergeant and with wry smile said, 'But this young man certainly isn't.' Ryan, not knowing what to make of this, remained silent while Hadleigh continued, 'Presumably the valuables stolen will need to be sold. Have you looked at the usual channels for distribution?'

'We've been speaking to some of the gentlemen who specialise in this area,' said Jellicoe.

'I suspect they're under surveillance. I can't imagine they'd be very forthcoming, otherwise.'

'They're not,' said Jellicoe, neatly dodging the question and moving on to another topic. 'Is there any possibility that your calling card may have found its way into someone else's hands?'

Hadleigh laughed, 'Well, Chief Inspector, as I always proclaimed my innocence, I think it better if I speak in the abstract rather than the specific. Let's assume that the calling card design did fall into someone else's hands, how is of less importance now. The design itself, which we both know was never made public, is easily replicable by any common or garden printer. This, of course, is conjecture, but there are any number of ways this could have happened: a leak at Scotland Yard, perish the thought, being one. The original printer could have supplied details of the design to a n'er-do-well, another. One of the unfortunate victims of the dastardly Phantom could've done likewise. You see there are any number of ways that this thief could have come by the design from the Phantom's calling card. But I'm sure that you've already begun enquiries along these lines, Chief Inspector.'

Jellicoe by means of the merest movement of his head confirmed Hadleigh's thesis.

# The Phantom

'Why would someone want to impersonate the Phantom?' asked Kit.

'Well,' said Hadleigh with a smile, 'Hypothetically, you understand, if I am the Phantom, and this is not an admission, then there are a number of thoughts that strike me. Firstly, perhaps someone wants to demonstrate that the good Chief Inspector caught the wrong man. This opens a wide field of inquiry, some of which might be embarrassing for my old friend, Jellicoe. Alternatively, it could be some fantasist. This would be quite a dangerous fellow I imagine, as who knows where such make-believe may lead?'

All the while Hadleigh was speaking, Kit found himself wrestling with an overwhelming certainty that their paths had crossed. Occasionally he would see a look from Hadleigh that confirmed this suspicion. But where? And when? The feeling was almost unendurable.

'This may seem like a strange question, but have we met before, Mr Hadleigh?' asked Kit, unable to suppress the question any longer.

Hadleigh laughed, 'If you remember, I was rather famous, or infamous, at one point, thanks to the Chief Inspector's efforts.'

This was a possible answer, Kit acknowledged, but he also sensed Hadleigh had deftly avoided a direct response. Rather than pursue the thought, Kit, with some degree of exasperation with himself, let it drop and allowed Jellicoe to continue the interview.

'How do you feel about the existence of this Phantom?'

'Well, if he is an impostor, then I imagine the real Phantom would feel both flattered by the imitation and quite pleased that someone else could take the fall for his crimes. Don't you think, Detective Sergeant?'

Ryan looked at Hadleigh in surprise. Until this point Ryan had been surprisingly quiet. Kit was not sure if Hadleigh was being polite and including him in the conversation or had another motive. The look on Jellicoe's face suggested he was of a like mind.

'Perhaps the real Phantom might be concerned an impostor could do something to tarnish his reputation, though,' said Ryan. Kit nodded to Jellicoe, while Hadleigh burst out laughing.

'Touché, young man,' replied Hadleigh. It seemed to Kit Hadleigh said this with something approaching relief. It was another thing to ponder. Jellicoe looked at Ryan without saying anything, but the twinkle was unmistakeable.

It became clear that the meeting was ending. Jellicoe stood up and rapped the door, which was opened by a guard. The farewells were warm on the part of Hadleigh and Jellicoe, the mutual regard undisguised. Kit looked closely at Ryan and Hadleigh as they shook hands. The impression Kit drew was of two men assessing one another and, overall, liking what they saw. Kit wasn't sure if Jellicoe had picked up on the undercurrent. He would check this a later, he decided.

Outside the cell, the three men walked along the corridor with Brickhill, who had returned to collect them.

'What did you think of Hadleigh, Lord Aston?'

'Fascinating. A very charismatic man. A lot to think about from that meeting.'

'Indeed,' said Jellicoe eyeing Kit closely.

'A cliché, I know, but he knows more than he's letting on,' continued Kit.

'Yes,' agreed Jellicoe, 'I had that feeling also. By the way, why did you think you'd met previously?'

'I'm damned if I can put my finger on why, Chief Inspector, but it was a strong feeling.'

Jellicoe nodded and then turning to Brickhill, and asked, 'Is it possible to see the other prisoner?'

'Of course, follow me,' replied Brickhill.

The four men reached the end of the corridor and descended a flight of stairs to a basement corridor. Kit felt his senses tingling. He wasn't sure if it was excitement, anger, or fear.

The corridor mirrored the one up above. The group went to the first door and the guard gave it a rap. The keys clanked noisily against the door. Finally, it opened, and Kit looked inside to see a very different type of cell. It was small, there was no window, just a naked light. Lying on the bed was a man. He turned over as the two detectives and Kit entered.

It took a few moments for Kit to register who the man was. Then he realised. He was staring into the face of Leonid Daniels.

Chapter 9

Judson Fish had been with Lady Agatha for longer than either of them cared to remember. She inherited him by marriage, following her union with the late Eustace, or 'Useless', Frost, as she called him. Often.

Lord Frost had passed away in 1911 in Agadir. A lifer in the diplomatic corps, Frost had spent many years in various posts in the Middle East and north Africa, arriving in Morocco days before the first German crisis. He believed, rightly as it turned out, this event heralded the birth of a new phase of German expansionism and that war was inevitable. Convinced that the German gunboat which had pulled into Agadir harbour, as he and Lady Agatha were taking a short break from his work at the embassy, was the first phase of his long-predicted war sadly proved too much for a constitution he had spent decades fortifying with rich food and vats of brandy.

Lady Agatha returned with Fish to England and set up home in Grosvenor Square, where they had resided these last nine years. Thankfully, her ladyship, although not necessarily blessed with the easiest of personalities, was at least quite low maintenance. Her relatives were few and friends fewer still. She entertained rarely, holidayed often, and confined her interests to occasional and quite devastating interventions in her family's affairs. In the case of her brother, and Kit's father, Lancelot Aston, affairs was certainly the operative word.

The lack of any real work to do in the house encouraged a certain torpor in Fish bordering on indolence. That and the fact that he was even more elderly than the mistress of the house combined to create a certain resentment when called upon to execute what few duties remained to him. Such as leaving his comfortable seat in the kitchen to answer the phone upstairs.

The phone was ringing insistently on this particular morning. He guessed it was someone who knew Lady Agatha as it rang for an inordinate amount of time. The caller clearly understood that he was no longer the lithe athlete of yesteryear and that his arrival to the phone would be measured in minutes rather than seconds.

Fish took to the telephone like a boulder to water. The shrill ring of the infernal device was always certain to produce a sinking feeling in the estimable butler's heart. This was because, in common with most people of a certain age, new technology brought out his inner Luddite. He hated the contraption and cursed the day Lady Agatha had been persuaded by that demonic Simpson woman to bring the evil device into her house.

'Lady Frost's residence. Miss Simpson, so nice to hear from you. Again. Lady Frost is having lunch. I shall inform her directly. Just a moment.'

Fish set the phone receiver down and went to the dining room. A minute later Agatha arrived at the phone.

'Hullo, Betty, what news?'

For the next minute Agatha listened and then said, 'I shall let Mary know and then we will plan our next steps. Good work, Betty.'

Replacing the phone, Agatha went into the dining room to apprise Mary of the news from her friend.

'Betty has managed to locate Caroline Hadleigh,' said Agatha excitedly to Mary, who was eating some toast.

'That's good news. I don't think the police will particularly like the idea of us visiting Miss Hadleigh but there's no reason why...'

'We can't follow her,' finished Agatha, 'My thoughts exactly. Let me write down the address before I forget.'

For the next few minutes, the two ladies outlined a plan of action.

'So, we're agreed. Alfred will take you to Eaton Square tomorrow and you can follow her on foot. Alfred can stay in touch with you at a distance. Did you have anything planned with Christopher tomorrow?'

'We'd planned on going to the Royal Academy and then lunch at the Ritz,' said Mary.

'Right, my dear, I suggest you rearrange that. Stick to the lunch but suggest visiting the Royal Academy in the afternoon. You're needed in the morning. Tell Christopher you're meeting Betty. This will be true, of course. And today, when will he be coming?'

'He said he'd come to me late afternoon, probably. I'll suggest we dine together here rather than going out.'

'Good idea. We can pump him for information on today's events,' replied Agatha, eyes alive. She was almost pawing the ground with excitement.

78

# The Phantom

Mary smiled at the elderly lady. When Esther had left to spend a week with Richard at his parents' house, she'd been worried about how things would be at Kit's infamous Aunt Agatha's house without her co-conspirator. The sudden turn of events was proving that every cloud might contain a golden goose.

The thought that life in London when Kit was not around would prove more amenable than she could have imagined also made her feel positively chipper. The chance to prove her skills as a detective, at such an early stage, was a marker she wanted to lay down for their future together. All in all, she reflected, this is turning out rather nicely. However, whether it was the curiosity about Kit's meeting with Scotland Yard and the Phantom himself, or simply the prospect of seeing him again, Mary felt excited about the evening ahead.

-

Leon Daniels was every bit as big as Kit remembered but his appearance had altered dramatically in the few weeks since Kit had last seen him. His eyes were black. There were cuts around both eyes and his face. Although Kit had little sympathy for the man, he was a cold-blooded murderer after all, he was appalled by the sight. However, he recognised that this treatment was probably inevitable both as retribution as well as a tactic to obtain information. Kit questioned its utility of the latter and the morality in the former.

One glance towards Jellicoe confirmed in Kit's mind that the Chief Inspector was no more comfortable about the treatment meted out to Daniels than he was. Kit wondered if Jellicoe was a supporter, or not, of capital punishment. There was little question, though, Leon Daniels was destined for the hangman's noose.

Daniels recognised both Kit and Jellicoe immediately. He was in agony. His body had been beaten severely and his head pounded from the pain. He nodded to them and smiled grimly.

'Mr Daniels,' said Jellicoe, much to Brickhill's chagrin and Kit's undisguised surprise, 'perhaps we should all sit down.'

Daniels nodded gratefully. It was too painful to stand.

'I won't ask you how you're being treated,' continued Jellicoe, clearly unhappy by what he was seeing, and equally intent on conveying a message for Brickhill. 'I will assume that you've not supplied the information requested.'

Daniels raised one eyebrow but remained silent.

'You'll doubtless remember Lord Aston.'

Daniels looked at Kit. There was neither hate nor resentment in this look. Kit realised that Daniels accepted his fate. He was a soldier. He took orders. These orders required him to kill. Implicit within the act of killing is the risk at that moment, or at some point in the future, of your life also being similarly imperilled. That time had arrived.

Once again Kit reflected on his own actions during the War. He'd killed men. He had ordered men to kill. The difference he believed, he hoped, was in the context. Those same men were trying to kill him; they were trying to kill his fellow soldiers; they were invaders. The victims of Daniels were, in this sense, innocent. However, sickened he was by the sight of Daniels, the man deserved no sympathy.

Kit nodded to Daniels, and then much to his own surprise, addressed him.

'I understand you speak English well.' This prompted no reaction from Daniels other than to continue looking at Kit. 'I presume you've been made aware that you were taking orders from two former British secret servicemen, one of whom, Kopel, had gone rogue.'

For the first time, Daniels acknowledged what was being said. He made one curt nod.

'The man you knew as Kopel is, in fact, Lord Olly Lake. He was a friend of mine. We were at school together. We grew up together. He's an enemy of mine now. An enemy of yours also. Of your country. You realise this, don't you?'

Silence. There was no reaction from Daniels to this. Kit gazed back at Daniels. It seemed there was no one else in the room. The only sound to be heard was the laboured breathing of Daniels.

Kit reached inside his coat to his breast pocket and took out a wallet. He opened it and extracted a small photograph which he handed over to Daniels. The big Russian looked from Kit to the photograph.

'What do you see?' asked Kit.

Daniels held the photograph up to his eyes. He moved it back a little so that his eyes could focus better on the image. The photograph showed four boys; all were around ten years old. There was also a man in the photograph. They were sitting by a pond. One of the boys was holding a toy. It was a three-mast sailing boat. The boy looked like the man before him in the cell. Beside this boy, was unmistakably the smiling figure of a young Kopel. Daniels handed the photograph back to Kit who placed it in his wallet and returned it to his breast pocket.

'You understand, don't you? He used you. He ordered you to murder innocent people. Innocent people, Mr Daniels,' repeated Kit more forcefully. Kit knew this had hit home. He pressed on. 'You were a soldier. You followed orders. But these orders were not enacted on behalf of your country. They were enacted on behalf of an organisation that wishes to undermine your country and mine. They are anarchists. We don't know what their objective is, but they are evil and must be stopped.'

Kit wanted to ask for Daniels' help. But how could he? Looking at the battered face of the Russian and asking him to help the people who had tortured him would have seemed like a sick joke. An act of hypocrisy. He realised the senselessness of torture lay not just in its illegality or even its immorality; quite simply it was ineffective. Perhaps Daniels could have helped the Intelligence Service find Olly. But that time was long gone.

There was no farewell. Daniels remained uncommunicative. Outside the cell Jellicoe glared at Brickhill.

'Was all that really necessary?'

Brickhill smiled cruelly and replied, 'Orders, old chap. Orders.'

Harry Miller opened the passenger door as the group, seen off by Hastings, walked back to the car. It was clear that Jellicoe was angry and Hastings, sensing an atmosphere, did not prolong the parting with any unnecessary chit chat.

Inside the car, Kit looked at Jellicoe and said, 'I don't like what's happened to Daniels any more than you, Chief Inspector, but you seem particularly angry.'

Jellicoe was silent for a moment and then replied, 'Principles aside, the plain fact is Daniels may be a killer, but he only did so because he was ordered. He had an opportunity to kill me but chose not to.'

'He was surrounded. Surely he knew he would be killed?'

# The Phantom

'No and yes. I've thought about that moment a lot, as you may imagine. There were several men with me; four were armed. He could easily have taken a couple of us with him. He chose to stop the killing. Oddly, if you think about it, he saved my life.'

Kit smiled and agreed, 'Well, in an odd sort of a way, I suppose you're right.'

-

Sally Ryan sat in the front room of the house. On a table in front of her sat a pile of assorted coats, trousers, skirts, and socks. Her fingers felt sore after a morning stitching together poor-quality clothes that were falling apart. Despite the dull ache, she liked the work. It was mechanical which meant she didn't have to think about it. Instead, her mind began to wander. To dream.

The sound of keys in the door made her start. Then she saw her husband walk in. Ryan looked down at Sally and saw fear descend on her, removing the colour from her cheeks and the life force in from her body.

'What's happened?' she asked, tears forming in her eyes.

Joe walked over to her, sat down, and put his arm around her. Outside the sound of rain began to beat heavier on the street and the windows.

'I was laid off Sal, but I've found another job already.'

'I don't understand,' said Sally, clearly upset by the news.

Ryan explained to her what had happened leaving out only the extortion by his new work colleagues. The news was a mixed blessing, they decided. It would be painful not to have her husband around in the evenings with the two children, but both recognised that working in the varnish factory was irritating Ryan's lungs, which had already been damaged by exposure to gas during the War. The money wasn't great, but they had just enough. Perhaps Ryan could find another job during the day.

'How's my boy?' asked Ryan.

'Sleeping. Wasn't so bad today.'

Ryan nodded. He went over to the bedroom and opened the door. Lying on the bed was his son. Ryan stood for a few moments and listened to the laboured sounds of the boy's breathing. The tell-tale whistling of severe asthma. He was joined at the door by Sally. They glanced at one another and then back to the boy. In some sense, their life was brutally simple. It was about survival. To get Ben through these few years and hope he could grow out of his illness. Taking the job was his only option.

Ryan turned away from the room and quietly shut the door. He held Sally as much to comfort himself as to comfort her.

'We'll be all right, Sal. Just you see.'

'Do you really think?' asked Sally.

'Yes, Sal. Really.'

Sally didn't look up at him, but he sensed her tears. He held her closer still. Maybe a second job was the answer. Something during the day. A little extra money.

# The Phantom

## Chapter 10

'Hello, darling,' said Kit walking towards Mary.

Mary smiled and knelt to stroke Kit's dog, Sam, and replied, 'Hello, darling,' to the terrier.

'Am I in the doghouse?' said Kit looking down at Sam nuzzling Mary.

Mary stood on tip toe and pecked Kit on the cheek.

'I haven't decided yet, Lord Aston,' said Mary looking Kit in the eye. She brushed a hair off the shoulder of Kit's tuxedo then knelt and picked up the ever-willing Sam.

'Yes, he is,' said Agatha arriving in the hallway. 'I think you've quite a nerve, young man, to leave this poor young lady behind as you swan off on a new case.'

Kit rolled his eyes and said, 'I'm not on a new case, Aunt Agatha. My involvement as of today is over. Chief Inspector Jellicoe is more than capable of handling this matter without my help.'

'How did you spend the day?' asked Kit over dinner.

Mary looked at Agatha before saying, 'We read a lot in the morning and we even tried to piece together a jigsaw puzzle. Unfortunately, there are a few pieces missing.'

This comment nearly made Agatha choke and she began coughing. Kit immediately poured her some water and gently patted her back. Agatha quickly regained control but gave

Mary a look that suggested that she warn her in future if she was going to be humorous.

Mary continued, 'After lunch we took a walk in the gardens. Alas the rain cut short our stroll, so we returned somewhat bedraggled back to the house to await my lord and master. Have a drink.' Mary poured some wine in Kit's glass and looked at him intently.

Kit noted the sardonic tone and ignored it. He glanced down at the wine then said, 'Trying to loosen my tongue?'

'I doubt she's going to try to seduce you in my house, Christopher, so please get on with it. What happened today with the police?' asked Agatha, impatience pouring from every pore.

Mary made a sad face which Agatha could not see but Kit interpreted all too hopefully. As an interrogation team they presented a highly effective, and certainly original, take on good cop, bad cop.

'Very well,' said Kit resignedly.

Mary's face lit up in a grin that made Kit wish they were alone, while Sam hopped up onto a chair to hear more. For the next hour Kit went through, in forensic detail due to the questions of the two ladies, the events of the day. This included the meeting with Leon Daniels. However, he refrained from describing the treatment of Daniels, partly from a desire to protect the ladies but also because of his feeling of repugnance and guilt.

Conversation turned to plans for the next day. Mary glanced at Agatha who put her hand up to stop Mary from saying anything.

'Christopher, do you mind if you delay your trip to the Royal Academy? Perhaps make it tomorrow afternoon? Betty

Simpson is coming over tomorrow morning. I believe she's keen to meet Mary.'

Kit looked at Agatha and then Mary. He smiled and said, 'Of course. Give my love to Betty.' Mary's face was difficult to read but Kit sensed something was afoot.

'Excellent. I'm sure Betty and Mary will get on winningly,' said Agatha. Then observing the fact that Sam had taken up a position on Mary's knee, a further thought seemed to strike her. 'Why don't you leave Sam here? You know how much Betty likes dogs. I doubt Sam will complain. Pass the salt, my dear.'

Sam by now was all but necking with Mary. Kit smiled and shook his head feigning exasperation with the little dog.

'Any chance we can swap places, Sam?' asked Kit. This brought a look of rebuke from Aunt Agatha, but Mary smiled, widened her eyes, and nodded imperceptibly. Changing the subject, Kit asked, 'Any word from the love birds in Sussex?'

'I gather Esther is unwell,' chipped in Agatha before Mary could say anything. Mary turned slowly to Agatha; her eyes narrowed. However, Agatha persisted, 'Yes, she may have to extend her stay, I understand.'

'I'm sorry to hear that. What's wrong?'

Mary felt like asking the same question. However, it was clear that the question was being addressed to her, so she turned to Kit with a smile and said, 'I'm sure it's nothing.'

'Let's hope so,' said Kit with concern.

Unnoticed by Kit, Mary and Agatha exchanged looks. The old lady gave a slight shrug and continued with her soup.

-

The rain had eased off as Joe Ryan made his way back to the factory. Darkness was drawing in, throwing a blanket over the streets. This did little to improve the beauty of the surroundings but increased Ryan's sense of ghostly unease as he walked towards the plant. A chill north wind was blowing. Snow was coming.

Groups of men were exiting from the facility. A few stragglers, like himself, were going in the opposite direction. He made his way through the same entrance from earlier and walked over to a group of men who were standing with Rusk. The group turned to look at Ryan but there was no welcome greeting, so Ryan did not offer any back. Instead, he stood with the group and waited.

Over the next few minutes, a couple of other men joined the group. Ryan was reassured to see their reception was no warmer than his. Soon, Ryan became aware that Rusk was counting the number of people. His mouth twisted into a peculiar grimace that Ryan took to be a smile.

'Stay here,' ordered Rusk and walked off in the direction of Johnny Mac's office. A few minutes later he returned alongside the towering figure of the Ulsterman. The man beside Ryan whispered to him, 'Big lad that one.'

Ryan nodded but said nothing.

'Are you new here?' asked the man. His accent was strange. Part British, part European.

'Yes. You?'

'Yes,' came the reply.

Johnny Mac surveyed the group for a few moments and then bent and whispered something to Rusk. As far as Ryan could tell, the comment seemed to amuse the shorter man. A quick scan of the other men's faces suggested they were all like himself, new to the job. They were a rough lot but overall, he judged them to be in the same boat as him. This was confirmed a few moments later.

'You men are very lucky to be here. Lose one job and then find one in the blink of an eye,' said Rusk. 'My name's Rusk, but you can call me sir.' He laughed humourlessly at his own joke. Even Johnny Mac looked unimpressed. He turned, glanced up at the giant beside him and shrugged.

'I'm Johnny. You can call me whatever you want,' said Johnny Mac. For the first time Ryan noticed that two of his top teeth, at the side, were black. A deep black. It looked like they had been painted rather than being a result of neglect. It made his appearance even more menacing. 'Rusk will show you the ropes.'

Following that short statement, he turned and walked away from the group, leaving Rusk. 'All right, I'll show you around.'

For the next fifteen minutes Rusk conducted a tour of the factory, explaining the process of making the products and the role of each machine. Although quite different from the varnish factory, Ryan quickly grasped that the key principles were similar. One part of the factory made the product; another part packaged it. Whether by accident or design, Ryan found himself paired with the man he'd spoken with briefly earlier. Rusk assigned them to packing the cigarettes as they came off the production line. After Rusk had left them to sort out the other men, Ryan held out his hand.

'Joe Ryan.'

'Abbott, Richard Abbott.'

Abbott was around forty and half a foot shorter than Ryan with relatively dark skin and jet-black hair. There was more than a trace of an accent. He looked up at Ryan with his moon eyes and explained a little of his background as the machine cranked into gear.

'My dad was English, my mum Austrian. I grew up in Vienna but moved over here when I was young,' said Abbott reading the mind of Ryan. Conversation was cut short as the machine began to spew cigarettes onto a conveyor belt. They looked at one another and made a start on with the job. Ryan had a feeling his arms would ache the next morning.

Ryan and Abbott chatted occasionally as they worked. He learned more about his colleague, almost as much from what he did not say as what he did. He sensed that Abbott had flirted with the other side of the law and perhaps had spent time in prison. He'd clearly not gone to France, but Ryan was not interested in why. At least the subject of the War was avoided. It was over. He was here. He didn't want to think about it anymore.

Aside from one short break for a snack, Ryan worked almost continuously with Abbott for eight hours. As he had surmised, his arms and wrists ached with the effort of packing the cigarettes.

The night shift ended around four in the morning. Ryan had never been much of a smoker but by the end of this shift he never wanted to see a cigarette again. The workers trooped into a line walking wearily away from the factory gates. Abbott fell in step with Ryan.

Abbott lit a cigarette and handed it to Ryan, then he lit one for himself, 'These managed to find their way into my pocket. Not sure how.' He laughed at his own joke. Ryan looked at the cigarette with disgust and then smiled at Abbott.

'Sick to death of these things,' said Ryan handing the cigarette back to Abbott. The little man shrugged and blew out the light, putting the stub in his pocket. 'Do you think they'll revolve people onto different machines? I'm not sure I can take that night after night,' asked Ryan.

There was a sly look on the face of the small man. It added little to his attractiveness. He was clearly pondering something. Finally, after glancing around to make sure no one was around, he replied, 'The only thing about where we are is that it might offer potential.'

'How do you mean?'

'I mean they can't keep their eyes on us all the time. What if a few cigarettes were to find their way into our hands? Just a few. We don't have to be greedy. I'm sure we could make a bit of extra money, don't you think?'

Ryan looked at Abbott. It was clear the little Anglo-Austrian was serious. It wasn't a bad idea. A little bit each night could build quite nicely. If they kept their wits that is. There had been no searches as they left the factory gates.

'What do you think?' persisted Abbott.

Ryan thought about his brother, a policeman. Not only a policeman, but one who was making rapid progress in the force. What would he think? This would only be an issue if they were caught. Was it worth the risk? Then he thought about young Ben.

'Yes, I think it's an idea,' replied Ryan, nodding his head.

They looked at one another and shook hands.

Chapter 11

*February 13ʰ, 1920: London*

The pitter-patter of rain on the window woke Mary. She'd hoped that her first dive into the world of surveillance would be made easier by benign weather. The gods of undercover detection were not going to be with her this morning. She rose from the bed and walked to the window. It was almost five in the morning. The lights on the street danced off the wet pavement. Yes, detective work was perhaps not going to be quite as glamorous as she'd first envisaged. On the bed, Sam was gently snoring. She walked over to the little terrier and gently stroked him behind the ear.

'Wakey, wakey. You've work to do this morning.'

Sam continued to snore.

'Men,' said Mary dismissively, moving towards the bathroom, 'you're all the same.'

Twenty minutes later she was met downstairs by Aunt Agatha and the chauffeur, Alfred. Neither Mary nor Alfred was, particularly, chipper, but Agatha was in fine fettle. Mary turned down the suggestion of breakfast. Alfred looked, as ever, like he'd eaten breakfast for three. Sam had finally woken and was keen to be fed and wolfed down bacon and sausage.

# The Phantom

'Well then, let's say goodbye,' said Agatha, keen to get everyone on their way and get herself back to bed, 'Best of luck.'

Mary and Sam followed Alfred out to the Rolls.

'Not the most inconspicuous,' said Mary sardonically. "Do you know where we're going?'

'Yes, ma'am,' replied Alfred, holding the door open for Mary.

The journey to Eaton Square was completed in a matter of minutes such was the eerie emptiness of the London streets. At Mary's suggestion, Alfred parked the car alongside a large Bentley. This gave them an unobstructed view of the road ahead and the front door to Caroline Hadleigh's town house with the added benefit of not looking entirely out of place.

It was nearly six and still night. Sam sat happily on Mary's lap as they waited. At one point a policeman strolled by and stopped to look at the car. He rapped on Alfred's window.

'Is everything, all right?' he asked looking at Sam and Mary in the back.

'Yes, constable,' replied Mary. 'I'm just waiting for the rain to stop and then I'll take my dog for a walk.'

'Very good, madam. It's an awful morning.' The policeman seemed satisfied with this explanation and went on his way.

Alfred looked in the mirror at Mary, something he had spent a large part of the journey doing, much to her amusement.

'Good thinking, ma'am.'

'Thank you. I was being honest. What an awful day,' replied Mary looking out at the rain falling steadily onto the pavement. As a rule, she loved the sound of rain. It was strangely therapeutic. However, the prospect of having to go out when it was so bad was about as appealing as a trip to the dentist.

In the distance, the booming notes of Big Ben indicated it was six o'clock in the morning. Mary idly wondered how people living near to the clock put up with the beastly sound.

And so, they waited. And waited some more. Sam fell asleep again. Mary looked down and envied him. She was beginning to worry this detective game was not as she had envisioned. Trailing master criminals, remarkable leaps of the imagination to connect the seemingly unconnected, and exciting shootouts seemed a million miles away from what she was doing at that moment.

At seven, Big Ben woke up Sam who looked around confusedly and began barking before remembering his attractive companion and standing on her lap pressing his face up to hers, perhaps in penitence at his over-reaction.

'Ma'am, the door's opening,' said Alfred, pointing towards the house under observation.

Mary glanced away from Sam. A young woman emerged from the house dressed in a long light brown mackintosh and flat shoes. She wore a head scarf but there was no mistaking her for someone older. She was in her early twenties and, even from fifty yards, very attractive. A strand of blonde hair fell from the front of the scarf. She walked down the steps and away from the parked car.

'What shall I do, ma'am?' asked Alfred.

'Let her walk to the end of the street. If she turns, then drive forward but remain out of sight.'

They both waited and watched Caroline walk straight ahead. Mary said, 'She might be heading in the direction of Sloane Square. When she gets to the next street move forward then park near to where she is now. I'll take Sam for a walk at this point. There are quite a few small cafes up ahead. We can't risk losing her.'

'Very good,' replied Alfred, and soon they were moving forward in the direction of Sloane Square. They stopped at the point Mary had suggested and she hopped out of the car with Sam.

The rain had stopped by now, but Mary was glad of her thick overcoat. It was very cold. Sam was wearing a stylish tweed coat but still seemed reluctant to walk in the decidedly chilly air.

'You really are a bit lazy, aren't you?' laughed Mary. Sam seemed to grumble in reply. 'I don't think you can buy doggie earmuffs old boy.'

Ahead, Caroline Hadleigh had slowed down as she passed a few shops. Mary checked her pace and bent down on a couple of occasions to pet Sam. In fact, Mary was now grateful that Sam was a bit lazy. Trying to keep a hold of him if he'd gone tearing ahead would have presented a problem or two.

Her quarry was back on the move and heading, as Mary had surmised, towards Sloane Square. Finally, she appeared to reach her destination which was a large café that Mary recognised. Mary walked past the café and saw it was fairly full. This made it more difficult for her to enter as she had Sam and it was not clear if dogs were allowed. Mary turned and saw Alfred was some way behind, stuck in traffic. This was a dilemma.

Mary crossed over the road to avoid being seen. From this position she could still monitor the comings and goings from the café. Meanwhile Alfred was gradually getting closer. Frustratingly, it was difficult to see Caroline due to customers sitting by the window. Another look towards the car. It was still too far away to be able to deposit Sam. One or two people were leaving now. Not Caroline Hadleigh, however.

Finally, Alfred's car was at a point where Mary could safely walk over and leave Sam while maintaining an eye on the café. She attracted Alfred's attention and motioned for him to pull over. Picking Sam up she jogged across the road between cars to Alfred.

Opening the rear passenger door, she dropped Sam into the back and instructed Alfred to wait. Closing the door, she made her way quickly to the café and entered.

There was no sign of Caroline Hadleigh.

Mary was shocked. Then she reasoned that she may have gone to the bathroom. Attracting the attention of a waitress she ordered a tea and then explained she needed to visit the cloakroom.

On her way there, a couple of women went past her, but neither were of interest. Once inside the bathroom the alarming fact dawned on her. Caroline Hadleigh was not there. She'd given Mary the slip.

-

Agatha and Betty looked at each other and then back to Mary. Kit's aunt asked the two questions on everyone's mind.

'How did she do it? And more important even, why? Was she aware she was being followed?'

'There's absolutely no chance you could've missed her when you were getting Sam into the car?' added Betty.

'None. My eyes barely left the café for a second. Furthermore, where would she have gone except further down the street? It would've been impossible not to see her.'

'Was she carrying a large bag?' asked Agatha.

'Yes, I was wondering about that afterwards. It could've contained a change of clothes because it was certainly a large enough bag.'

'This is very interesting,' said Agatha, 'And it definitely puts a new complexion on the case.'

Betty's eyes lit up and she said, 'Well, in that case I may have something else that will interest you. I did some digging into Miss Hadleigh and I found out from an acquaintance that she was expelled from one of her schools when she was in her teens.'

'Do you know why?' asked Agatha.

The smile on Betty's face grew wider and she leaned forward, 'Stealing.'

The room grew silent as the three ladies considered the implications of Betty's revelation. Finally, Agatha gave voice to the thought shared by everyone.

'A kleptomaniac?'

'Very possibly,' replied Betty. 'Now, having heard about Miss Hadleigh this morning, I think we have enough evidence to continue our surveillance.'

'But how?' asked Mary.

'I have an idea,' responded Betty.

'Go on,' said the other two ladies in unison.

'You and I shall return to Eaton Square, Agatha, and spend the rest of the afternoon there to await Miss Hadleigh's return.'

Agatha looked at Mary and said, 'Good idea, but how do we get there and where do we wait? We'll need the car and Alfred's away to his film studio. I don't know about you dear, but I for one don't fancy standing outside in the cold. Quite apart from this, it would look distinctly odd.'

'I can drive,' suggested Betty brightly. 'I've driven cars before.'

'No harm to you, my dear, but a Rolls Royce isn't any car,' pointed out Agatha, 'Even I am wary of driving it.' Mary smiled at the two elderly drivers, but she also felt proud of them.

'Nonsense. I'm sure we'll manage,' replied Betty, oblivious to the undisguised scepticism of her two companions.

'What shall I do in the meantime?' asked Mary, not sure whether to be amused or alarmed at the prospect of the elderly Betty negotiating London traffic in a Rolls Royce.

'Stick to your plans with Christopher for the moment. There's no point raising any suspicion. Your fiancé, unlike most of the male sex, is no fool.'

-

The Ritz dining room was humming with activity. All around Kit and Mary, the serving staff machine purred with efficiency. Rich people eating even richer food in sumptuous surroundings.

'Are you sure you don't want a sweet?' asked Kit looking down at the space on the table where Mary's dessert should have been.

'Would you have me like one of those ladies that Rubens, or his assistants, liked to paint?' responded Mary, with a mock frown.

'No, I rather like you as you are. Your discipline is to be admired. In fact, I rather look forward to spending many a happy hour admiring the results of your discipline,' said Kit tucking into his dessert with relish. This proved too much for the Spartan warrior in front of him, and she deftly removed the spoon from Kit's hand and tried some for herself.

## The Phantom

'Not bad,' said Mary, handing back the spoon and wiping some cream from the side of her mouth with her finger in a way that made Kit consider seriously booking a room there and then.

The momentary and blissful distraction over, Kit asked Mary, 'How about we skip the Royal Academy today and head over Whitehall direction?'

Mary brightened at this idea, 'The London Conference. Can we get in?'

'We might be able to see some of the stir. I doubt we'd get into the committee rooms though.'

Miller collected the couple on Piccadilly and Kit told him of the change in plan.

'Very good, sir.'

A few minutes later Miller dropped them off on Whitehall. They walked towards a building where a small crowd was assembled. There were policemen standing outside the building watching the various groups. A handful of men and women were holding up banners demanding Kurdish independence. A small group nearby had similar placards related to a Jewish homeland. Dark-suited men of varying nationality entered and exited from the building straight into waiting cars. The level of security seemed somewhat disproportionate to the threat suggested Mary. Kit smiled; recent events had shown him that danger could come from the least expected places.

'Isn't that your friend Spunky over there by the entrance?' said Mary pointing towards the building.

'Good Lord. So it is,' said Kit, laughing. He started to wave hoping to attract Spunky's attention. Eventually Mary walked over to a policeman and pointed to Spunky. The policeman gladly obliged and went over to Kit's friend.

'I was just about to do that,' said Kit.

'Yes, I thought I'd save you the bother,' replied Mary archly.

Spunky arrived with a delighted look on his face. Kit's friend was tall, and certainly striking, with an eye patch in one eye, courtesy of the War and a monocle in the other. His features were completed by a pencil-thin moustache which made him look handsome, ridiculous, and brigand-like by turn. Not that Spunky cared a jot.

'I say, bloodhound, this is a stroke. I was meaning to get in touch with you. Mary, so good to see you,' said Spunky, 'May I kiss the bride-to-be?'

'You may and while you're at it you should tell your friend to get a move on before I become an old maid,' pointed out Mary as Spunky, not waiting for a response, planted kisses on both cheeks, continental style.

'Are they letting any of the general public in?' asked Kit.

'Certainly not,' replied Spunky, 'Come this way.' Spunky led the couple up to the same policeman who had helped Mary and said a few words. Moments later Kit and Mary were through the cordon and standing on the steps of the building.

'I don't have a lot of time, Kit. Are you free tomorrow morning to pop over to Holland Park?'

Kit looked at Mary, who smiled and nodded. This surprised Kit, but Mary just shrugged innocently. Kit's thoughts on why Mary was being so reasonable were interrupted by a commotion behind them. George Curzon, 1st Earl Curzon of Kedleston, former Viceroy of India and now the Foreign Secretary for His Majesty's Government, was bounding down the steps with a face like thunder, one policeman in tow. He stopped briefly as he spotted Kit before thinking better of it and walking on.

Mary looked up at Kit, frowning, 'Something else you neglected to tell me?'

'Yes, forgot that bit,' admitted Kit, grinning sheepishly like a schoolboy caught red-handed in the tuck shop. Changing the subject, he turned to Spunky and said, 'Why are you here? I thought you left spying to the boys on the factory floor.'

'I do, dear boy, I do. But as it's on my doorstep, I thought I might pop along and see if I could pick up some useful titbits.' Spunky had a genius for logistics and could turn talk of widgets into detailed analysis of the military-industrial economy. His interest in obtaining this information from primary sources, himself, was limited. He much preferred analysing the information obtained by others.

Kit smiled at his friend. The smile, Mary noted, seemed sympathetic rather than mocking. This was confirmed a moment later by Kit's cryptic question.

'Have you seen any old French friends?'

Spunky's face seemed a little rueful for a moment, 'No. Sadly, no sighting on that front.' Mary stored this away for further inquiry later. 'However, where one door closes another opens, so to speak. I've been up at Dawn a lot recently,' continued Spunky, looking at Kit directly.

Mary detected the trace of a smile, or at least an attempt to hide a smile, on Kit's face. Another question was heading her future husband's way. A couple of minutes later, Spunky had to leave. Kit and Mary bid farewell and descended the steps.

'What did you friend mean, up at Dawn a lot, by the way?' asked Mary.

'Early morning walks?' responded Kit to her query, walking a few feet in front of Mary.

Mary speeded up to fall in step alongside him.

'Look me in the eye, Lord Aston, and say that,' said Mary laughing. By now Kit was laughing also.

# The Phantom

## Chapter 12

*February 14<sup>th</sup>, 1920: London*

Mary woke groaning as the five o'clock alarm blasted a rather pleasant dream involving Kit, a punt, and a secluded spot underneath a willow tree out of her head at an inopportune point in the narrative. She trooped blindly to the bathroom muttering words that were all too lady-like when men were not around to declare them unladylike.

Alfred was waiting downstairs twenty minutes later looking, if it were possible, even more bleary-eyed. Agatha was pippedness personified in a hideous patchwork dressing gown and hairnet.

'Come on then, get weaving,' urged Agatha, as she saw Mary come down the stairs. Agatha and Betty reported the previous evening that Caroline Hadleigh had returned around four o'clock the previous afternoon, along with what they agreed was a bag large enough to contain a change of clothing. Both had come through their reconnaissance mission unscathed fortified by what Mary suspected was a significant amount of gin.

'You're more than welcome to take my place,' said Mary, rubbing her eyes.

'No time for prep school repartee,' replied Agatha, 'Come along now.' Agatha hustled Mary and Alfred out of the house before closing the door, shaking her head, and saying, 'Young people.'

At this point Fish appeared, also in a dressing gown.

'Ah Fish,' said Agatha, 'A cup of tea would be wonderful.'

'Very good, milady,' replied the elderly man with as much spirit as he could muster.

-

Rather than stay too long in one place, as they had done the previous morning, Mary ordered Alfred to park in a different location, confident that Caroline would probably follow a similar route. Around six thirty, a figure emerged from the front door. Mary used her opera binoculars to confirm it was Caroline Hadleigh. As expected, Caroline headed towards Sloane Square. This time, however, she was carrying a small suitcase rather than a bag.

Mary trailed behind in the car, only getting out as they neared the same café. The morning was bitterly cold but free from rain. Taking a risk, Mary followed right behind Caroline and took a seat with her back to her quarry. Acting on a suggestion from Betty, Mary was wearing a pair of reading glasses and a beret. As disguises went, it was just about one step removed from a false nose and moustache but there hadn't been time for anything more elaborate.

She overheard Caroline order tea with toast. When the waitress came over, Mary did likewise. The order arrived quickly as the café was still not very full. Mary was able to keep an eye on Caroline using the reflection from the glass front. Outside it was getting brighter. Her earlier impression of

Caroline as very attractive and of a similar age to herself was confirmed.

When Caroline finished her breakfast, she stood up and went to the counter to pay. Then she went down a small corridor to visit what Mary remembered was the bathroom. Mary leapt up and went to the counter to pay her bill.

The bill paid, Mary left the café and signalled to Alfred to make ready to pick her up. A minute or two after Mary had left, Caroline Hadleigh also exited the café. Only she wasn't the same as the one who had entered. Gone was the blonde hair and light-coloured mackintosh. In its place was a dowdy, seemingly older woman with dark hair and a tweed overcoat. Mary would never have recognised the young woman were it not for one thing. The suitcase.

By now, Mary was in the car and able to observe Caroline unseen. The traffic was beginning to build, however. At one point they came to a standstill. Mary watched in frustration as Caroline began to edge ever further ahead. And then they realised the reason for the hold up. Two cars had collided up ahead. Mary could have screamed. Caroline was nearly out of sight.

-

Melbury Road runs from Kensington High Street along the western perimeter of Holland Park. Dozens of red brick Victorian houses and apartments lined each side of the street. Few realised, and even fewer would have welcomed, the fact that it was home to Britain's embryonic Secret Intelligence Service, led by the shadowy figure of Mansfield Cumming, otherwise known as 'C'.

It was in this highly suburban environment that Aldric 'Spunky' Stevens plied his trade. His office overlooked

Holland Park, which was a relative compensation for having to move away from the centre of London. The compensation being the opportunity to enjoy the endless procession of young ladies promenading in the park. However, those days were over for the time being. The weather had turned a little inclement which discouraged the daily beauty parade, and now he only had eyes, well one eye, for the attractive young secretary to 'C', Dawn.

It was Dawn who led Kit up to Spunky's office following their arrangement the previous day. After Dawn had left the two men alone, Spunky indicated to Kit not to say anything.

'Wonderful girl, Dawn. Without her, I'm convinced this place would fall apart. Keeps the old man on his toes,' said Spunky a little too loudly.

Kit nodded in understanding, 'Yes, clearly very efficient.'

Spunky leaned forward and stage whispered, 'Keeps more than the old man on his toes, I can tell you.'

Kit closed his eyes and held his palms up thereby missing a series of hand gestures from Spunky unlikely to be found in any mime artist's repertoire unless they were French. This made Spunky chortle even more. When Kit raised the subject of Leon Daniels, though, the atmosphere changed.

'I saw the Russian chap, Daniels, yesterday.'

'So, I gather. What brought you out there?'

'I have to say Spunky, he was in a pretty poor state,' replied Kit, ignoring the question.

'He'll be in an even worse one when he's dangling at the end of a rope,' pointed out Spunky.

'Yes, no doubt, but this is the law of the land, whatever one may think of it. However, I'm pretty sure that the same law does not endorse torture.'

# The Phantom

'No,' conceded Spunky, 'But we both know it goes on. And don't tell me you had no idea what his fate would be.'

'Seeing it first-hand is another thing. It's inhuman. Torture makes us no better than the people we're supposed to be defending the country against.'

'Enhanced interrogation, old boy,' said Spunky by way of correction, 'is necessary. Who knows what other covert cells Russia has operating in this country? We must be able to defend ourselves. The Bolsheviks aren't playing by Queensbury rules, y'know. They've killed people in our country before and they'll do it again. And again. You may not like it, but it won't change anytime soon.'

'Well, I don't like it, Spunky. It's not...'

'Cricket?' said Spunky with one eyebrow raised.

'No, definitely not cricket. Nor is it what I believe this country should stand for. That probably makes me a fool but there you have it.'

'Anyway, on a happier note, your unscheduled appearance may have had an impact,' said Spunky.

Kit looked surprised and said, 'Really? How so?'

'Do you still have that old photograph of us by the lake with you?' asked Spunky. Kit retrieved it and handed it to Spunky, who smiled nostalgically. 'A bit sentimental of you to keep it in your wallet.'

'Yes, I know, but it was such a wonderful time. I looked at it often when I was in France. It kept me sane, I think. To know there was another world out there that had sunshine and friends and possibilities.'

Spunky handed it back and said, 'And ladies. Anyway, I think it fairly convinced Daniels that Olly had hoodwinked him. He began to talk about Olly and the other chap Fechin.

You were right, they did bump him off. Incompetence. Olly ordered it along with the other killings. Daniels claims not to know why, which I believe, incidentally. He's just a foot soldier.'

'And Roger?'

'I think Daniels has pretty much confirmed he was duped by Roger into thinking he was working in a covert cell in Britain. He fed Roger a lot about the way *Cheka* were set up in a broad sense, but he had no knowledge of other cells working in the country.'

'And the killings? What was Roger's involvement in those?'

'He was not involved apparently. He handed over the reins to Olly who was the prime instigator of what happened.'

Kit nodded and felt a wave of sadness engulf him. Sadness for the loss of his former commanding officer, sadness for the circumstances that led to his death, sadness for not seeing that Ratcliffe had slowly been driven mad by years of leading a double life. A life that led him to be unable to distinguish between reality and fantasy. He wondered if such a fate befell all those who spent their lives undercover, not just acting but *becoming* the person they had to portray to the outside world. He was glad to be out of it.

The conversation moved off the recent case. Kit had the feeling his friend was probing him, indirectly, about why he had gone to the prison. As there was no reason, he could see not to admit it, he confirmed the original purpose of the visit had been to see the Phantom.

'Why is the Phantom in a special prison used by our people?' asked Kit.

# The Phantom

Spunky smiled and pointed out, 'He's the Phantom. He'd walk out of any other prison, old boy. Why the interest in Hadleigh?'

Kit told him about the evening of the theft, on the eve of the London Conference.

'You were there?' exclaimed Spunky, 'I'm very impressed. So, Jellicoe's back on the case, then?' asked Spunky.

'Looks like it. He caught Hadleigh originally if you remember.'

Spunky shook his and said, 'Had no idea. Stout man, obviously.'

Kit smiled. This was the very highest of praise, just one step behind being a good egg. Or was it the other way around? Kit could never remember.

'Yes, he's good. He has a young sergeant with him now who appears to be his protégé,' added Kit.

'Well, the more the better, I say. Fewer criminals, means more men in prison which means more girls at a loose end, grateful for a bit of Stevens...'

Kit put his palms up to stop Spunky in mid flow, lest his eloquence take him towards schoolboy alliteration and oblique references to his undoubted credentials for the fairer sex. This intervention managed to bring Spunky back on subject.

'What's the latest on the conference?' asked Kit.

'Well, I'm not sitting in the room obviously. My role is more akin to eavesdropping in the corridors of power, or peace in this case. Usual story, bit like Paris. Us, the Frenchies and the Italians all have an agenda in the Middle East which is based purely on our respective national interests. Well, the Italians probably don't care. I think they're on holiday,' added

Spunky before continuing, 'But it's probably not in the long-term interests of the region.'

'What do we want?' asked Kit.

'Well, as long as we can protect our oil interests in Mosul, we're of a mind to leave the rest to the French and the Americans to sort out, particularly Constantinople. We'd be happy for them to do our dirty work in keeping seaways open, means easier access to India.'

'What do the French want?'

'What does any Frenchman want?' This appeared to amuse Spunky immensely before he added in a more serious tone, 'They've finally woken up to the potential of the region for oil. It took them long enough. Winston and the rest have been on this like a rat through cheese for a long time now.'

'There were a lot of protesters outside I noticed,' said Kit.

Spunky nodded and said, 'The region is a powder keg of different ethnic and religious groups. Still, better they're all together in one place, I say.

'Where are you and Jellicoe with the case?' asked Spunky, returning to the subject of the Phantom.

'I'm no longer on it, insofar as I was ever a part of it. It's a police matter,' said Kit, a little more ruefully than he would have liked.

Spunky smiled sympathetically, 'Want me to pull a few strings, bloodhound?'

'No, I want to spend the time with Mary, not chasing after criminals. After what she's been through, I think we need to be together.'

On this matter Mary and Kit were not quite as one. The extraordinary activity of Caroline Hadleigh in the morning had duly been reported to the other two members of the investigative team.

Mary had related how her tracking of Caroline had nearly gone awry once more. Having almost lost her quarry, Mary had been forced to demonstrate why she had been the sprint champion at her school for six years, literally, on the trot, with a mad dash that had by turns, nearly knocked an old gentleman into the road, resulted in a near collision with a man on a bicycle and a possible world record in the sixty-yard dash.

She'd eventually caught Caroline as she turned into Sloane Gardens. Making a note of the house number, she waited for twenty minutes for Caroline to reappear before dark clouds suggested the best plan was shelter and warmth.

'We'll have to get you into that house, Mary,' said Agatha when Mary had finished.

'How do you propose I get in there? As a maid? And what do I tell Kit? I mean he and I have plans over the next few days,' pointed out Mary.

'You'll have to bail out, I'm afraid. No option. Needs must and all that.'

Mary looked troubled by this idea. 'I see that but what shall I say? Don't forget, it's St Valentine's Day. I imagine my intended would be keen that we spend it together. Besides which, I'm not keen on lying to Kit. It wouldn't exactly set the right precedent for our future together.'

'Oh nonsense, a good marriage is built on deception. What would be the point of trust otherwise?' said Agatha, which settled the matter in her mind, if not entirely in Mary's.

Betty glanced askance at Agatha. Mary merely frowned and then a thought occurred to her, 'We need a credible excuse. We don't know how long will be needed.'

'Good point and I think I may have a solution that fulfils both your need not to lie to Christopher and allows us time to put together our case.'

'Go on,' prompted Mary.

'If you remember, my dear,' said Agatha, leaning forward licking her lips, 'I laid the foundations already by suggesting Esther was unwell. I think you should ask Esther to extend her stay in Sussex claiming a fictitious illness. You, of course, shall visit to provide nursing. I seem to recall, young lady, you have some experience in such matters.'

Mary smiled sheepishly at Agatha.

Betty continued where Agatha had left off, 'You should see Kit today as planned. Anything otherwise on St Valentine's Day will arouse suspicion. Break the news about Esther. In the meantime, Agatha and I will apply ourselves with assiduity to securing you a position in the household.'

'Do you think you can?'

'Leave that to us,' said Betty with a surprising degree of confidence.

At that moment Fish appeared in the room. He looked somewhat ill at ease. Agatha looked up at him and said, 'Well come on, Fish, out with it. We're all friends here, I'm sure.'

'There's a gentleman to see Miss Simpson. A police constable.'

Mary eyed the two elderly women. Neither looked surprised so much as guilty. Agatha glanced at Betty.

# The Phantom

'Ahh, they did say they would pay us a visit, dear,' said Agatha to Betty, and then addressing Mary she added, 'I forgot to mention. Our trip in the car was not without incident.'

'What happened?' asked Mary, her brow furrowing.

'Well, Betty managed to get us to Eaton Square without any problems. However, it was rather a long wait,' said Agatha.

'So, I brought along something to sustain us,' continued Betty. "I thought that some brandy would do the trick. The car was rather cold.'

'It did more than the trick dear, you were one over the eight,' admonished Agatha, although not unkindly. 'If you hadn't stumbled at the young man's feet, he'd never have known.'

'Yes, it was unfortunate timing, I grant you. Still, the young policeman was remarkably good about it. Clearly recognised breeding when he saw it.'

'He clearly recognised you were too whiffled to drive if you ask me.'

Betty ignored Agatha's jibe and continued, 'Anyway, he kindly brought us home.'

'The young policeman?' asked Mary, a smile growing on her face. The two ladies had withheld this incident in their brief update earlier. 'Is there anything else you haven't told me,' continued Mary in the manner of a schoolmistress.

Betty seemed oblivious to the situation, but it was clear that Agatha was somewhat embarrassed that they had been found out.

'Well, this is the interesting part of the story, Mary,' said Betty, 'The young detective had just come from Caroline Hadleigh's house.'

Mary was stunned by this news, 'But this changes things somewhat. If they're investigating Caroline, then should we be interfering in a police matter?'

'That's the point, Mary,' replied Agatha, 'The way he said goodbye to her on the doorstep suggested to me that either investigation techniques have changed or...'

'Caroline Hadleigh's sweetheart is a detective,' concluded Betty, 'Excuse me, hello constable. 'Betty stood up to receive the policeman, who was standing at the dining room door.

Agatha looked at Mary and said gravely in a stage whisper, 'I don't think Christopher really needs to know of this unfortunate incident, Mary. I don't want him to think Betty a bad influence.'

'I quite understand,' said Mary with as straight a face as she could manage under the circumstances.

Chapter 13

*February 13th, 1920: London*

Early morning. It was still dagger-dark. The sun would not rise for another three hours. Sheets of sleet curved craftily into the faces of the workers as they left through the factory gate. Each cold drop stinging their faces beat a reminder of their place in life. A lorry went past them, narrowly avoiding a puddle by the side of the pavement. This brought up an ironic laugh for those who had narrowly escaped a soaking.

Ryan turned and watched the lorry pass. It turned into the factory, causing workers to skip out of the way. A few grumbled in appropriately undiplomatic language. The driver didn't look like he was in a mood to stop for anything least of all an inattentive pedestrian.

'Unusual,' commented Ryan.

'What?' asked Abbott.

'The lorry. Deliveries and collections are usually during the day, aren't they?' observed Ryan.

'Who knows?' replied Abbott in his curious mid-European accent. He looked at Ryan with his big moon eyes, a trace of irritation, 'You shouldn't worry about these things.'

The two men, for better or worse, were work mates. Ryan would not have chosen Abbott nor, he suspected, would

115

Abbott have chosen him. But they were bound together now, after only a few nights, by their secret.

Ryan had thought about Abbott's idea. Stealing cigarettes and selling them on the black market was hardly lucrative but it was possible to make some money. Each created hidden compartments in their trousers and shirts. Each evening, the plan was for Ryan to hand over their swag and Abbott would sell it wherever he could. They split the profits sixty-five, thirty-five in favour of Abbott. Ryan was relaxed about this. Although both men shared the risk, Ryan did not have the wherewithal for selling. They hurried to a building which provided a degree of shelter against the weather.

'Quickly,' ordered Abbott, looking about nervously.

Ryan emptied his pockets and handed over close to one hundred cigarettes. Enough to make some money but not so many to raise suspicion. Swiping so many cigarettes over eight hours was not so difficult, they'd found.

'That's it,' said Ryan, checking his pockets one last time.

They went their separate ways into the darkness.

-

Harry Miller walked into Kit's room and opened the curtains. Outside the sky was grey and rain fell with a depressing swagger, bouncing off the street, saturating the air and splashing anyone unwise enough to be outside defended inadequately by an umbrella.

'What's it like?' asked Kit from a underneath pre-Cambrian number of blanket layers.

'Wet. Whether its sleet or rain, it's hard to tell, sir,' replied Harry placing a cup of tea by Kit's bedside table.

Kit finally surfaced and had a sip of the tea. He wasn't quite sure what the day held for him. Mary had told him the

The Phantom

previous evening that she was going to Sussex to tend Esther. The prospect of her leaving, if only for a few days, was grim indeed. The last couple of weeks had been the happiest of Kit's life.

'How was your evening off?' asked Kit with a grin.

Without looking at Kit, Miller removed a tweed suit from the wardrobe and placed a recently ironed shirt with it. He glanced at Kit and replied, 'Oh, it was a pleasant evening, sir. Thank you.'

Kit probed a little further, 'Must have been a lot of couples around.'

'Yes, we couldn't get a seat anywhere.'

'We?'

Miller turned to Kit and grinned guiltily, 'You should be a detective, sir.'

'Chance would be a fine thing, Harry.'

Miller looked at Kit while brushing down the jacket, 'I'm sure something will turn up. Is there nothing new on the diamond robbery?'

Kit shook his head resignedly, 'I don't know. Chief Inspector Jellicoe is handling it now. I couldn't ask you when we were in the car with Jellicoe, but what do you think of the Phantom? Professionally speaking, of course.'

Miller grinned. He had once been a cat burglar. This was before the War. The conflict had ended what had been a reasonably successful career. The subsequent meeting with Kit and the offer of employment merely cemented what would have been his wish anyway, to end this career before the police ended it for him.

'My dad was always talking about him. He used to cut out newspaper stories of his robberies. I think he was trying to

117

understand how he went about it. There was a lot to admire and learn. Of course, when it turned out that this chap Hadleigh was a toff, well my dad felt let down and threw the cuttings in the fire.'

'Why was that?'

'I think his view was that we'd never be invited to the houses he was able to rob, sir. Mr Hadleigh was probably a friend of his victims and knew what to look for and where to find it. Me and my dad and Dan never had that luxury unless we were lucky.'

'Yes, I can see the problem,' added Kit, 'You'd have limited knowledge of the target which meant you had to lower your sights on what you could nab.'

Miller laughed. It never ceased to amaze him, his master's fascination with the underworld and his complete lack of censure towards him over his past.

'None of this is to detract from Mr Hadleigh, of course. The man was a genius. He could crack safes all right. Just because you know where the loot is doesn't mean you're going to get it. What's that thing you say at golf, sir? None of the robberies was a gimme.'

This time Kit laughed.

Miller continued, 'And the Belgravia robbery. Well, we talked about that one for weeks, when he was chased over the rooftops by the 'rozzers'. He didn't always swan in through the front door carrying bubbly.'

'True,' acknowledged Kit. "I'd forgotten about that robbery. Just around the corner. Although wasn't there some doubt if that was him? They didn't find the card.'

'It was him all right, sir. We all thought there was something going on between him and Lord Ravensdale's wife.

# The Phantom

She knew it was him and hid the card. If you remember, sir, the lady in question was somewhat younger than her husband. She was at the court every day during the trial.'

This made Kit smile, 'Interesting theory.' Very interesting, thought Kit and quite plausible also. 'There were a number of ladies present throughout the trial if I remember.'

'Indeed, sir. Must be something in the daredevilry that attracts the ladies,' pointed out Miller with a grin.

'This was your own experience, Harry?'

'I couldn't possibly say, sir.'

Kit looked at Miller archly and then his thoughts returned to his own lady. The thought of not seeing Mary was weighing on him a little and it was barely eight o'clock in the morning. The next few days were going to drag. This much was certain. However, looking on the positive side, it showed how much his life had been turned upside down by a girl of twenty-one. If he was not discombobulated, he certainly wasn't completely recombobulated either.

Miller seemed to read his mind and asked, 'Are you seeing Miss Mary today?'

'Unfortunately, no. Apparently Esther is unwell down at Richard's place, so Mary is going down to act as a nurse.'

'She'll know all about that, sir,' said Miller with a grin.

Kit laughed, 'I know. So that leaves me at a loose end, today. I think I'll lunch at Sheldon's. You can have the afternoon off if you like just in case there's anything from yesterday you wanted to follow up on.'

Any comment Miller might have made was interrupted by the arrival of Sam who came scampering into the room and hopped up onto the bed to lick Kit 'good morning'. Having completed his salutation to Kit he turned to Miller and barked loudly.

'In a good mood,' said the two men in unison.

-

Mary rose from the bed and went to the window. It was light, in a manner of speaking. A grey shroud in the sky was doing a splendid job of absorbing every particle of light. The sound of rain against the window and the stinging cold of the room made her dive beneath the bed sheets again, glad she didn't have another morning of tailing a suspect. Agatha and Betty had other plans.

She lay back in the bed and wrapped the blankets around herself tightly. The thought of one day snuggling up next to the warm body of Lord Kit Aston almost made her giggle. How she wished she could do it now. She happily played with this thought for a few moments. The danger of indulging herself in these dreams was the sense of impatience that arose simultaneously. Only two months ago the thought of marriage was as far from her future as lion taming. Such is the madness of love. Such joyful madness.

Her mind went back to the hospital, that day when the orderlies had brought Kit in. Just another poor soldier with another horrific injury. A man more likely to die than survive. Yet survive he had.

Most of the nurses had been aware of him. There was a sense of mystery owing to the three identity cards with different names and nationalities. There was also the story of how he had been saved from the middle of No Man's Land. And of course, there was no denying his beauty. A face so refined and god-like it seemed an absurd joke he should be found amid such brutality and dehumanising ugliness.

# The Phantom

The question of his origin, German or otherwise, was laid to rest after he awoke. When he had spoken, his voice, as well as his manner, had more than lived up to his looks and confirmed his country of birth. To find such refinement in the pitiless context of a military hospital, near the front, was rare. Mary had felt drawn to him from the start.

But the hospital was a never-ending conveyor belt of misery. The terrible consequences of man's inhumanity were fed through daily. The ward was not a place to recuperate. You were patched up and sent away. Day after day. But this was the life Mary had volunteered to live, for reasons, that even now, she could never quite explain.

It certainly was nothing so banal as rebellion. But nor was it a vocation. She had left nursing six months after the War had ended. She and Esther had dealt similarly with the grief of losing their father.

At first the pain of loss had inevitably shredded the secure life they had both known. Denial was impossible. So many had lost fathers, sons, and brothers. To deny would have seemed an insult to their sacrifice. Instead, a prolonged period of anger followed that resolved itself, Mary realised, in a desire to *do something*. Both she and Esther decided that life could no longer continue at Cavendish Hall as it once had. Each, in their own way, went to war.

A machine gun rattle of rain against the window brought Mary back to the here and now. She rose and made herself ready for breakfast. Downstairs she found, as ever, Agatha up and attacking the day with gusto. Betty had arrived also. Events were about to move forward rapidly. This was confirmed as the two elderly ladies looked up expectantly at Mary's arrival.

'Take a seat, my dear, Betty has some wonderful news.'

Betty certainly looked like she had wonderful news. Her eyes were bright, and she looked, as far as its possible for a septuagenarian to look, like a teenage girl desperate to share the latest jape with her friends. Betty leaned forward, as did the others, and reported the latest.

'As you know, I spoke to a lot of the girls and found out who lived at the address Caroline Hadleigh visited in disguise. The house belongs to an American banker who lives there with his wife. Herbert Rosling, not sure if you know him.' The two ladies shook their heads. 'Anyway, he's been over here for a few years, certainly since before the War, and heads up the London office of the Anglo-American Bank. I gather Mrs Rosling is something of a harridan which has resulted in a high turnover of domestic staff.'

'Well done, Betty,' commented Agatha, and Mary nodded in agreement.

'There's more, trust me,' replied Betty. 'It turns out that Flora Atwood's maid has a sister in service there as a house maid. I spoke to the young lady in question and she told me that she is terribly unhappy.'

Agatha clapped her hands in delight, 'You didn't?'

'I most certainly did. I told Flora's maid that I would offer the young lady five pounds to leave her position immediately and I also offered to find her another more suitable position, which I have, incidentally.'

'Bravo,' cried Agatha, 'You know what this means, Mary?'

'Yes, I should get down there as soon as possible and offer my services. Can you write me a reference, Betty?'

Betty took a letter out of her handbag and handed it to Mary, saying, 'Already done.'

# The Phantom

Mary took the letter from Betty and read it over. She grimaced good naturedly at one point, 'Mary Tanner?'

'Yes, couldn't resist it. Well, I mean, Kit was banging on about this nurse for a year before you finally met again.'

'He was?' asked Mary, happily surprised.

'Can we get a weave on please,' interrupted Agatha, 'How are you with accents? Your voice is too refined to be a maid's.'

Mary demonstrated that she could easily pass as a Londoner but without being too pearly queen.

'Jolly good,' complimented Betty, 'You have a definite facility. The stage's loss...'

'Thanks,' said Mary smiling. Then she frowned for a moment, 'I'll need a disguise. What happens if I meet someone I know, which is unlikely, but we should be prepared.'

It was Agatha's turn to look triumphant. She went to the dresser at the side of the room and extracted from the drawer a blonde wig.

'Try it on.'

Mary put the wig on. It was clearly new and styled fashionably.

'I say,' said Betty admiringly, 'You really are quite a beautiful girl.'

'Thanks,' replied Mary and then glancing wryly at Agatha said, 'Just as well my hair was quite short.'

Agatha pretended not to notice Mary's remark and picked up a shopping bag and brought it over to Mary.

'I had one of the maids go to Marks and Spencer. She's as undernourished as you,' said Agatha looking disapprovingly at Mary.

'Don't listen to her, Mary. Kit's a very lucky man,' said Betty.

Mary laughed and took the bag from Agatha.

'I'll go upstairs and get changed.'

Mary left the two ladies. Betty turned to Agatha and said, 'I hope we're doing the right thing. Still, she seems full of enthusiasm.'

'Of course, we're doing the right thing. This may help break the case wide open. The police are getting nowhere if the papers are anything to go by. Jellicoe is coming in for a bit of criticism this morning.'

'Yes, I did see that. I wasn't just referring to the general. Specifically, it seems that Mr Rosling considers himself a bit of a lady's man.'

'How old is he?' asked Agatha.

'Nearer sixty than fifty, I understand.'

Agatha harrumphed, 'Well, I hardly think Christopher has anything to worry about on that score.'

'Of course, Agatha, I'm not suggesting for a minute that Mary would ever be interested, but I understand it's more a case of wandering hands and liberties,' replied Betty meaningfully.

Agatha thought for a moment and then said, 'I haven't known that young lady long, Betty, but I would not like to be in the man's shoes who tried anything untoward with her.'

'Tried what?' asked Mary re-entering the room replete with frumpy tweed suit and blonde wig.

Agatha and Betty looked at one another. However dowdily dressed she may have been, she was stunning.

'Your new boss,' said Agatha.

# The Phantom

'Ah,' said Mary smiling. 'I think I understand you. I'll deal with him, don't worry.'

'Good girl,' said Betty.

At this moment Alfred knocked on the door and entered the dining room. Mary turned around to him and said, 'Morning, Alfred.'

Young Alfred reddened at the sight of the blue-eyed, blonde vision before him. His first attempt at speaking was a dismal failure, being dumbstruck became a choice not an outcome.

'Close your mouth, Alfred, there's a good boy,' said Agatha.

Chapter 15

Sheldon's, in the heart of St James in London, was a private club in which elitism and snobbery didn't so much walk hand in hand as get chauffeur driven to the front door. Kit had been a member of the club since before he was born. This was courtesy of the rule that allowed children of members to have automatic right of entry assuming they had the great good fortune to be born a chap rather than a lady.

Although Kit had never felt entirely comfortable in such a frivolous context, a feeling exacerbated following his return from the War, there was no denying the exceptional kitchen and a library that was well stocked with fine books and even finer brandy.

The wood panelling walls were an art lovers dream, if one's taste ran to horses, hounds, and fields. Occasionally the board of the club dealt with proposals, and even generous bequests to upgrade the quality of the art. These requests were dealt with summarily. Sheldon's would never stoop to the vulgarity of Renaissance art; not now, not ever. Consequently, Titian was less likely to adorn the walls of the club than a portrait of a recent Derby winner.

Such conservative tastes left Kit's head shaking but also amused him greatly. He briefly considered the apoplexy that might accompany the installation of work by Picasso, or, his recently acquired friend, Duchamp.

Lunch was, as ever, a marvel and had allowed him to catch up with one or two compatriots from the War. Although the club had more than its fair share of silly asses, this was more than compensated by the presence of some men who had fought alongside him in Flanders. If they knew of his secondment to Russia, they never alluded to it, nor to his injury. No one came back from the War uninjured. Everyone in the club had experienced loss of someone they knew.

As Kit sat in the library, he heard raucous laughter emanating from the dining room. It was a group of young men he'd seen earlier. Perhaps three Englishmen and, what sounded like, an American. At a neighbouring table, looking a little displeased, Kit spotted Lord Wolf chatting with a small group of men. At the same moment, Wolf also noticed Kit and excused himself from the meeting. He stood up and walked over to join him.

'Hello, Kit, I think I recognise that post meal glow,' laughed Wolf, patting his own stomach.

'It is rather special here, Anatoly is a marvel,' agreed Kit shaking Wolf's hand. 'Any news on the necklace?'

Wolf's face darkened, 'You've seen the papers?'

'Yes,' replied Kit, 'They seem to be giving Jellicoe a hard time. No mention of the Phantom yet. I suppose it's only a matter of time.'

'I know you have a high regard for him, Kit, but I have to say I'm not impressed. They have no leads, no clues, nothing. It seems to be drifting like they're waiting for something to happen.'

Kit's sympathy lay with Jellicoe. He liked the Chief
Inspector and certainly did have a high regard for his
capability. It seemed to Kit that both the newspapers and Wolf
were doing Jellicoe a disservice. The police could only follow
certain lines of inquiry such as speaking to known felons and
fences. If the diamonds had not appeared on the market or
had found their way into an individual's hands directly from
the robber, there was little Jellicoe could do. This was a crime,
unlike other crimes, where the imprint was clear but the trail
completely obscure.

'Kit, I know this is probably unfair to ask of you, but would
you be able to speak to this chap Jellicoe? He doesn't seem to
want to keep me informed. Yesterday I spoke to his sergeant.
I had the distinct impression Jellicoe was avoiding me.'

'I can't imagine he would do that, Peter,' responded Kit.

'Well, he may have been angry. I must admit I spoke to
the Commissioner regarding this matter,' admitted Wolf.
There was something in his tone which suggested to Kit he
had regretted his actions.

'I'll see what I can do.'

'Thank you, Kit. I shall leave you and return to the music
hall in there,' replied Wolf indicating the party of young men.
Kit smiled sympathetically and returned to reading the
newspaper. Half an hour later, Kit went down the steps of
Sheldon's and was met by Harry Miller in the Rolls.

'Where to, sir?'

'Scotland Yard, I think, Harry.'

-

Mary spent most of the journey to Sloane Square staring
out the window, quietly amused by Alfred's fascination with
her. It took her mind off the slight nervousness she was

128

feeling. What she was about to embark upon was uncommon. She would go undercover rather as Kit had done in Russia, only this time to catch a criminal. She wondered what Kit would make of it all. He would just have to get used to it, she concluded. She hoped he would.

Her thoughts then turned to Caroline Hadleigh. If it were true that she was the new Phantom, Mary found herself torn. On the one hand it would be quite a coup to catch a criminal, a kleptomaniac even, who had evaded the law for six months. On the other hand, she was a young woman like herself. Her father was in prison and her mother was dead. If she was the Phantom, Mary wondered what could possibly be driving her to take such risks. Was she trying to clear her father? Or was nature merely taking hold? Mary was less sure of this. But the prospect of finding out was intriguing and exciting in equal measure.

She glanced up at Alfred just in time to see his eyes dart away. The impact on Alfred was clear. She wondered if this would create problems in the interview with the housekeeper, Miss Carlisle.

Alfred drove up into the square and found a spot at Mary's instruction to set her down. It was far enough away from any shops or cafes to avoid being seen, but close enough to the house so that she did not get soaked by the never-ending drizzle.

Exiting the car, Mary walked around the corner to the house. It was nearly nine in the morning, just in time for her appointment. The red brick house was five stories high, with an exuberantly tasteless Palladian-style set of pillars adorning the front door at the top of half a dozen steps. To the right of these steps was another set of steps leading to the basement floor. This was for the tradesmen and staff.

Mary hesitated for a moment then moved to the right and descended the wet metal steps slowly, fearful of falling. She knocked on the door and waited. Finally, it opened, and she was greeted by a woman Mary guessed to be anywhere between fifty and ninety. Her hair was tied back tightly into bun with a small net enclosing it. She was never going to be mistaken for a ballerina though. Her pinched expression registered immediate disapproval of Mary. An auspicious start, she thought with amusement.

'Mary Tanner,' announced Mary.

'Miss Tanner,' said Miss Carlisle, who sounded as if she did, in fact, come from the city just south of the Scottish border, 'I'm glad to see you are prompt.'

You certainly don't look it, thought Mary, following the housekeeper inside to a large kitchen. Looking around, she felt a pang. It reminded her of Cavendish Hall. The cook turned around and smiled at Mary who returned her smile. The cook, at least, seemed friendly and reminded her of Elsie. It must be all the lovely food they get to make and eat every day. Why wouldn't you be happy, she reflected.

They sat down at the dining table. The cook came over and introduced herself, 'Hello, my name is Rose.'

Mary shook hands and smiled, 'Hello, I'm Mary.'

'You sound as if you're a Londoner.'

'Yes,' said Mary, before deftly moving away from any conversation about where, exactly by saying, 'And you're from Yorkshire, if I'm not mistaken.'

'Born and bred,' confirmed Rose. 'Would you both like a tea?'

# The Phantom

Mary looked at Miss Carlisle who nodded curtly to Rose. The cook turned away and said sardonically, 'That'll be a yes then.'

Miss Carlisle looked with ill-disguised irritation at Rose who walked to the large Aga stove that dominated and warmed the kitchen. Then she returned her interrogative gaze to Mary.

'References?'

Mary handed over a letter written by Betty without saying anything. Already she felt the best strategy for winning the job would be to say as little as possible. With people like this, being seen and not heard wasn't just a distinct advantage, it was part of the job description.

The housekeeper read through the letter and then returned it to Mary. Betty's reference had clearly done the trick. There was an almost imperceptible softening in the unimpressed exterior of Miss Carlisle, although she didn't seem altogether impressed either, mused Mary.

'Well, how long have you been in service?'

'Three years, Miss Carlisle.'

'What have you done?' pressed the housekeeper.

Mary listed a few lady's maid and house maid activities that she had been personally responsible for. They matched, for the most part, what she had done in France at the hospitals.

'Do you know the requirements of the role here?'

'No,' admitted Mary.

'You will conduct all of the housemaid duties you mentioned before and assist Rose, when needed, in the kitchen. Do you understand?'

Mary smiled and nodded.

'When can you start?'

'Any time but I shall need to collect my belongings from Miss Simpson's house.'

'That can be arranged. For the moment, you'll need to change. There is livery in the cupboard. Pick something in your size. It's all clean. I'll introduce you to Mr Grantham, the butler later and Miss Hannah, who is Mrs Rosling's maid, for the moment, until Verna returns from honeymoon.' The last comment was made as if she was chewing a troublesome wasp.

'Very good, Miss Carlisle,' replied Mary rising.

'One other thing, Mr Rosling's nephew is staying with us. He's a young man and his manner is decidedly American,' said Miss Carlisle with something approaching a shudder, 'which is to say highly familiar. Such familiarity should not be misinterpreted nor encouraged. Am I clear?'

'Yes, Miss Carlisle,' responded Mary. This was new news. She wondered what the young man would be like. Mary suspected that this was potentially a complication. She hoped she would not have to deal with any *droit de seigneur* ambitions the young man might have when it came to female members of the staff.

'I should also add that Mr Rosling, although no longer a young man is, shall we say, of a robust manner.'

Mary nodded at Miss Carlisle's flailing attempt at euphemistically describing a man with overly libidinous proclivities but said nothing. This was becoming more complicated by the minute. Although not vain in any sense, Mary was not unaware of her own appeal. Working in the field hospital had been a daily exercise in fending off the advances of doctors, soldiers and, on occasion, some nurses. Luckily her manner, whilst not prurient, nor stand-offish, was sufficiently forceful to avert any serious misconduct or embarrassment. She briefly considered if Kit had ever had to deal with unwarranted attention from women in the course of his work as a spy. She concluded, unhappily, it was probably different for men.

Miss Carlisle led Mary to get changed and soon she was clad in a manner like Polly back at Cavendish Hall with a long black cotton dress and a white pinafore. She looked at herself in the mirror and pondered what Kit's reaction would be to seeing her dressed thus. This made her smile. Perhaps something to store away for the future. Miss Carlisle met her outside the changing room.

'Come this way. You'll start with the bedrooms. Make the beds and tidy the rooms. That should take you up to lunch time when I can introduce you to the others. The Rosling family are all out this morning and won't be back until late afternoon. Follow me.'

Making beds, thought Mary, this detective lark isn't all beer and skittles. She wondered what Kit was doing at that moment. Playing schoolboy games in his club no doubt.

## Chapter 15

Although Kit felt certain that the recent shared experience with the Chief Inspector had meant they had developed an acquaintance of sorts, he still felt distinctly uncomfortable about seeing him again. Unquestionably, he felt at loose end without Mary and wanted to fill his time. However, this mission was one part imposition and two parts messenger-boy from Lord Wolf. The latter was a means to an end and might help achieve the first object, that of getting involved in the case, although it ran the risk of doing exactly the opposite.

At the reception desk Kit asked to see the Chief Inspector. He sat in the reception area and waited for a few minutes. Then he saw Detective Sergeant Ryan. The young detective made his way straight towards him. Kit rose to meet Ryan and they shook hands.

'Lord Aston,' said Ryan, 'I'm afraid the Chief Inspector is with the Commissioner now. Can I help?'

'I quite understand. I only came on the off chance he might have a spare few moments. I was hoping to get an update on the case. In fact, if I'm being honest, I met Lord Wolf earlier and he was somewhat disappointed with progress. I'm here at his behest although I must admit to curiosity about the latest.'

Ryan nodded gravely, 'Yes, sir, we're aware that Lord Wolf is displeased.'

'Yes, I had a feeling you might be. I tried to reassure him that you were the best men to be investigating this but, well I'm sure you can imagine.'

In fact, Ryan could not begin to imagine what the loss of a diamond necklace worth tens of thousands of pounds might feel like. Unwittingly, the look on his face may have betrayed this for he saw Kit grinning back at him.

'Perhaps not everyone has had a diamond necklace stolen,' said Kit. 'Are you able to tell me how things are going? I promise I will be circumspect in what I tell Wolf.'

Ryan nodded, and the two men walked outside into the afternoon air. The rain had eased off, but the cold lashed their faces.

'We have no new leads, which is the problem. Anything we've had has turned out to be a dead end. The diamonds haven't surfaced in any of the usual places. Nobody seems to know anything or, at least, is saying anything. It all feels like it is news to everyone.'

'Have you mentioned the Phantom?'

'No, the Chief Inspector is still adamant that we shouldn't. As far as he's concerned, the Phantom is in prison. Any mention of him is a distraction or, more likely, misdirection by the real criminal.'

Kit nodded in agreement. He thought so too but it still troubled him as to why the robber would go to the trouble of printing and leaving the calling card and, more pertinently, how he obtained a card that was in every respect identical to Hadleigh's.

'Have you any theories on how the new Phantom came by an identical card? This might be the key.'

'Well, it's certainly been troubling the Chief Inspector. We investigated the printer, but he went out of business years ago. I think he's dead now, anyway.'

'And there's no other potential source for these cards?'

'I understand all of Hadleigh's cards were either seized or destroyed from both his house as well as the printer's. That includes the printing plates. This was before my time, obviously.'

'Of course,' replied Kit eyeing Ryan. One of the things Kit realised about himself was his ability, as he grew older, to deceive more easily and to comprehend when someone was lying to him. The very nature of his work in Russia was to live a lie, to recognise its form, its texture, and its tone. This was a matter of survival as much as it was a tool of the trade. When Ryan replied to him, Kit's senses tingled. Something in the young detective's manner told Kit he was either lying or more likely, not telling the full truth.

The two men turned and walked back in the direction of Scotland Yard. When they arrived at the steps, Kit said, 'Thank you for sharing this, sergeant. Would you be kind enough to let the Chief Inspector know I called. I think you can tell him what you've told me. He'll want to know and I'm sure he won't mind.'

Kit returned to the car.

'Anything new, sir?' asked Miller.

'No, they're floundering somewhat. No clues, no lead, nothing.'

'None of the stolen items have surfaced?' By the tone of his voice, it seemed extraordinary to Miller.

# The Phantom

'Apparently not,' replied Kit.

'Well, either there's a new fence that no one is aware of or the person stealing the jewels doesn't really need to sell them.'

'I agree, Harry, it's a very good point. Hadleigh was a gentleman thief. It could be we have another.'

'Not a lot they can do then,' pointed out Miller. 'It sounds like they need a break badly. No trail, no catch the criminal.'

Kit nodded and added, 'And this is the nub of the problem for the Chief Inspector. They need a break. In my limited experience, these things usually come from the area one least expects.'

-

Nearly two years nursing in France meant Mary was more than capable of managing a handful of bedrooms. She moved methodically through each room changing sheets, cleaning floors and windows, tidying clothes away. It was almost a surprise how quickly it all came back to her. The memory in her arms, muscles and sinews acting independently of thought, with an economy and speed that was almost gratifying. Almost. It was also deadly dull, and Mary was keen to meet up with Caroline.

Each bedroom was large and, she noted with disbelief, Mr and Mrs Rosling slept separately. This situation was certainly not going to be the case for her and Kit. She stopped for a moment to consider the delightful prospect of spending the night in Kit's arms before the sound of Miss Carlisle's footsteps jolted her back to the job in hand.

There were some photographs of the family in Mrs Rosling's bedroom. Out of sight from Miss Carlisle, Mary picked up the pictures to study the family members. Mr Rosling appeared to be in his fifties. Beyond a certain point she found it difficult to be precise. He had a well-manicured beard with flecks of grey around the chin which twinned nicely with the grey at the sides of his head. Rosling's eyes were his most distinctive feature. They were hidden under bushy eyebrows, which made him quite compelling. She nicknamed him Svengali.

Mrs Rosling looked every bit as imperious as Aunt Agatha or Aunt Emily. Her dress was as fashionable as it was obviously expensive. Notwithstanding her apparent manner, she appeared to be quite a bit younger than her husband. Mary would have said she was in her early forties. Her hair was still long but done with some awareness of current style albeit with an innate conservatism.

There were no photographs of nephew Rosling, but it was clear when she was tidying his room that he was quite a tall gentleman, and every bit as untidy as she assumed the *weaker* sex to be. One thing that Mary noticed on his tuxedo was a strand of hair that suggested either a man of bohemian appearance or, more likely, fast out of the gate when it came to the fairer sex.

After less than two hours she had completed her task and descended the back stairs to the servant's quarters. Miss Carlisle's demeanour was a little more relaxed having seen Mary's work. If there were any complaints, Mary hadn't heard any.

Rose greeted her with a big smile and handed her a cup of tea. At least one person in the staff was friendly, thought Mary. There was a knock on the door of the kitchen and in walked Caroline Hadleigh.

Caroline looked at Mary in surprise and then glanced at Miss Carlisle.

# The Phantom

'Miss Hannah, this is Miss Tanner. She's taking over from Gibson.'

-

'So, what was she like?' asked Betty as she, Mary and Agatha sat around the dining room table in Grosvenor Square later that afternoon. Mary frowned a little and spent a moment to collect her thoughts. There was so much to take in, distil and discuss.

'It was difficult at first to gain an impression, I was so struck by her ridiculous disguise. I mean it was patently obvious that it was a disguise. I was amazed no one could see through it. She's wearing a wig to hide her blonde hair, which is ironic, given I'm doing the opposite. The glasses are obviously meant to hide the fact that she is quite beautiful. They fail abysmally of course. I wonder if the young Mr Rosling, or indeed the elder, has spotted this fact yet. If they're half the men I think they are, I'm sure they'll have noticed. Her voice is certainly not what one would describe as working class. She's made little or no effort to hide that she's educated.'

'How was she with you?' asked Agatha.

'Polite but wary. There was something, but I couldn't put my finger on it. It seems we will room together tonight, so I may have a better opportunity to get to know her.'

'Do you think she's planning a job? Perhaps your arrival has upset the proverbial apple cart? She may be sore at you for this,' pointed out Betty.

Mary nodded in agreement and said, 'Yes, I wondered about that also. Anyway, we shall see. Right ho, I think I'd better get a shake on. They'll be expecting me back soon.'

'Good idea, I'm sure Helen has packed your things now,' said Agatha, rising from her seat.

They exited the dining room and, as Agatha had forecast, two suitcases sat in the entrance hall. Noticing Mary's surprise at the two unfamiliar bags, Agatha said, 'I took the precaution of buying slightly less expensive bags than the two you brought originally, Mary. Your bags might've aroused suspicion.'

-

Miss Carlisle seemed relieved when Mary reappeared at the Sloane Gardens house in the early evening. However, she made no comment on this and said to Mary instead, 'We'll go up in a few minutes to meet Mr and Mrs Rosling. I'm not sure if their nephew has returned. He keeps strange hours.' The way she said the final part of the statement suggested, unsurprisingly, disapproval.

Caroline Hadleigh was not around so there was no chance to renew her acquaintance. Rose, however, was and asked her if she had eaten anything. Mary admitted she had not adding that the stew in the pot smelled awfully good.

'Sit down,' ordered Rose, 'I'm sure you've time to have a spot of dinner. There's hardly a pick on you either. You young girls, I really don't know.'

Mary laughed. It was clear Caroline had been at the receiving end of a similar admonishment from Rose. Miss Carlisle didn't look happy about the arrangement but, as so often, she deferred to the common sense of the cook rather than her own more mean-spirited inclinations.

The stew was every bit as nice as the aroma had suggested it would be. Even Elsie would have been hard pushed to improve on it. Or, perhaps, the hard work of the day had meant she had built up a healthy appetite. Only her innate good manners prevented her from wolfing down the delicious meal.

# The Phantom

When she'd finished, she offered to wash the dishes, but Rose wouldn't hear of it telling her to think of her hands. This comment meant nothing to Mary, but she nodded sagely anyway. A few minutes later Grantham, the family butler, appeared.

'Miss Tanner, the family are ready to meet you now.' It seemed he was every bit as formal as Miss Carlisle. Something in his seeming piety reminded her of Curtis, her own butler. She smiled at the thought of him back at Cavendish Hall.

A few butterflies appeared in Mary's stomach as she followed Grantham up the stairs, with Miss Carlisle following just behind. They arrived in the main entrance hallway and went from there to the drawing room. Grantham knocked lightly on the door and went in when he heard an American voice.

'Enter.'

Mr and Mrs Rosling were sitting in the drawing room. Neither turned around to look at the new arrival. For a moment Mary was surprised and then she remembered who she was supposed to be. As she walked towards the couple, she wondered if she had always been so rude. It was possible. Although as a rule she would acknowledge the servants when they were in the room with her, she realised it was by no means certain she did so every time. A feeling of shame descended on her momentarily and an aspiration that she would never do as the Rosling's had done in the future.

Miss Carlisle walked to a certain spot, not quite in the centre of the room. She stopped and remained silent, waiting for one of the Roslings to speak. Finally, both looked up. Each registered Mary with a degree of shock, which had Mary smiling inwardly. It required no mind reader to understand what they were thinking.

'You're Gibson's replacement?' said Rosling.

'Yes, sir,' replied Mary. For fun, she accompanied this with a delicate curtsy, tying desperately not to laugh. This seemed to please the elder Mr Rosling. The first hurdle had been cleared. She recognised this was the lower of the two hurdles, however. From the moment she'd entered the room, it was clear who the master of the house was. The master spoke.

'Name?' demanded Mrs Rosling in a tone of voice that suggested she had guessed exactly what her husband's view of the new arrival would be and wasn't happy about it, no siree.

'Tanner, ma'am,' replied Mary.

'Where have you come from, Tanner.'

Mary took her through the pre-arranged story, careful to be brief. The fact that she had conveyed the information efficiently without excess of detail seemed to impress the lady of the house. She nodded to Miss Carlisle. Mr Rosling saw this tacit communication and sought to regain some degree of control of an appointment he would, of course, have little say over.

'Yes, well, very good. You can go,' said Mr Rosling, pretending to return to his newspaper. Carlisle looked at Mary and indicated with a jerk of her head to exit stage left immediately.

Happy that the cattle parade was over, Mary needed no second invitation and sped like a gazelle to the door. As she opened it, she bumped into someone coming in. The someone in question was six feet tall and a male of the species. The young man quickly informed Mary and had his arms around her slender waist in the blink of an eyelid as if to stop

# The Phantom

her falling over. Mary suspected this was the younger Rosling. Not bad looking either, she thought.

'I'm sorry,' said the young man in a voice that was as delighted as it was certainly unapologetic. He quickly released Mary but the smile on his face couldn't have been wider than if it started in Norway.

Mary returned the young man's gaze for a moment before remembering she was not Mary Cavendish, and then shot out of the room without saying anything. The meeting with the two Rosling men confirmed in Mary's mind that their interpretation of her role in the house would almost certainly be wider-ranging and more eclectic than the narrow remit envisaged by Miss Carlisle and Mrs Rosling. The wisdom of Caroline in dressing down was looking increasingly astute, even if her purpose was to rob them.

A little later that evening, Mary assisted Grantham in serving dinner. Much to Mary's surprise, the Americans also dressed for dinner. Perhaps they were not as uncivilised as her reading novels on the wild west as well as occasional visits to see moving pictures by D.W. Griffith had led her to believe.

Thanks to Rose's sterling work, the dinner menu would have gone down just as well in a Parisian salon never mind with three emigres from the new world. An onion soup was followed by a cold salmon first course. The main course was duck with a sauce Mary had never seen before. It smelled delicious. Mary hoped there would be some left over at the end.

Conversation around the table was surprisingly lively and piqued Mary's interest. In Britain one rarely talked of commerce or politics over dinner when women were present. Mary resented this and felt excluded from subjects she felt just

143

as qualified to comment on. Here, the three Americans talked of nothing else but business and politics, including Mrs Rosling. For all her petty pretensions to be a *grande dame*, she was clearly an intelligent, formidable woman. Mary also found herself admiring the level of respect afforded by her companions for her opinions.

The most interesting part of the evening for Mary came when they talked of Mr Rosling's impressions from the London conference. Unsurprisingly, Mr Rosling's views were forthright.

'It would be funny,' said Mr Rosling, 'If it weren't so transparent how Britain is trying to lock France out of access to oil.'

'Typical British trick,' replied the young man before remembering the presence of the two English servants.

This brought a stern look from Mrs Rosling, but Mr Rosling ignored him and carried on.

'The more I see of the Europeans negotiating together, the more I think that their time is up. The new world will be our world. Mark my words, America's time is coming. Europe and all their damn, sorry, Isabelle, colonies will go the way of the Greeks and the Romans and the who knows what.'

'I think you've hit the nail of the head, uncle,' continued the younger man. 'I've been to this gentleman's club with some of my pals, Sheldon's. You have to see some of these people to believe them.'

Mary resisted smiling at the mention of Kit's main club in London. This'll be interesting, she thought.

'It's full of the old lords, their silly ass sons and military types that sent tens of thousands of men walking into a hail of lead.'

# The Phantom

'It's not so long ago we were doing the same, Whittaker,' pointed out Mrs Rosling.

Whittaker? Mary immediately covered her mouth lest they see the amusement that Rosling's name caused her.

'They certainly didn't learn from us then,' added Rosling senior. 'That makes them damn fools in my eyes, sorry Isabelle.'

The rest of the evening confirmed Mary's fears regarding their interest in herself. Both Rosling men were on their best behaviour, obviously keen not to tip their hands too soon, especially in the presence of Mrs Rosling. However, men in these matters have as much proficiency at disguising their intentions as an army that has ceased its three-day artillery bombardment and follows this by the blowing of dozens of high-pitched whistles. The overt ignoring of Mary by the two men was understood and apparent in Mrs Rosling's permanent scowl over dinner.

However, the evening did throw up one piece of information that Mary was keen to share with her accomplices in Grosvenor Square. Mrs Rosling was wearing a spectacular diamond necklace.

-

The sound of crying woke Joe Ryan from a deep slumber. Initially he thought it was young Ben and then he realised it was Sally. He immediately rose from the bed and went to the living room. His wife looked up at him with tears staining her face.

'What's wrong, Sal?' asked her husband.

'Sorry, Joe. I didn't mean to wake you.'

Ryan looked at the time and saw it nearly four in the afternoon.

'I'd have been getting up anyway, love. What's wrong?'

Sally dried her eyes and tried to regain her composure.

'I was just looking at Ben outside. He's with Alice and some of the kids, Grace from number eleven is keeping an eye on them. He just sits there, like he hasn't the energy to play. All the kids are so nice to him, but he doesn't seem to have the energy to respond. It breaks my heart, Joe, it really does. What's going to 'come of him?'

Ryan hugged his wife tightly. He thought about this often. This was something he could not share with his wife. She needed his strength. He needed to convey a certainty he did not feel. His own fears he buried deep within. If they ever surfaced it would enfold his family in a darkness which no light would ever enter.

'He'll get better, Sal. He will. When I was a young 'un I knew loads of kids who had asthma. They coped. Ben isn't any worse than they were. You'll see, Sal.'

These words had their usual effect. How true they were was another matter, but this wasn't the issue Ryan had to deal with in that moment. Keeping his family's spirits up was paramount. He had enough to deal with at work without any additional burden.

Two hours later Ryan was standing opposite Abbott at the conveyor belt waiting for the waves of cigarettes to arrive.

'I think I've found someone who is interested in taking bulk from me. We'll earn less for the snout, but he can pay,' said Abbott.

'As long as he has the money, that's fine,' replied Ryan. He was about to add something else when Abbott moved his head slightly to indicate someone was coming.

'All right?' said Johnny Mac looming over them both.

146

# The Phantom

'Yes, boss,' replied the two men in unison.

'You want to stay here or move to another part?'

'Fine here, boss,' said Abbott but not too quickly, 'How about you, Ryan?'

'Me too, boss,' added Ryan more casually than he was feeling. The big Ulsterman always gave the impression that he was as likely to stab you as pat you on the back.

Johnny Mac nodded and walked away without saying anything. Ryan looked at Abbott and asked, 'What do you think that was about? '

'Nothing, I'm sure. But to be safe, we'll lay off the snout tonight.'

'D'you think they suspect something?'

'Let's not get caught out if they do.'

'I agree,' nodded Ryan.

The rest of the night went as slowly as ever. Both men's senses were on heightened alert for either Johnny Mac or, his Rottweiler assistant, Rusk. Neither spoke much over the course of the shift. Neither had to, it was clear that they were under surveillance. Both were scrupulous in not giving any appearance that they were aware of this. At the end of the shift, Rusk called the two men over.

'Follow me,' said Rusk curtly.

The two men glanced at one another and followed Rusk into Johnny Mac's office.

'Wait here.'

Rusk went out and returned a few moments later with Johnny Mac.

'Take off your coats,' said Rusk. Both men did so and handed them to Rusk. A quick inspection followed revealing no cigarettes.

Johnny Mac nodded to Rusk to hand the coats back. Taking a risk, Ryan stepped forward and held his arms up by his side. Neither Rusk nor Johnny Mac moved, both seemed confused.

'Do you want to search me?' asked Ryan, keeping his tone neutral, neither mocking nor fearful, although he certainly was fighting a battle to avoid trembling.

Johnny Mac turned and walked out of the room without saying anything. Instead, Rusk shook his head and said, 'Get out of it.'

Ryan and Abbott made their way out of the plant silently. When they were outside, Abbott risked a triumphant laugh. Ryan remained quiet. They had managed to avoid detection, but it was a problem now. This potentially lucrative side-line was now closed off.

'What's wrong?' asked Abbott, eyeing Ryan closely.

'I don't see what there is to celebrate.,' replied Ryan gloomily.

'We live to fight another day, Ryan. We don't be greedy; we keep our heads down and we earn their trust.'

Ryan nodded. This made sense, but his sense of impatience was almost overwhelming as he thought of his boy. His mind began to wander to those dark places where hope was extinguished, and anxiety grew; he felt a nudge from Abbott.

A lorry pulled into the cigarette factory. Abbott pulled Ryan in a different direction and they walked towards a different part of the road to get a better view of what was happening at the back gate of the factory.

Looking through the fence, they had a clear view of the lorry backing onto the dispatch doors. Both doors were open.

# The Phantom

Johnny Mac and Rusk loaded a dozen boxes containing forty boxes of cigarettes onto the lorry. They closed the doors of the lorry and banged the side. A moment later the lorry took off. The whole process had taken less than a couple of minutes.

Abbott looked at Ryan with a grin as unattractive as it was wily.

'Well, if I didn't know better, I'd say our bosses have their own little racket going on.'

Chapter 16

*February 16ʰ, 1920: London*

Kit woke a little later the next morning. The feeling of emptiness hit him immediately and was almost palpable. When Mary returned, he resolved that they should fix a date for the wedding as soon as possible. He would suggest it take place at Little Gloston, the village near Cavendish Hall, with Reverend Simmons presiding. This would have the dual profit of making Mary happy and irritating his own family. He realised he had never personally told them he was engaged. Perhaps he would just let them find out from The Times. Another task for when Mary returned. Any sense of contriteness was momentary as Miller brought in his tea.

'Plans for today, sir?'

'Pining, I think, with a dash of self-pity,' said Kit.

'Very good, sir. Shall I bring you a revolver?'

'Yes, nice and quick, that's the trick.'

Miller smiled sympathetically and asked, 'Have you thought about going down to Sussex yourself? It wouldn't take long. You could be there in two to three hours.'

'I've already suggested this,' said Kit glumly. 'I mentioned it to Mary on the phone last night, but she said she'd be back very soon.'

# The Phantom

In fact, the phone call in question had been as brief as it had been, on reflection, perturbing. It was clear she did not want him to speak with either Richard or Esther. She was also a little too quick in moving the conversation on to the case and away from discussion of Esther. Although it was only a minor niggle, it was not something he disregarded altogether. Kit had relied on these spider senses to save his life on many occasions. He decided he would press her on this later.

All of which still left him somewhat at a looser end than he would have liked. If he was not exactly disgruntled, he was hardly very gruntled either. He had always hated inactivity. The spate of cases over the last two months had fed his need for excitement and mental stimulation. The last year had hardly allowed him to draw breath.

A year previously, he'd been in France, averting a potential assassination attempt on the British Prime Minister; from there he went to India, once more at Spunky's request which meant yet more exposure to murder and the dangers facing the empire.

He suspected his fiancée was going to prove every bit as immune to inactivity as he was. There would be no respite with this young lady around. This presented a happy dilemma for him. He recognised that his desire to protect Mary from danger would go down like champagne at a funeral. These thoughts were broken by Miller asking him of his plans for today.

Without thinking he replied, 'Probably Sheldon's for lunch.'

-

Mary woke to the sound of Caroline Hadleigh's alarm clock. The previous evening, Mary had fallen asleep before

Caroline had returned from attending Mrs Rosling, meaning she hadn't had time to get to make any conversation with her new roommate.

'Hello,' said Mary brightly, sitting up from the bed, 'I'm glad you've an alarm clock. I left mine behind.'

Caroline laughed. It was an agreeable sound.

'It would wake up the dead. Sorry if you found the ticking too loud. I'm usually so zonked from the day I'm out for the count pretty quickly.'

'Same here,' replied Mary rising from the bed, 'I was bedding the night away as soon as I lay down.'

Caroline grinned, 'Well first day behind you. What did you make of them?'

Mary frowned a little before replying, 'They seem very serious, Mr and Mrs Rosling, that is. Young Mr Rosling looks like he could be a little too much the other way. Perhaps I'm being unfair, but I think he could be a handful.'

Caroline shook her head and smiled, 'No, I think you're being entirely fair. Look Miss Tanner, I must tell you something in confidence.'

This was interesting. Mary wondered if she would admit who she was. She leaned forward and said, 'Mary, please call me Mary.'

'Mary be careful with the two men. They both,' Caroline hesitated for a moment.

'Take liberties?' suggested Mary with a smile.

'Yes,' said Caroline, not sure of how to interpret Mary's light tone.

'Thanks, Miss Hannah,' replied Mary.

'Charlotte,' interjected Caroline.

# The Phantom

'I'll be fine, Charlotte,' continued Mary. 'I don't like it if men think they can do as they please with me just by grinning inanely and uttering ridiculous flattery. I can be polite but firm when I need to be.'

'I'm glad you said that Mary,' nodded Caroline, 'Believe me, you'd come off worst. Miss Carlisle won't have it and nor will Mrs Rosling.'

'I don't blame her. For all her grandiose manner, I found myself quite impressed with her. She's quite formidable.

Caroline nodded her head, 'Yes, formidable is the word. But in a good way. She's very smart.'

Mary had a feeling that she was going to like Caroline more than her role might allow. She moved on to more practical matters.

'Do you need to go to the bathroom first or shall I?'

'Do you mind if I go first? Her highness will be expecting me in about fifteen minutes. The servant bells aren't working well so I like to make sure she doesn't have to ring for me.

Mary gave a flamboyant wave of her hand which made Caroline laugh as she left the room. Good start thought Mary. Unquestionably, if Caroline Hadleigh really was the new Phantom, bringing her to justice might not be much fun.

It was with such unhappy thoughts that Mary spent the morning helping serve breakfast to the elder Roslings and then tidying their rooms. After finishing Mr Rosling's room Mary stepped outside and ran, once again, into the younger Rosling. Mary doubted this was pure chance. The young man used the opportunity to put his arms around Mary's waist, before quickly releasing her with a sheepish smile.

'Excuse me, sir,' said Mary, in an effort to remain neutral when her instinct ran more towards moderate violence bordering on actual bloodshed.

'No, my fault entirely,' laughed Rosling. 'It's Tanner, isn't it?'

'Yes, sir,' said Mary.

'Is there a first name to go with Tanner?'

'Yes, sir,' replied Mary, then after some hesitation, she added, 'Mary.'

'Well, I don't quite go in for the formality of my aunt and uncle so if it's all right with you I'll stick with Mary. I must say, I think you're a swell addition to the staff.'

'Thank you, sir,' responded Mary, turning to walk away. As she did so she was aware of the young man lightly brushing his hand against her the base of her back. She ignored it and walked ahead without breaking her stride. This undercover business was proving more difficult than she had imagined.

-

The morning for Sir Nevil Macready had started off with an argument with a senior level mandarin, was followed by spilling tea on his trousers, just missing the old horsebox. He felt sure things were unlikely to improve anytime soon. The principal evidence for this was the upcoming meeting.

In the normal course of events, raking a subordinate over the coals was one of the perks of the job. After all, what would be the point of being the top man if you couldn't enjoy a good bawling out on occasion? This was all fine if the object of your righteous indignation was a fatheaded ass. Unfortunately, for once, the object of ire for the Commissioner of the Police for the Metropolis, was very far from being either fatheaded or any other 'headed, for that matter: he was one of Macready's best men. Worse, for the Commissioner, he entirely sympathised with the problems his Chief Inspector was facing.

He thought about his own upcoming posting to Ireland. Dealing with a bunch of Irish rebels seemed a more enticing task than facing a combination of the British press and the aristocracy up in arms over the theft of a few trinkets. Expensive trinkets, admittedly.

There was a brief knock at the door. Macready looked up as Jellicoe entered his office. With some embarrassment they went through the usual formal greetings before Macready wanted to hear of their progress.

'Any good news, Jellicoe? I could really do with some. I think you could also.'

Even if Jellicoe had good news, it wouldn't have been evident from the mournful expression on the Chief Inspector's face. However, even by Jellicoe's exceptional standards of solemnity, Macready could see that little or no progress had been made. Jellicoe made his report, which was as succinct as it was bereft of new news.

Macready nodded wearily. Then he shook his head. Jellicoe had done, or was doing, everything humanly possible. But it was clear the current situation was untenable.

'Look, Jellicoe, you know that I trust you and more importantly, I have confidence in you. But we need to shake things up a little. This stasis can't continue. The wolves are howling. At me I might add. That means either we change our approach or, regrettably, our personnel.'

Jellicoe was surprised that matters had moved to this point and said as much. It would be professionally embarrassing to be removed from such a high-profile case.

'I need a little more time, sir. The few leads we have we've followed up. We are literally treading sand.'

'We no longer have time. I've a few angry 'nobs raising merry hell in the chamber. They want action.'

'I wouldn't advise mentioning the Phantom, sir. That would make things worse.' This applied as much to the Commissioner as it did for him. Both knew any revelation about the calling cards would exacerbate the situation further without any material gain.

'You have forty-eight hours, but in the meantime, I'm briefing a backup team.'

'Not Bulstrode, sir.'

'Bulstrode.'

'You know my views on Bulstrode, sir,' said Jellicoe. His face took on, if possible, an even an even more dejected *mien*.

In fact, Jellicoe had never actually stated any view about the Detective Inspector, but Macready didn't need to be a psychic to know what his opinion would be.

'You probably deplore his methods,' responded Macready.

'He's a thug, sir.'

This was as precise as it was difficult to argue against. The high correlation between Bulstrode's successful convictions and confessions obtained by vicious beatings, had anyone bothered to check, and Jellicoe had, was certainly not due to chance.

'I'm afraid I've made my decision,' said Macready. This was clearly not a happy choice for him, either.

'Can we at least delay until the forty-eight hours have elapsed?'

'He started this morning. I suspect he'll be in your office now.'

# The Phantom

-

Kit took a seat at his usual dinner table by the window. He looked outside and thought of Olly Lake. The two of them had often lunched together at Sheldon's. The gradual decline of Olly into alcoholism had been so cleverly staged, it had taken him in completely. His mood sank as he thought of his former friend. As wonderful as the last few weeks had been with Mary, his mind sometimes returned to his youth, school, and his life before the War. He knew he and Olly would meet again. The prospect of this left a sickening feeling in the pit of his stomach.

Rather than dwell on Olly, he thought about Mary. Her manner had been evasive, certainly, but was he being paranoid? Thinking along these lines was also dispiriting. He badly wanted her back. It had only been a day since her departure.

His mood was lowered further by the arrival of the same loud group as yesterday. They set up camp near Kit's table which meant he could enjoy the breadth of their erudition and repartee. It was going to be a long afternoon. He thought for a moment about getting up but was halted by the arrival of the waiter with one of Kit's favourite dishes, asparagus soup. There was no choice but to endure, with fortitude, a situation that was, otherwise, unendurable: loud Americans eating nearby.

Kit glanced at the four men. Two of the young men were English and were swivel-eyed bleaters of the first rank. One of them was familiar to Kit, the son of a Viscount, like himself. He was likely to be a member. It was possible the Americans were also members as Kit had noticed, recently, an increase in

157

fellows from the New World amongst the hallowed ranks of Sheldon's.

The volume of their conversation was inversely related to its quality. Each of the group, intent in outdoing one another in their stories related to success with the opposite sex, succeeded only in proving how insubstantial they were. One member of the group caught Kit's attention. He was the leader. Well made, and clearly wealthy, he was as loud as the others but seemed less eager to please. Kit suspected an underlying contempt for the people he was with.

At a certain point it was his turn to share with the party his tale of success in the mating game. He leaned forward rather needlessly as his voice carried across the dining room like a scream at midnight.

'Guys, we have a new maid in the house.'

This brought guffaws from the others. One of the Englishmen said, 'Is the previous one off to have the sprog?'

The American waved his hands downward, 'Hear me out guys. Anyway, I think you'd have to ask my uncle about the other one, but anyway.' This created more chortling from his listeners.

'What's she like?' asked the other American.

'Most gorgeous looking dame I've seen in England so far.'

The party began to clap at this pronouncement. By this stage a few of the other diners were beginning to grow impatient with the young men. Finally, a waiter came over to them and requested they lower their voices. Apologies, sincere or otherwise, followed.

'Go on then,' said the young lord, after the waiter had departed.

# The Phantom

'She's young, very slim and so pretty she'd make one of these old generals in here turn German with the flutter of an eye. She's pretending to play hard to get but I think she's game.'

'What's her name?'

It came out of the blue. As much as Kit did not want to listen to the conversation, it was unavoidable. And then he had heard the name.

'Mary Tanner.'

Three thoughts raced through Kit's mind in an instant. The first one was that Mary Cavendish and Mary Tanner were two different people. This was discounted quickly as the second thought hit Kit: was this Mary and if so, what was she playing at? A final thought followed. Why had she misled him?

Reluctantly Kit listened to the rest of the American's story. The maid had arrived the previous day. This tallied with Mary's trip to Sussex. The description matched Mary, save for the blonde hair, which could easily be explained by a wig. The narration by Rosling veered off into territory that almost had Kit marching over to the table and handing out a thrashing to the young man there and then.

Kit quickly finished his meal and went to the head waiter. Rather than complain directly, he asked for the names of the men at the table. The head waiter would draw his own conclusions from this. Next, he went to the General Manager at Sheldon's and obtained the address of the young man he now knew to be Rosling. He also found out a little bit more of the background of the young man following a few calls to friends in commerce and the civil service.

An hour after overhearing the conversation between the young men, Kit and Harry Miller were sat in a car near the house in Sloane Gardens. Miller was apprised of the situation. It seemed to Kit this made sense practically as well as from the point of view of trust: they were potentially going to be embarking on a long watch. Over the next few hours, each took turns sitting in the car while the other took a break.

Night fell like black ink on wet paper, weeping gradually downwards from a sad sky. The Rosling family returned at different times over the course of early evening. Yet there was no sign of Mary. If Mary was, indeed, acting in the capacity of a maid, she would not be free until near ten o'clock. This would mark the end of dinner freeing servants either to relax, go to bed or, as Kit hoped, take a walk.

In fact, there was one other option which Kit had not considered until it happened.

# The Phantom

## Chapter 17

The Commissioner's prediction that Bulstrode would be waiting for Jellicoe when he returned to his office was a little way off the mark. It was early evening before Bulstrode descended on the office like a black cloud. He did so in tandem with his sergeant, Wellbeloved, who wasn't, never had been and cared not a jot if he ever would be.

The timing of the arrival, just as the Chief Inspector was about to leave, seemed deliberately aimed at irritating Jellicoe. In this regard, Jellicoe's instincts were more acute than the Commissioner's. Unlike Jellicoe, neither Bulstrode nor Wellbeloved had families, therefore they were more likely to work late into the night. The benefits of this were twofold, and readily appreciated by the minority of senior officers who had facilitated Bulstrode's rapid rise through the ranks to the current glass ceiling.

Firstly, crime was an activity that tended to be executed at night rather than during the day, if only for the desire of criminals to avoid being detected in the act. Less obviously, but of equal if not greater importance, the reduction in manpower during the evenings gave the detective duo free rein to employ their robust interrogative techniques to the full.

The greeting between the two policemen had a polar quality: low in temperature, bereft of life and unlikely to witness either warmth or life anytime soon. There was no handshake only a nod and a brief introduction of the two men to Ryan.

Ryan looked at Bulstrode. They'd never met but his reputation not only preceded him, it was manifest in the short, squat, bull-necked man before him. His red face suggested, accurately, a temperament that was as unruffled as an Italian facing a German who has insulted his mother.

Bulstrode's partner in crime detection, Wellbeloved, was of middling height, leaner with a sharp face and an eye that was closer to beady than bright. Ryan didn't need to pick up on the body language of Jellicoe to form an instant dislike and distrust of these men. This was consolidated by Bulstrode's first comment accompanied, as it was, by the bronchial cackle of Wellbeloved.

'Macready wants us to hold your hand, then.'

'So, it would seem,' responded Jellicoe neutrally. This appeared to have more of an effect on Bulstrode than his original comment had on Jellicoe. Ryan noted this and realised the way to play Bulstrode was not to rise to the man's needling manner. A glance between him and Jellicoe was sufficient for master and protégé to understand this.

Bulstrode turned his attention to Ryan, hoping for more purchase from his brand of wit. 'Shouldn't you be at school, son?'

'I left school to join the army, sir,' replied Ryan with a smile. 'I'll go and retrieve for you the case file and would you gentlemen like a tea?'

Jellicoe allowed himself a smile, not that anyone would have known.

-

# The Phantom

It wasn't a falling out exactly. They stood in front of one another and glared their disagreement. In the scheme things it was nothing but there was a lesson in there had he chosen to see it. But he was desperate.

'I still think it's too big a risk,' said Ryan sulkily.

'You saw the way they searched the coats they'd never look where you've put them. They won't even search, anyway. See if they do.'

'It's me that's taking the risk, not you,' pointed out Ryan though gritted teeth. He glanced up to see if anyone could see their *contretemps*. Thankfully the sound in the factory meant no one could hear, and they appeared to be out of the eyeline of anyone working on the factory floor. Johnny Mac and Rusk were in the office.

By continuing to argue the point rather than refuse point blank meant, as Ryan slowly realised, he was merely delaying the moment when he took the risk. The noise of the factory and the heat inside felt oppressive and Ryan's head began to swim with the fear he was feeling. Facing the Germans was one thing: you expected to catch one. If he was never exactly inured to the feeling of going up top he had, at least, found an accommodation with his maker.

Now the stakes had changed. He had family now. It was no longer just him. To lose his job would be a disaster. But they needed the money. The new job wasn't enough. The two men remained silent for another few minutes, each left to their own thoughts. Finally, Ryan relented.

'All right.'

A few yards away in the office, Johnny Mac and Rusk were having a conversation along similar lines.

'You're sure you saw them?' asked Johnny Mac doubtfully.

'I did, they must've had wind of it. I'll search their coats again tonight,' replied Rusk.

Johnny Mac was silent for a few moments. He was amused by the idea of the two men thinking they could pull a fast one on him. Didn't they know who he was? Clearly not. A lesson might have to be handed out to them.

'Leave them.'

'Leave them?'

'You heard,' said Johnny Mac irritably, 'Give them a day or two, don't go near them, don't even look at them. Ignore them when they leave, don't acknowledge them when they arrive. Let them think the coast is clear. Let's see what happens then.'

'Then,' said Rusk smacking his fist. He didn't need to add anything else.

'One other thing,' added the big Ulsterman as Rusk turned to leave. 'Have them followed. I want to know more about them. Where they live, what they do. They'll have to sell them sometime. Find out where. Ask around if you must. Who's buying?'

Rusk nodded in agreement, not that he had any choice but to agree. There were few men that Rusk was afraid of. Johnny Mac was one.

-

If Harry Miller was surprised to see Mary emerge from the basement steps wearing a blonde wig, he was too discreet to draw attention to it. Whatever the colour of her hair, she was striking. However, the blonde hair, in Harry's humble opinion, made her quite a head turner.

'Sir'

Kit, who was reading a paper glanced up and saw what Miller saw.

# The Phantom

'Interesting,' was Kit's only comment. They both watched as Mary crossed the street. She appeared to be heading towards a big car. 'That's Aunt Agatha's car if I'm not mistaken. Harry, do you think you could get us back to Grosvenor Square before Mary?'

Harry had already started the car and moments later they were on their way. Miller risked a glance in the mirror and saw Kit was smiling.

'This should be fun,' said Kit enigmatically.

They arrived, as Kit had directed, well before Mary. Kit got out of the car and went up the steps while Miller moved the car away from the front. Fish appeared a few moments later. He looked surprised at seeing Kit.

'Hello, Fish old chap,' said Kit moving inside before the old butler could make any excuse for the lady of the house. 'I'll just pop in to see Lady Frost.'

In the entrance hall, Kit could hear his aunt's voice and that of another lady. He made straight for the drawing room, with Fish trying to keep up behind him. A knock of the door and in he went. Agatha and Betty looked up at Kit standing in the doorway.

'Hello, Aunt Agatha,' said Kit disingenuously and then he walked over to Betty and kissed her on the cheek. 'Good to see you, too, Betty. Now what are you ladies cooking up?'

'Christopher,' said Agatha regaining her composure, 'what are you doing here?'

'Can't a chap visit his favourite aunt out of the blue?'

This raised Agatha's suspicions immediately. She realised the game was partly up and said, 'Well, as it happens, it's fortunate you're here, because Mary is on her way back to us as we speak.'

'Indeed, how fortunate,' said Kit. He seemed anything but surprised.

'Young man,' said Agatha, now completely in command of her senses if not exactly the situation, fell back on her default tone of voice in situations such as this: righteous indignation. She didn't for a second think it would work but it was worth a try. 'I will not be spoken to in that tone of voice.'

'Aunt Agatha, I'm not sure I know what you mean.'

At this point the door opened and into the room walked a de-wigged Mary Cavendish.

'You're back, darling,' said Kit rising from his seat.

Mary's eyes narrowed, 'And you're here too, darling.' She looked at Agatha and Betty, but they were clearly as shocked as she was. Rather than take the high hand, she adopted a tactic, even less subtle, used by the distaff side of the species, through the aeons to avoid either the censure or the wrath of the less intelligent sex. She put her arms around his neck, looked him in the eye and kissed him gently on the lips.

If Kit had been truly angry, forgiveness would have been immediate and sincere. In fact, he was highly amused by the turn of events and happily reassured by Mary's first instinct in avoiding reproach. It augured well for the future, he noted.

'Sit down, my love,' said Kit, finally disengaging himself. 'I think you ladies owe me an explanation.'

Mary now looked more amused than shocked. She looked at the other ladies and said, 'Who wants to begin?'

Agatha recognised that it was for her to enlighten Kit on what they had been up to. She reached down to the newspaper and held it up for her nephew to see. The article on the recent spate of robberies was circled.

'We've cracked the case, Christopher,' announced Agatha.

# The Phantom

'Possibly,' added Mary.

It's not easy to state offhand what the last thing Kit thought his aunt might say, and it would still have been a close-run thing. For example, if Agatha had stated her intention to marry Fish, the butler, due to the arrival of their baby in autumn, this might have edged it. Just.

In the event, Kit managed to splutter, 'Cracked the case?' Kit looked at the three ladies. It was clear they were in earnest.

'It's true, Kit,' said Agatha with eyes gleaming.

The evening was proving to be full of surprises. Aunt Agatha had never referred to Kit as anything other than Christopher. He looked at his elderly aunt. She appeared to have shed at least twenty years with the excitement. It was abundantly clear they believed they had a break in the case.

'Go on.'

'Caroline Hadleigh,' proceeded Betty, 'is working at the Rosling household. In disguise I might add.'

'We followed her,' added Mary.

'Yes, we felt that the apple doesn't fall far from the tree. There's no reason why the daughter couldn't have learned from her father the tricks, so to speak, of the trade,' continued Betty.

While Kit couldn't stop himself looking amused, which earned a frown from Mary, he also felt a swell of pride. It was certainly plausible. After a few moments, he replied, 'Well, you're certainly to be congratulated on uncovering something which, at the very least, appears suspicious. We need proof though. This may not be available until Miss Hadleigh makes a move. That's if she makes a move.'

Mary was well past the point of hoping they were wrong. She trusted her instincts normally and they were telling her Caroline was not a criminal. She looked at the time.

'I need to return. They'll wonder where I am.'

Kit looked stunned by this and said, almost angrily, 'You most certainly are not. This man Rosling is a cad and from what I'm hearing appears to be very interested in you. Who knows what he might do?'

'I'm rooming with Caroline Hadleigh, so I doubt he'll do very much.'

This did not mollify Kit, 'He'll choose his moment. What if you and he are alone?'

'Well,' said Mary, pausing for a moment to think, 'he is rather good looking.'

'Tall too,' pointed out Kit, grimly.

'Broad shoulders,' added Mary, brightly.

'And an arrogant fathead,' continued Kit.

'Utter,' agreed Mary.

'My dear, Kit's right,' said Betty, 'We can't have you put yourself in harm's way.'

'Thank you everyone,' replied Mary rising from the table, 'I appreciate the concern and I will do my utmost to avoid an unpleasant situation arising. Now, I do need to get back.'

Mary's tone, pleasant and calm also brooked no argument. Kit realised that this was something he would have to become used to. It was part of who she was. He was as much in love with her spirit as he was attracted by her beauty. To object now would possibly carry the day but it would lose something greater. He looked at Mary. In the look was an appeal but also an admission of defeat. She returned his gaze and nodded reassurance.

The Phantom

'Harry Miller or I will be stationed outside the house on a twenty-four-hour basis.'

'I can ask Alfred also,' suggested Agatha, 'This way you'll have immediate transport if you feel imperilled by this young hooligan.'

This was a sensible compromise. Mary walked out of the room with Kit.

'At least let me take you back to Sloane Square.'

Mary looked up at him wryly saying, 'Climb into the car of a young man, unaccompanied. What about my reputation, sir?'

With the door to the drawing room closed and Fish not in the vicinity, Kit decided to test Mary's commitment to her reputation. Blissfully, it seemed, his fiancée's defence of principle was less steadfast in deed than word. However, such stolen moments, Kit realised, only increased the pain of separation he was bound to feel when she returned to the Rosling house.

Chapter 18

*February 17<sup>th</sup>, 1920: London*

It was midnight when Mary returned to her room. She opened the door as quietly as she could but then realised Caroline was still awake, reading in bed. In fact, she was reading in German, noted Mary. There was no reason why Mary should have been surprised by this, but she was.

Caroline looked up and said with a grin, 'Hello, what have you been up to?'

Mary laughed conspiratorially. There was little choice but to admit some of the truth. She said to Caroline, 'Promise you won't tell? I have a sweetheart. I went to see him.

Caroline put down her book. This was more interesting. She grinned and asked, 'What's he like?'

Mary needed no second invitation to describe Kit.

'He's good looking. No, make that very good looking. Tall, smart, kind and very funny. He was in the War. A captain.' At this point she stopped as thoughts went through her mind of the awful injury he had sustained and what she had seen of the other men in her care. Tears stung her eyes.

'Was he hurt?'

Mary nodded and looked down, unable to speak.

# The Phantom

'It doesn't seem to bother him, though. It was part of his leg. It certainly doesn't bother me. I just want to be married to him,' admitted Mary with utter sincerity. It was best to stick to the truth and, in this regard, Mary didn't have to act. Before Caroline could ask any other question about Kit, Mary thought it best to redirect the conversation. 'Do you have a sweetheart?'

Caroline hesitated before answering.

'You do, don't you?' continued Mary, hoping this would help her open up.

'Yes,' admitted Caroline sheepishly, 'yes, I do.'

'What's he like?'

'Well, bit like yours. He was in the War, survived unscathed. Doesn't talk about it much, but then we've only been going together a month or two.'

'Do you like him?' asked Mary.

Caroline looked a little troubled though. Mary guessed she did like him. However, falling in love with a policeman was somewhat fraught with difficulties if your profession was burglary.

'I'm sorry, Charlotte, it's none of my business. I think you do like him though,' suggested Mary smiling.

Caroline nodded after a few moments, adding simply, 'Yes, I do.'

Then stop stealing jewels, screamed Mary, albeit inside her head. It was now clear to her that she liked Caroline Hadleigh very much. There was a spirit as well as a vulnerability that she could discern but also empathise with. Her father was in prison, a mother no longer alive; there were no siblings that she was aware of. Caroline was very much on her own and Mary found herself desperately hoping that she was not the

171

person that she, Agatha and Betty suspected her to be. The lights went out, but it was a few hours before sleep came to Mary.

The next morning both had to rush to get ready as they'd overslept by twenty minutes. Each giggled as they danced around the small room dressing and tidying as they went.

'No more late nights,' said Mary grinning.

'I know, come on, Mary, we're going to be late.'

They fell out of the room together and rushed towards the kitchen to have a quick breakfast. Before they entered, Caroline stopped Mary and said, 'Be careful of young Mr Rosling. I don't like the way he looks at you. If he tries anything, just shout. I'll come running. With a heavy object.'

Mary nearly burst out laughing. Then, taking a moment to compose herself, she nodded thanks and they both walked in together to face the inevitable disapproval of Miss Carlisle.

The granite face of Miss Carlisle made it clear that censure was facing the two young women as soon as Grantham had finished his breakfast. They ate in silence and then the two girls were saved, quite literally, by the bell. Two of them.

'Mr and Mrs Rosling. Seems their bells are working again. We should still get them looked at. I still think something's not quite right with them.' said Grantham rising to his feet.

'Miss Hannah, you'll have to finish that later. Best get up and see what she wants. I'll attend to Mr Rosling.'

Caroline glanced sympathetically at Mary, who remained impassive save for a slight crinkling around the eyes. Rose, recognising a distinct chill in the air emanating from a Carlisle direction, came over and asked Mary to help her prepare the breakfast for the family. Mary leapt from her seat and winked at Rose, who grinned broadly. This left Miss Carlisle looking like a wasp had set up home in her undergarments, with its in-laws.

Mary relayed the food up from the kitchen. Grantham was no longer up to the job of lapping around the house like a miler. The first to come down to breakfast was Mr Rosling. He was dressed in a dark suit. At first, he took no notice of Mary apart from requesting a coffee. As she came over to serve him, she felt his hand touch high up on her leg.

'How are you finding things, Miss Tanner?'

In any other circumstances Mary would have enjoyed pouring the hot coffee over the misbehaving man. However, for once, discretion became the better part of temper. She finished pouring and stepped back.

'Miss Carlisle and the staff are very welcoming, sir. Will there be anything else?'

Rosling looked neither abashed nor, seemingly, prepared to acquiesce too soon. Instead, he smiled and said, 'I'm glad to hear it, Miss Tanner, please stay a bit longer.'

For the next few minutes, Rosling made conversation with Mary, asking about her background and life before arriving at the house. He did so in a manner that, it seemed to Mary, was highly practiced, wholly disinterested and calculated purely to allow Rosling the chance to gaze at Mary under the protective cloak of an innocent dialogue between master and servant. By the time Mary finally escaped she had formed a deep dislike of Rosling and a great sympathy for his wife.

-

Outside in the street, Kit arrived to take over from Harry Miller who had selflessly volunteered for the night shift. Miller felt stiff from the hours sitting in the car. And cold. It would take a week to heat up again. A warm bath and a long sleep were the order of the day.

'How was it?' asked Kit, as he climbed into the car. He smiled sympathetically as looked at Miller who was clearly in some discomfort, 'You'd better return to the house. Bath and bed would be my suggestion.'

'Nothing much to report sir,' said Miller. 'Mr Rosling, the elder, left about ten minutes ago. I haven't seen any sign of the young man or the lady of the house.'

'Good,' said Kit enigmatically. He had some modest plans regarding the young buck.

A few minutes later Miller was in a taxi heading back to the apartment in Belgravia. Kit sat in the car with his terrier, Sam. For the next hour there was little or no life around the house and, disappointingly, no sign of Mary. He guessed she would be cleaning the rooms at that this point.

Around ten in the morning, the young American left the house. He began to head in Kit's direction. Kit climbed out of the car immediately with Sam on a lead, lowered his hat, and walked towards Rosling. Pretending to be distracted by a noise on the street, he deliberately banged into the unsuspecting Rosling, using his cane to help trip the American. Rosling crashed to the ground, heavily. Restraining an impulse to cheer, Kit offered apologies as profuse as they were insincere. Rosling, however, was unsurprisingly irate and began shouting at Kit. Never one to duck a fight, Sam entered the fray and gave Rosling a piece of his mind as the American was rising from the ground.

'And get that goddam dog of yours under control,' shouted Rosling. This was red rag to the terrier who increased the volume of his discourse and even threatened to bite Rosling

# The Phantom

the younger. Kit swiftly intervened lest his jape became something more serious.

'You're quite right, sir. So sorry. Sixths, that's enough,' admonished Kit, waving his finger at Sam. This caused the little terrier to stop immediately and turn to Kit with a confused tilt of the head. Kit tipped his hat and moved on swiftly before Rosling could say much more. Seconds later they were around the corner and out of sight. Kit risked a peek at how Rosling was. Unhappy certainly but mostly unhurt seemingly. When the coast was clear, Kit returned to the car, at least reassured of Mary's safety for the time being.

Just before midday, Mrs Rosling appeared with a young woman with lank, brown hair badly hidden under a cheap hat. She wore spectacles which made it difficult for Kit to gain a true idea of her features. However, Kit had no doubt he was looking at Caroline Hadleigh. Less than quarter of an hour later, Mary emerged from the basement steps. At street level she looked around and spied Kit. She crossed the road and made her way to the car.

Kit opened the door to her and said in a cockney accent, 'How much, darling?'

'You couldn't afford me,' replied Mary impassively before adding, 'But as I'm in a good mood.' She climbed into the car and proved to be as good as her word. A few minutes later, when Kit came up for air, he noticed Sam looking at them both with curiosity.

'Don't look, boy,' said Kit to the little dog before turning back to Mary, 'Where were we?'

-

Sally Ryan gently nudged her husband as he lay in the bed. It was lunchtime, which meant Joe's breakfast was ready. He

175

looked up at her, smiled and then groaned. She stroked the side of his face with her hand.

'Rise and shine.'

He pulled her down on top of him which made her giggle.

'Stop,' ordered Sally, 'Uncle Ben's outside having some lunch with our Ben, he'll hear us.'

'Let him,' replied Ryan but alas Sally was not having any of it. She escaped his clutches and ironed out the wrinkles on her dress. She didn't seem too indignant, however. A few minutes later Ben was joined by his brother.

'Hello, Ben.'

Ben nodded glumly back to Joe.

'What's wrong?'

'It's this new case. We're getting grief from up above. They've brought in a couple of other coppers. Hateful people. Thugs.'

'You all are, sure,' replied Joe Ryan with a grin.

'You're funny,' replied Ben Ryan sourly. 'The old man's livid although he won't say anything. Another day and we'll be off the case completely unless we get a break.'

Sensing his uncle was unhappy, little Ben crawled over and attempted to climb up on his uncle's knee. This put a smile back on all their faces.

'Time you had one of your own, Ben,' said Sally knowingly.

'What's going on?' asked Joe Ryan, 'Am I missing something?'

'He has a sweetheart, hasn't he?'

Ben Ryan looked up at his sister-in-law and laughed, 'Last time I tell you anything. You're a real grass.'

# The Phantom

'About time too, Ben. You're a good-looking lad and smart. Lots of girls would love to be with a bloke like you.'

However, the look on his brother's face suggested this was not a subject he wanted to elaborate on. A look from Sally confirmed it was best to drop it for the moment. Instead, the conversation turned to the new job although no mention was made of the secondary revenue stream Ben and his work colleague were developing.

After lunch the two men walked towards the bus stop. Joe was heading in a different direction, so he crossed over the road and waved as his brother stepped onto the bus and headed back towards the city. The sun shone down on him, but it was bitterly cold. He shivered involuntarily for a moment. He turned to a man that had joined him at the bus stop and smiled.

'Brass monkey weather, this.'

The man nodded in agreement but remained silent. A few minutes later, the man reached inside his pocket and took out some cigarettes. He offered one to Ryan who shook his head and smiled, pointing to the cigarette box.

'I work for that company.'

This time the man smiled. It probably wasn't the best idea. What teeth he had were like dark stumps, and not long for this world.

'Really? You don't say.'

## Chapter 19

Whatever one may have thought of Johnny Mac and many, to be fair, did not hold him in the highest esteem, there was no question that he was a hard worker. His values were few and self-serving. However, one of these values was a willingness to put a shift in.

He took pride in little. He was too honest, oddly, to acknowledge anything other than the fact that he was bad, but he knew he was a hard worker. He accepted what his old pastor had often tried to instil in him with a leather belt: he was going to a hell. Not that he cared much about this. Strangely the prospect of being in the company of wailing and gnashing teeth proved oddly prophetic for the exuberantly violent Ulsterman. Although, perhaps not in the way the good pastor, as evil a man as had ever walked the earth in Johnny Mac's expert view, would have had in mind.

Johnny Mac had always been big. By thirteen he was well over six feet, weighing in at thirteen stone and getting bigger. His size, as well as a certain moral flexibility when it came to the use of physical force, soon brought him to the attention of both the police and the Ulster Volunteers, a paramilitary group formed in 1912 dedicated to keeping Ulster out of the clutches of a Catholic-dominated Ireland.

# The Phantom

In many other countries, membership of a group whose *modus operandi* was targeting one section of the local community for violence, might have resulted in imprisonment. Johnny Mac was feted and promoted. Often. His natural predisposition towards brutality allied to an undoubted charisma borne of an evident streak of sadism, saw a rapid rise through the ranks of this quasi-terrorist organisation.

That he avoided jail was a tribute both to an innate street sense as well as the fact that, for practical purposes, the Ulster Special Constabulary and the paramilitary Ulster Volunteers were one and the same thing. In fact, due to the high overlap in their personnel, never mind objectives, the police and the para-military group made official what everyone knew anyway, by merging in 1919. This was long after Johnny Mac had felt it time to relocate. The War was over and, unlike many of his UVF colleagues who had served, Johnny Mac felt it safe to make a career move.

The decision to uproot had been a difficult one. He loved his country. For him, Ulster was God's Own Country. He was a Protestant by birth. He accepted what many of his fellow soldiers believed fervently, that Ulster held a special place in the heart of God. However, unknown to those same colleagues, Johnny Mac was surprisingly agnostic for a foot soldier of Protestantism.

Ever honest, it seemed to him a plainly ridiculous proposition to reconcile the extreme violence he meted out on a frequent basis to Catholics and faith in God. He noted, with some cynicism, many of his fellow warriors had no such problem. He was fine with this. It meant that he could get on with the real business in hand.

Crime.

# Jack Murray

The odd thing about crime, he discovered, was its intrinsic pluralism. Johnny Mac's victims and, sometimes, associates came in all sizes, shapes, genders, and creeds. By day Johnny Mac might be beating the be-jays us out of a Catholic who had strayed into the wrong area, by night he might be working with other Catholics, earning money on the black market. Had he thought much about it, the black economy, which linked the north and south of the island as well as the two religions in a common purpose, was the one true manifestation of Ireland's unity.

Although he feared no man, Johnny Mac accepted he was a prominent target. Literally. Being virtually a foot taller than most meant he was unmissable in a crowd. It was inevitable he would become a focus for republicans. As the price on his head began rising at an alarming rate, he decided the time had come to leave his beloved Ulster.

A move to the mainland, he recognised, would offer new opportunities to expand his criminal horizons. As the republican net drew tighter, he hastened to London. Belfast was becoming a no-go area for him as soldiers of both religions, trained in killing returned from the trenches. They were an altogether tougher prospect than the usual assortment of hard men who had avoided the War.

One final, and relatively lucrative, raid on a village post office provided the pin money to set up comfortably in London. He invested his money wisely: principally property and stolen goods. Dabbling in the black market, plus his inability to avoid excessive violence, soon brought him to the attention of those who could deploy this proficiency to best effect. The criminal underworld.

# The Phantom

And they liked what they saw: a man with sadistic inclinations, brutally uninhibited by any sense of morality apart from an honest dishonesty and the work ethic of the religion he was born into. Once again, in a short space of time, Johnny Mac rose through the ranks to assume wide responsibilities in the serious business of crime.

Frank self-appraisal had long since occasioned Johnny Mac to accept that his gifts were better utilised as a senior rather than a leading figure in an organisation. He was happiest giving and carrying out orders within a remit defined elsewhere. The elsewhere, in this case, was one Charles 'Wag' MacDonald, the head of the Elephant and Castle Gang, or the 'Elephant Boys'.

Few people had ever earned Johnny Mac's full respect. Wag was one. It wasn't just that he'd given up crime to fight in Flanders; the risks in this endeavour surely outweighed the pleasure to be gained from the unhinged violence of war, in the Ulsterman's view. The unnecessary risk to life and limb was also a question mark against him. However, outweighing this was his admiration for the brilliance McDonald had demonstrated in uniting various family factions, reducing gang warfare in the city, and exploiting the business potential of nightclubs and, particularly, horse racing. Wag McDonald transformed skirmishing factions into a single, cohesive unit that linked up with Billy Kimber, another criminal kingpin from the Midlands.

It was late afternoon and Johnny Mac trooped into Wag's office, located at the back of the Duke of Wellington, a pub on Waterloo Road frequented by McDonald and his brothers. There was no greeting when he arrived. McDonald wasn't a man for small talk. He walked in and sat down in front of the boss. Wag McDonald was in his thirties but could have been older. Dressed well in a shirt, tie, and waistcoat, he looked like a boxer working part time in bank.

'You wanted to see me, Wag?' asked Johnny Mac after a minute of silence had passed.

More silence followed as McDonald continued to study the notebook in front of him. Then he wrote a paragraph on the book. Finally, he looked up, past Johnny Mac to the man stationed at the door. Johnny Mac looked at the notebook with curiosity.

'You keepin' a diary, Wag?'

McDonald glowered at the smiling Ulsterman before looking up at the man standing at the door and ordering, 'Bring him in.'

Johnny Mac turned around and was somewhat surprised to see the new arrival. The initial surprise was that he did not enter under his own steam so much as land on the floor. The second surprise was his face.

Abbott was never the best looking of men, but the vicious beating which had recently been administered made him almost unrecognisable. Both eyes were swollen, with cuts and abrasions around his face and a bloodied mouth which probably sported even fewer teeth now.

Johnny Mac reluctantly moved his gaze from the fascinating spectacle that was Abbott back to McDonald for an explanation.

'He ate something that disagreed with him.' Johnny Mac waited for the punchline. 'Wal's fists,' laughed McDonald. 'He tried to sell some snout in the Temple Bar. Snout from your factory.' He pointed at Johnny Mac for added emphasis.

# The Phantom

Johnny Mac laughed mirthlessly and looked down at the pitiful figure of Abbott.

'That was mistake. Silly boy, what are you?'

Abbott groaned in reply. It seemed he was just about alive.

McDonald looked Johnny Mac in the eye, 'You knew nothing of this?'

'No.'

McDonald nodded. He believed the Ulsterman because he saw no good reason why anyone would be stupid enough to go into one of his pubs and try and sell cigarettes to one of his men, inadvertently, unless he was a lone operator, and a stupid one at that.

'He says there's someone else. He said this person made him do it.'

'Who?'

'Wyan or something. It's difficult to make someone out when their mouth is full of teeth.'

'I've found that also. Best to start on the body and work your way up slowly, like,' suggested Johnny Mac.

'Good point. You hear that, Wal? Listen to this man, he knows what he's on about. Who's this Ryan?'

'They're both on the packing. Probably where they stole the stuff,' replied Johnny Mac.

'It was a rhetorical question, Johnny. Deal with him. Make a point to the rest of the boys there,' said McDonald, 'I mean it.'

'We have a problem then,' commented Johnny Mac in a manner that was marginally more casual than the can-do tone his boss was wanting to hear at that moment.

'I pay you to take away problems, Johnny. D'you hear what I'm saying?'

183

The Ulsterman held the palm of his hands up.

'Hear me out. We were aware that Ryan and Abbott were up to something but when we searched them the other night, we found nothing.'

McDonald looked unimpressed, but Johnny Mac indicated he was not finished.

'So, I had both followed. Abbott went home then afterwards he went to the Temple Bar where he was a naughty boy.'

'You knew he was selling snout?' asked McDonald.

'Yes, I found out earlier. Anyway, I haven't finished. Ryan went home and didn't come out again until early afternoon. So, he's not the seller.'

'I don't care,' said McDonald angrily, 'Get him in here. You don't seem to understand this, Johnny. They know we're creaming off cigarettes from the factory. Abbott told me he saw the lorry.'

This seemed to stop the Ulsterman in his tracks for a moment. McDonald had the happy inner glow of triumph that a boss feels when he has put a troublesome subordinate back in his box. However, this was to be short-lived.

'And you're not listening to me, Wag,' insisted Johnny Mac, 'Ryan had a visitor. My man recognised him. He's in the job.'

'He's already been to the rozzers?' exclaimed McDonald angrily.

'Wag, the copper is his brother. He's obviously not one of yours.'

McDonald put the heel of his palms to his temple. The situation was spinning out of control and he needed to think.

# The Phantom

'I can still bring him in,' suggested Johnny Mac finally, 'Find out what he knows. But then we must finish it. That'll bring a lot of problems when his brother gets involved.'

McDonald glared at Johnny Mac. The Ulsterman had a smile on his face. The effect was always somewhat distracting. McDonald never could understand why a man would paint his front teeth black. Bloody Irish, he thought, although never said. This was probably for the best as the Ulsterman would have been deeply offended by being called Irish.

'So? What's your solution then, Johnny?'

'You need to call in some favours.'

Then a smile spread across McDonald's face as he understood where Johnny Mac was heading. He nodded and said, 'I'm think I'm with you now. Maybe it's time some of my people started to earn their money.' He looked meaningfully at Johnny Mac.

'Precisely, Wag. This is exactly the kind of problem they need to take away.'

## Chapter 20

It was late afternoon when Kit handed over watch duty to Alfred. He thanked him again for his support. Quite what the rotund young man could contribute to the physical safety of Mary was up for debate. If anything, he suspected Mary would be a better bet than Alfred. Hopefully matters would not arrive at such a hazardous point. Kit looked in amusement as Alfred arrived with a bag full to the brim of sandwiches.

'Keeping your strength up, Alfred? What do you have there?' asked Kit with a smile.

'Bacon, sir. I'm a somewhat partial to a nice bacon sandwich,' replied Alfred.

Or six, thought Kit.

'I've asked Mary to bring you out some food if she gets a chance. I was worried you would get hungry. Unnecessarily, it seems.'

Alfred laughed, and admitted, 'I never turn down nice food, although I'm not too keen on eggs, to be honest.'

Kit tried hard to avoid looking at Alfred's rather large stomach and wished him well. He confirmed Harry Miller would take over around seven thirty for the night. With that, Kit left Alfred to his observation tasks and went in search of a taxi to take him back to Belgravia, judging it too cold to go on foot.

# The Phantom

Inside the car, Alfred settled down to what he hoped would be an uneventful afternoon of surveillance. He lifted from the passenger seat a fine pair of binoculars and surveyed the house. Nothing much seemed to be happening, so he began to test the power of the glasses on houses further away. The potency of the glasses was immediately apparent as he looked from one bedroom window to another. If the room was lit up it was possible to see quite a bit through the sash windows in the square. From time-to-time people would stray into view. A couple arguing. A young woman dancing. A middle-aged woman alone: she seemed sad. What, at first, had seemed to be a bit of a bore was soon transforming into something infinitely more interesting.

Around six thirty, a light came on the in a dining room at the front of the house. First a butler appeared, followed by a blonde maid. The maid was wearing a black outfit that clung enchantingly to an evidently slim figure. When she turned around, Alfred realised he was looking at Mary. For the next few minutes, she moved in and out of sight. This was somewhat frustrating for Alfred, like listening to beautiful music on a radio which occasionally loses its frequency.

At one point, Mary reappeared in view. Clearly, she had spilled something on the front of her white pinafore. Alfred, watching her hands slowly rub the front of her outfit, experienced a level of excitement he would have dreamt impossible not three hours previously. He shifted position several times as the delicious spectacle he was viewing up close, thanks to the miracle of magnification, sadly reached its climax.

Mary disappeared for a moment and then reappeared walking towards the window. Alfred found himself looking

187

directly into her blue eyes. Those eyes narrowed for a moment into a frown that caused the young man's heart to manage the improbable feat of missing a beat whilst racing like he was sprinting after a bus. Then, all too soon, she swept out of view.

For the next five minutes, Alfred yearned for Mary to return. This felt like a significant moment in his young life. He had enjoyed the vision in the dining room on several levels that he did not understand. To have it so cruelly removed felt close to a bereavement.

The separation was, thankfully, ended by the delightful arrival of Mary to the car. She leaned down close to the driver's window. Only a pane of glass separated Alfred from the almost hallucinatory beauty of this young woman. As desperate as he was to kiss the enchantress, he realised this would have several consequences the worst of which was the certainty of missing out on the food parcel she was carrying.

As ever, Alfred's stomach ruled his heart. He opened the door and Mary handed him the food.

'Can't stay. Enjoy.'

Alfred opened the paper and found chips and what looked like lobster. He closed his eyes and breathed in the aroma of the food and tried to recapture the image of the previous moment so that he would never forget.

-

It had been a waste of a day in Jellicoe's view. Several hours spent with Bulstrode and Wellbeloved reviewing the case notes was as disheartening an experience as he could remember. Their inclination towards more savage methods of interrogation was one thing but, with a realisation bordering on epiphany, the reason they employed this approach was because they had the collective intellect of a tomato.

These faults allied to a general deficiency of character, an absence of morality and a heightened suspicion that there were no depths to which they would sink left Jellicoe and Ryan both feeling thoroughly dispirited from their morning's work. Jellicoe had been tempted to join Ryan when he went to see his brother for lunch.

The plan of attack, which Jellicoe worried they meant literally, was to revisit all the known fences for jewels and to apply greater rigour. The Chief Inspector remembered with a shudder Bulstrode's smile when he said, "rigour".

It was with something approaching ecstasy that, late in the afternoon, Jellicoe heard of Lord Kit Aston's arrival at Scotland Yard asking to see him. Bulstrode heard this with amusement.

'Hobnobbing, are we?' asked Bulstrode sardonically.

'Something like that,' replied Jellicoe rising his from his seat and walking to the door.

Ryan looked up at him hopefully, but Jellicoe indicated to stay. He felt a pang of guilt at doing this, but it was impossible to know if the meeting with Aston would be useful or not. On the one hand there was no doubting Aston's intelligence, his intuitive sense of people and, most importantly, his ability to connect seemingly disparate pieces of information. However, he represented a class to which Jellicoe was not a member, and never would be. The jewel robberies were a threat to this class and Aston had been used once, however reluctantly, as a messenger to communicate this fact.

Jellicoe greeted Kit warmly in the lobby area and asked him to come through to an office. The policeman looked at

Kit wryly and asked, 'What brings you along today, sir? Is there another message to communicate?'

Kit exhaled and looked at Jellicoe with a degree of embarrassment, 'I'm sorry about that, Chief Inspector, it was a favour and I hoped it would ease some of the pressure.'

Jellicoe showed Kit into a room and they sat down. He glanced at Kit and said, 'The Commissioner has invited a couple of other men to join the investigation and take a lead.'

Kit looked at the Chief Inspector. It was often difficult to tell if he was happy or gloomy about any given situation.

'Is this a positive development?' asked Kit.

'Bulstrode, the new man, and his partner, Wellbeloved, have achieved good results in the past. Their approach is, shall we say, robust.'

'I think I take your meaning, Chief Inspector,' replied Kit. 'I wonder if you are interested, in that case, if I offer a suggestion on another possible avenue of enquiry?'

Jellicoe did smile at this point and nodded, 'I would be interested in your thoughts, Lord Aston, certainly. We could do with something new.'

'To your knowledge, did the other houses that were robbed employ a young woman in the days leading up to the robbery?'

Surprise registered on the Chief Inspector's face followed by a nod.

'Yes, Lord Aston. In the first two robberies, this was the case. The third at Lord Wolf's, there were many servants hired for the pre-conference party, men, and women. But, certainly, in the first two cases a young woman was brought in as a maid. The description differed on each occasion but the woman or women in each case were judged to be in their early twenties, respectable and all disappeared after the robbery. We didn't publicise this for the reason I suggested earlier. We could not obtain a consistent likeness. May I ask how you arrived at this conclusion?'

Telling the good Chief Inspector that the possible break in the case was the result of the investigation of two elderly women and his fiancée struck Kit as not being very sensible. Instead, he opted to check one other point that had been nagging him.

'Before we go into that, may I ask you another, related, question. How did the young women obtain these postings? Was it the same agency who placed them?'

'In the first two cases, their predecessors left very suddenly. Coincidentally, the household received a flyer detailing the existence of an agency dedicated to placing experienced servants in houses on either a short term or long-term basis. This agency was called Holland Placements. Of course, when we went to visit them, it was an abandoned office in Clerkenwell. We followed up by checking printers in a wide vicinity, but no one admitted to having done the print job on the flyer.'

'Is this unusual? I mean, would a printer have any reason not to admit they'd created such advertising?'

'None that I can think of unless they feared being implicated in the crime. What are you driving at?'

'I'm not sure. It just strikes me that this is a very well-planned operation. On the one hand you can, presumably, pay off a servant to leave a job. You go to the trouble of printing flyers about an employment agency then place someone on the inside.'

'Ryan and I feel the same way. It appears to be bigger than simply a lone burglar. But, if I may, do you have any information on this young woman or women?'

Kit thought for a moment and then decided to press ahead.

'I think I may know who the young woman is. I've no proof, of course. I also know where she is employed now.'

Jellicoe was unquestionably smiling at this point. His faith in Kit was fully restored and, for a moment, he felt a pang of guilt at the impression he must have given earlier.

'Would you mind waiting here, sir? I think I will bring Sergeant Ryan in on this.'

Kit waited in the office and reviewed what he was about to do. Having Mary working on the inside was causing him anxiety. He believed that young Rosling was capable of anything, especially with staff. Of the elder Rosling he knew little but suspected few would be immune to the charms of someone like Mary. However, by involving the police, was he throwing an innocent young woman to the wolves? He trusted Jellicoe and Ryan, from what he had seen of the young man. The other policemen sounded ghastly, and it would be better for all if the case achieved a swift conclusion.

The two policemen entered the office a few minutes later and sat down in front of Kit.

'Sergeant Ryan, I'm pleased to see you again.'

Ryan smiled and nodded but made no reply. Jellicoe turned to Ryan and said, 'Lord Aston may have information on the jewel robberies which he's going to share with us now.'

Jellicoe and Ryan turned expectantly to Kit.

Kit looked first at Jellicoe and then turned to Ryan and said, 'As I was explaining to the Chief Inspector earlier, I think we all believe there is a connection between the arrival of a young woman as a maid and the recent robberies. I think I may know who the young woman is. She is currently working under an assumed name and in disguise at a house in Sloane Gardens.'

Just as Kit was about to elaborate, the door burst open. The three men turned around to see Bulstrode and Wellbeloved walk into the office.

'Hello, gentlemen,' said Bulstrode, 'I hope we're not missing anything.'

Jellicoe looked up in shock at the new arrival. He took a moment to compose himself before saying, 'Bulstrode, may I introduce Lord Aston.' His voice was steady but there was no question, he had been startled.

Kit stood up and shook hands with the two men. Jellicoe's reservation about Bulstrode were not difficult to comprehend. He had a face even a mother would struggle to love. One look at the two men and Kit made an immediate decision.

'I'm a close friend of Lord Wolf, this so-called Phantom's third victim. He asked me to pop in to see Jellicoe and find out what progress had been made.'

Out of the corner of his eye, Kit saw a trace of a smile on the otherwise solemn face of the Chief Inspector.

'Well, Lord Aston,' replied Bulstrode, 'You may convey to his lordship that the case is under new management and that we will expedite a conclusion. This has been dragging on long enough.'

'Bravo, Chief Inspector, that's the spirit,' responded Kit enthusiastically. He pumped his fist also, hoping it would not guild the proverbial golden goose. 'I'm sure Lord Wolf will be delighted to hear that Scotland Yard are finally getting their act together on this case.' Even Ryan was struggling to stop smiling but for very different reasons from the beaming Bulstrode and well pleased Wellbeloved. 'You see, Jellicoe, this is exactly the kind of attitude we need if we're going to capture this despicable villain.'

At this point Kit took out a notebook and said to Bulstrode, 'Forgive me, but what did you say your name was again? My hearing isn't quite the same since the War.' There comes a point in any man's life when it is necessary to lay it on a bit thick. Kit hoped he hadn't exceeded the limit, but the look on Jellicoe's face was slowly becoming beatific.

'Bulstrode, Samuel Bulstrode and this is Sergeant Alex Wellbeloved.'

'Thank you, Bulstrode. I shall convey all that I've heard to Lord Wolf. He will, no doubt, be pleased to hear that we may soon have some, badly needed, momentum. Take note, Jellicoe, old chap.'

'I shall, sir,' said Jellicoe, gamely getting into his role as the hapless flat foot.

'You too, Ryan,' added Kit, beginning to enjoy himself.

Having said his piece, Kit rose, which forced the policemen to do likewise. He shook hands with the four men and made his way out of the office into the corridor leading to the entrance lobby of the building.

'Glad someone here appreciates what we do,' said Bulstrode as the four men returned upstairs.

Ryan remained silent, but he noticed that Jellicoe, a man whose face he was beginning to read well, looking unusually un-solemn. At the door to their office Jellicoe showed him the reason why. In his hand was a piece of paper. The same type of paper as Kit's notebook. On it were written the following words:

# The Phantom

*Meet me outside at 7pm.*

Chapter 21

There was no sign of Abbott when Ryan arrived at the factory. He deposited his coat in the cloakroom and made his way to the usual spot only to find two other men there. An icy fear gripped him. The prospect of losing a job, even one he didn't like, made him feel sick. Instantly he regretted agreeing to partner with Abbott and steal the cigarettes.

Rusk saw Ryan's arrival and followed him as he walked towards the packing area. The look on Ryan's face was a picture of dismay. It was obvious he thought he was going to be fired. In Rusk's view he should have been. After a few moments he called over to Ryan to come to the office. There was a look on Rusk's face that Ryan did not like. If cruelty had a face then Ryan was looking into its cold, black eyes.

'Johnny wants to see you.'

Ryan followed Rusk away from the factory floor to Johnny Macs's office. Any explanation on Abbott was clearly going to have to wait until he saw the Ulsterman. As it happened, Johnny Mac smiled when he saw Ryan. The fact that his smile was as scary as his frown because of the two painted teeth was not as reassuring as it might have been. Not that Johnny Mac had any yearning to soothe anyone.

'Sit down, Ryan,' said Johnny Mac, ignoring any pleasantries. As usual.

# The Phantom

Ryan did as he was bid but remained silent. He was scared, not for himself, not physically. He'd encountered worse than these two men and survived. If it came to it, he'd give a better account of himself than they might guess. The anxiety was the prospect of losing his job. He stayed silent not to appear tough, but because he was sure his voice would betray his fear.

Johnny Mac and Rusk both looked at Ryan for longer than a few moments, doubtless they were trying to unnerve him. Oddly their tactic rebounded. Instead, Ryan began to feel a swell within him. Anger. He'd felt it towards the Germans. He felt it towards the enemy. Right now, the two men before him were the enemy. The anger he felt was cold, not hot. It was his way. It had helped him survive hell. He would survive this whatever they tried to throw at him.

Perhaps the change in Ryan's self-belief became apparent. Years of looking into men's eyes seeking to frighten them had made Johnny Mac especially attuned to fear. The anger lit something discernible in Ryan's eyes. The moment passed, and Johnny Mac began to speak.

'You've been a naughty boy, haven't you?'

So, they knew.

The rage in him died immediately. He'd been found out. He was guilty, all right. They could fire him and be entirely justified in doing so. Perhaps once more, the Ulsterman saw the change in Ryan, Rusk certainly did.

'Not so tough now, Ryan, eh?' taunted Rusk.

In fact, once again, in a blink of an unguarded comment, Ryan's courage came flooding back. If they thought were going to toy with him like a cat, they had another thing coming. Johnny Mac, as ever, read the change and glanced irritably at Rusk.

197

'Abbott was caught selling snout down at the Temple Bar by one of Wag McDonald's men.'

Ryan's first thought was: *idiot.*

Idiot, idiot, idiot. He felt like screaming in frustration. For himself but particularly for Abbott. Of course, he'd heard of Wag McDonald. Who hadn't heard of the 'Elephant Boys' in south London? This was another level of threat for him. He wondered if the two men in front of him were members of this infamous gang. In fact, was the whole operation part of a criminal empire?

'He says it was your idea,' continued Johnny Mac.

Ryan's face betrayed his immediate reaction to this blatant lie from Abbott. He couldn't bring himself to reply and instead gazed back at the grinning Ulsterman.

'Did you steal snout?'

Ryan exhaled slowly. He could deny everything, but they wouldn't believe him. He could admit it and give them grounds to fire him. His mind was a blur of weighing the options.

'Yes, I stole some snout, but it wasn't my idea. I went along with it.'

There, he'd admitted it. If they fired him, so be it. Lesson learned. An expensive lesson. If they tried it on with him, he'd give some back. He tensed his muscles waiting for the physical intimidation to begin.

It didn't.

Johnny Mac was silent for a few moments.

'Get back to work,' said Johnny Mac finally, 'Rusk will show you what to do.' He turned to Rusk and with a slight nod of his head dismissed both.

# The Phantom

Jellicoe and Ryan exited Scotland Yard ten minutes apart so as not to arouse the suspicion of their colleagues. Jellicoe left first. He walked out of Scotland Yard but saw no car. This made sense as Kit's Rolls might attract attention. Pushing on ahead, he walked around the corner from the police headquarters.

Ryan followed a similar route and caught sight of Jellicoe standing at the roadside. Almost on the dot of seven, a taxi appeared. Kit caught sight of the two policemen and ordered the taxi to execute a U-turn. The road was quiet, and the driver negotiated this without any difficulty.

Jellicoe and Ryan jumped in and they set off to the Sloane Gardens address given by Kit to the taxi driver. Beside Kit was Harry Miller and introductions were made. After these had been completed, Ryan looked expectantly at Kit but a shake of the head and a glance towards the taxi driver indicated any further discussion would have to wait.

A few minutes later the cab pulled up alongside Kit's Rolls Royce situated outside the Rosling household. The four men disembarked from the taxi and went to the Rolls. Inside Jellicoe saw a rather pudgy young man finishing a sandwich. The young man looked up a little guiltily at Jellicoe and Ryan. Despite their plain clothes, there was no mistaking them for anything other than policemen.

Further introductions were made. Then Kit asked Alfred, 'Is the Rosling family all together?'

'No, young Mr Rosling hasn't returned, but his aunt and uncle are there and the two ladies. They also had a visitor, but I couldn't see him. I'm not sure if he's gone yet.'

Kit nodded and then thanked Alfred for his help. As this was the handover with Harry Miller, Alfred was supposed to take the taxi just vacated by Kit and the men. However, prompted by the arrival of the policemen and the prospect of something happening, he asked to stay.

Kit looked at the rotund young man and smiled, saying, 'Of course, Alfred. The more the merrier.' Perhaps there was more to Alfred than met the eye, and there was certainly a lot of him for the eye to meet. Kit explained the situation to the policemen.

'I've brought you here because I've reason to believe it may be the target for the next robbery.'

'How did you arrive at this conclusion, Lord Aston?' asked Jellicoe.

'It's a long story and frankly I can scarcely believe it myself. Suffice to say there are two young women in the house now. Both recently employed. One is my fiancée. She's working undercover to keep an eye on the second who we believe, might be the young woman you are looking for.'

'What is her name, sir?' asked Ryan.

'Caroline Hadleigh, sergeant,' replied Kit. As he said this, he saw the colour drain from the young sergeant's face.

Jellicoe looked astonished also and asked, 'Are you sure?'

'Quite sure,' replied Kit.

'If you don't mind me asking, how?'

It was Kit's turn to look uncomfortable. The question was, entirely reasonable, the answer, scarcely rational.

'My fiancée and two of her,' Kit hesitated for a moment as an image of Aunt Agatha and Betty Simpson hove into view, 'collaborators, suspected Miss Hadleigh.'

This had Jellicoe looking querulous, which Kit had some sympathy with. Ryan remained grim-faced as Kit continued in a manner that would later have him shaking his head in embarrassment, 'My fiancée has suffragist sympathies.' He wisely decided to quit this train of thought while he still had some credibility left.

'So, if I can summarise,' said Jellicoe, 'this is a surveillance operation. The house belongs to a Mr Rosling, is that correct?'

The surveillance operation was for Mary's protection. However, Kit felt it best not to add this ingredient into an already spicy dish.

'Yes, it's a gentleman named Herbert Rosling, not sure if you know him. He heads up the London office of the Anglo-American Bank.'

Jellicoe shook his head for a moment, searching his memory. Finally, he looked at Kit and said, 'There was an American called Rosling at the London Conference on the Middle East.'

'Same one I believe, according to Mary. Not sure if that makes any difference, as the thief may be after Mrs Rosling's rather large diamond necklace.'

Ryan seemed to wake up from a daze at this point and asked Kit, 'You say, "thief", do you mean Miss Hadleigh, sir?'

'I don't think we can be sure, sergeant. There may be innocent reasons why she has taken a position in this house, although her motives for doing so in disguise are, to say the least, unclear. It certainly looks suspicious.'

Ryan nodded in agreement. It was damned suspicious, he thought. His mind burned with possibilities: fear and no little anger making an unpleasant prism with which to refract the evidence.

Jellicoe quizzed Kit a little more on Rosling but it was clear there was not much more to add to the story. Kit decided to avoid mention of his earlier encounter with the younger

American. It was clear to Kit while he was talking to the two policemen that each seemed troubled by the revelations. There could be any number of explanations and Kit felt sure it was beyond merely professional embarrassment at missing a potential lead. Finally, Jellicoe appeared to reach a decision which explained the sense of foreboding on his face.

'I think we must share this with Bulstrode and Wellbeloved. Without wishing to offend sir, this requires a proper police surveillance.'

'Sir,' replied Ryan, clearly agitated, 'They'll just bring her in, and you know their methods.'

'I'm all too aware of their methods, sergeant,' said Jellicoe resignedly, 'But for better or worse, they are working with us now.

Kit looked at both policemen. He wasn't sure if he should feel relieved that the matter would be taken out of Mary's hands, worried that she would be angry at such an event or, more obliquely, a concern about the arrival of the two new policemen, who were clearly disliked, and how they would progress matters. His thoughts were broken by Jellicoe who looked at Ryan and suggested, 'I think you should stay here, and I will return to Scotland Yard.'

Ryan was more than happy to stay but he could not hide his displeasure at the steps proposed by the Chief Inspector. After Jellicoe had left to find a taxi, Kit looked at the young sergeant.

'I'm curious, but was Miss Hadleigh questioned before?'

'Yes, sir,' replied Ryan. Kit said nothing, so Ryan continued, 'I questioned her after the first jewel robbery when it was apparent the thief was using the Phantom's calling card.'

# The Phantom

'Was this to find out if some cards had not been found from the original investigation?'

'Exactly, sir,' responded Ryan, 'The original printer of the cards is dead now, as you know, and the business was closed down. I think there is a haberdasher there now. According to the Chief Inspector, no other cards were found when the premises were searched after the first investigation.'

'When did the printer die?'

'In 1915, sir. Cancer apparently.'

Kit mused on this for a moment and said, 'Still, there was time after the investigation finished to print new cards, if someone required them.'

'Indeed, sir, but why would someone do that? And why wait five years? We have the Phantom locked up.'

'Unless it really is his daughter, sergeant. I have the sense you don't think so.'

Kit's intuition, unlike his nine iron, rarely missed the target. Right now, Sergeant Ryan was all too convinced that his girl was the Phantom. His heart began to thump against his chest like a drum. The car was cold, but he felt sweat tickle his forehead as he became gripped by a mixture of fear and disappointment. He had to fight back an overpowering urge: the desire to run into the house and warn Caroline.

Aware that Kit was looking at him strangely he answered, 'No, Lord Aston, I don't think Caroline's a thief but, I agree, it's very strange.' Regaining his composure, he added, 'Perhaps we need to go back to the original Phantom investigation. Who else might have seen the calling cards?'

Ryan's words seemed to startle Kit, but the highly unusual detective nodded in agreement after a few moments, 'It's a good point, sergeant. The Chief Inspector says they were never made public. However, this doesn't mean the designs couldn't have leaked for a whole host of reasons. The question is, who would have access to see the cards, the wherewithal to organise these robberies and the capability to execute them?'

In the front seat, Harry Miller and Alfred sat listening in fascination for entirely different reasons. The idea of a female thief seemed extraordinary to Miller but then, as he reflected on the War, women had proven themselves to be every bit as good as men in filling in for those who had gone off to fight.

Alfred, meanwhile, was desperate on three fronts. Firstly, he regretted not bringing his notebook so that he could jot down his ideas as he listened to the three men in the back. He was also beginning to feel a little peckish, again. By now, in any normal circumstances, he should have been home with his feet up, enjoying his supper. More pertinently, it would have allowed him the opportunity to pay a visit. Right now, he was at bursting point.

As Kit and Ryan were chatting, a taxi pulled up outside the Rosling household. Ryan alerted Kit to the arrival, 'I wonder what's going on here?'

The question was answered a few minutes later when the front door opened, and a couple descended the steps.

'Looks like the Roslings are having a night out,' commented Ryan.

Kit nodded. He was looking closely at Mrs Rosling and what she was wearing.

'Is something wrong?' asked Ryan, noting how Kit was staring at the couple as they climbed into the taxi.

'I'm not sure, sergeant,' replied Kit. Then more to himself, 'This might be a good night for a robbery.'

# The Phantom

## Chapter 22

This day was proving to be one major hassle after another for Wag McDonald. He looked down at the man who, it seemed, was chiefly responsible for introducing so many complications into his life. On the ground Abbott lay a whimpering mess. McDonald was almost tempted to whimper also because things were certainly a mess.

The cigarette operation was a nice earner for very little effort and could, if managed properly, run for years. The key was to avoid being greedy and nicking just enough to avoid suspicion. Young men were always wanting to get rich quick. Slow and steady. That was your man.

Now, there was a strong possibility that the police were aware of this activity and he had a problem on what to do with Abbott. Lurking at the back of his mind like a flasher in a park at midnight was the thought that Johnny Mac was either losing it or, worse, no longer to be trusted. The Ulsterman would be a very big problem, literally. And all because of some idiot getting greedy and selling some snout in a pub. Yes, Wag McDonald felt like whimpering. A criminal empire pieced together from the factions of south London was potentially at risk.

Rage boiled within him and he walked over to the prone Abbott and snarled, 'You've really messed up my day, son.'

# The Phantom

Abbott groaned. McDonald wasn't sure if this was in sympathy, sorrow or if he was sore from the various broken ribs and cuts. On reflection he felt it was the latter. Without thinking, he kicked Abbott causing further moans from the injured man. McDonald had never been one who subscribed to the view that it was bad form to kick an injured man when he was down. He nodded to his brother, Wal, to come over.

'We need to tidy this up a bit. Get rid of him.' Wal looked surprised by this. His brother shook his head, 'I don't mean that. Can't we give him something to do down at the track? Keep him out of trouble for the moment. Tell the boys to keep an eye on him, mind.'

-

Johnny Mac sat in his office. He was also unhappy about the situation. Ryan was a problem. Continuing to use him was a dangerous game but the alternative was worse. His brother would know where he was working. The prospect that he knew of the other operation did not bear thinking about. This would have to be confronted sooner or later.

From time-to-time Rusk made his presence known to Ryan, without saying anything. The objective was intimidation. To be fair it was working quite well but not through any lack of physical courage on Ryan's part. It was clear to Ryan they knew that he knew about the other operation. The question Ryan was weighing up was whether to come clean on this or to play stupid. In a list with very few limited options, this was distinctly unappealing. For the moment, it would be better to keep things close to his chest.

The noise in the factory was close to deafening at times. Conversation was impossible unless you were within a few feet. The new job assigned to Ryan was mostly solitary. Clearly trust had been broken. He was not to be allowed near anyone else until Johnny Mac and Rusk were sure of him. This was unlikely to be any time soon. It would have disappointed the two men to learn that Ryan actually enjoyed not having to interact with anyone. His own company was all he wanted for the moment. He would have thanked Johnny Mac in any other circumstance

The workers around him, a bit like himself, lacked a certain refinement. However, most looked like they would break the law without batting so much as an eyelash. Ryan was obviously no blushing innocent on this score either, but he reconciled his conscience with an image of his young son. This resolved any moral ambiguity he unquestionably felt, or would feel, in the future. Keeping his boy alive was the only thing that mattered.

His eyes hardened as he thought of the child. Just at that moment Rusk was passing and saw the look on Ryan's face.

'What do you want?' snarled Rusk.

'What do you want?' said Ryan glaring angrily back at Rusk. This caught the little man by surprise. A slow smile crossed his face.

'Get back to work.'

Ryan did so. He resolved to keep his head down and give them nothing more to complain about. The years in the army had taught him when to take orders as well as when and who to confront. Johnny Mac was out of the question, but Rusk was another matter. He might even enjoy that.

-

'We'll be late,' said Rosling, entering his wife's room after a brief knock. His tone was curt. Twenty years of marriage had reduced conversation between them to a combination of implicitly barbed comments, mutual directives, and sometimes impressively informed conversations about business or current affairs. To be fair, the latter formed most of their discourse, mostly to the benefit of the husband.

Although any attraction he once had for his wife had died gradually in the icy tundra of her personality, he was never less than awestruck by her intellect. If he was not the most obvious candidate to support the aspirations of the suffragette movement, Rosling would happily have put his wife on the board of the bank, such was the respect he held for her acumen. The attraction may have died but mutual esteem was high. It even made those occasional moments of disagreement an interesting challenge for rather than a manifestation of hostility.

'They will expect us to be late. It's courtesy on our part,' responded his wife fixing an earring. Beside her, Caroline Hadleigh, put a pin in her hair.

Finally, Mrs Rosling stood up and turned to face her husband. Duty called for Rosling to proclaim how beautiful she looked and to take her hands and demonstrate his undying affection. He did so with a practiced ease but also with enough sincerity to make it seem less like a ritual than a mark of respect between the two leaders.

'Are you not wearing the diamonds tonight?' asked Rosling, as he noticed a gold necklace around her neck: a crucifix.

Mrs Rosling glanced at Caroline and then at her husband before saying, 'I think such a show of wealth would be inappropriate given that we are with the Archbishop tonight.'

Rosling laughed sardonically, 'The church is never backward in showing off its wealth, my dear.'

'My point exactly.'

Rosling smiled and nodded. He looked at her again with a respect and affection that was undisguised. She was a formidable woman. A man such as he could have no better partner. As they walked out of the room together, they discussed what, if anything, Rosling could gain from the evening in return for what the Archbishop would, no doubt, be asking for the church.

As they descended the stairs, Rosling spotted Mary waiting at the door with Grantham. As much as he tried, it was impossible not to allow his gaze to travel up the slim figure of the new maid. She helped him with his coat, as Caroline did the same with Mrs Rosling.

'The cab is outside, sir,' said Grantham.

Neither spoke as they walked outside into the moon-cold night. Rosling took his wife's hand and they descended the steps together slowly, fearful of making any slip that might cause them both to fall.

-

Mary glanced at Caroline as the door closed. Caroline's face broke into a grin. They both moved towards the stairs leading to the servant's quarters. As they descended, the grins became a fit of giggles.

'I rather think Mr Rosling is smitten, Mary'

'I wish he wouldn't be so obvious. I think men are like dogs, sometimes. You can see their tails wagging.'

'I'm sure she knows,' replied Caroline.

'Why does she put up with it?'

'They do get on well, you know. It's strange, I know, but they seem to have reached an accommodation.'

# The Phantom

'I'll never do that,' said Mary, 'God help the man who thinks he can look at other women and be with me.'

Caroline regarded Mary for a moment before saying, 'Somehow I don't think you need worry on that score, Mary.'

They reached the kitchen and conversation stopped immediately. Miss Carlisle sat at the kitchen table while Rose prepared a meal for the servants. She looked up at the new arrivals. They were smiling conspiratorially. She knew she would never know the source of their amusement. Was it her? Someone or something else? After only a day or two they were more intimate than she would ever be with them. They liked one another. That was plain enough. A wave of sadness swept over her. She did not have that closeness. It was something which she no longer felt capable of giving or comfortable in receiving. It had never been her way.

The two young women in front of her had an easiness of manner, a youthful vitality, and a natural beauty, even Miss Hannah, that could not be denied. By dint of her role, or more likely, her life, Miss Carlisle was imposing and awkward in equal measure. Had it always been so, she wondered? Was there a moment in time when another path might have made her into someone different? Both girls had sweethearts. This much she knew. There had been no one in her life.

As the two girls fought hard to suppress their smiles, Miss Carlisle felt like crying. In a moment she would reflect on later, with surprise, she wanted to tell the girls to leave. Not because she was jealous, nor because she felt she was being mocked. She felt neither of these dark emotions, or at least not at this moment. She wanted to tell them to choose another way of life. Service was safe, but it was an escape from life, from experiencing the world yourself. And the world was very different now for young women. There were choices. A bell sounded on the wall causing everyone to look up. Then another. And then another.

'I thought everyone had left,' said Miss Carlisle irritably.

'They have,' replied Caroline.

Grantham walked into the kitchen, also, at this moment and said, 'I think Mr Headley must have fixed the bells.'

'I'll go up and see if he'd like a cup of tea or something to eat, it's quite late now,' suggested Caroline, rising from the table. She looked at Miss Carlisle. A curt nod of the head provided confirmation that she could leave.

'Don't be too long,' shouted Rose as Caroline went through the door, 'I'm serving the dinner now.'

Caroline smiled and replied, 'Just start without me, please.'

-

About ten minutes after the departure of Mr and Mrs Rosling the front door opened again. This time a small, bearded man came out wearing a bowler hat and carrying a bag.

Kit turned to Alfred and asked, 'Is that the man who came earlier?'

'Yes sir, I'm certain,' said Alfred. 'It's the same man.'

The man walked to the bottom of the steps and looked in both directions before choosing to walk in the direction of the car where Kit sat with the other men. As he drew closer, they could see he was wearing spectacles. Underneath his coat he wore overalls. The bag looked like something a workman like a plumber or an electrician might carry. As he passed, he looked at the Rolls first and glanced inside on his way past.

Kit smiled and said, 'It probably looks a little suspicious all of us in this car.'

212

# The Phantom

The others laughed in agreement. Although there were many other fine cars on the street, the Rolls was very distinctive. In this sense it was the perfect cover for surveillance. Kit looked at the small figure of the man recede into the distance before turning a corner and going out of sight.

Something seemed out to place to Kit, but he couldn't quite grasp what. He turned to Alfred and asked, 'When did the man arrive?'

'Around five, sir,' said Alfred.

'Can you remember from what direction he came?'

'No sir, I may have been distracted,' replied Alfred. In fact, he had been finishing the lobster and chips that Mary had brought out and had, only by chance, seen the man arrive. Alfred decided not to say this. There seemed to be a lack of heroism in such an admission and Lord Kit Aston looked every bit the noble hero of one of the penny bloods he loved reading. Another less-than-heroic admission would have been the state of Alfred's bladder, which was reaching danger levels.

Kit looked out the window and began tapping furiously on the door. Something was not quite right. Ryan looked at Kit and then to Harry Miller. Miller shrugged.

'Sir, is something wrong?'

'Yes, but I can't put my finger on it. That man. It's wrong. What we saw was wrong.'

Miller smiled at Ryan. His boss was about to make a breakthrough. He'd seen it before. The tenseness, the frustration, the anger followed by the revelation.

And then it seemed to hit him. Kit turned to Alfred and asked, 'Alfred, when the workman arrived, did he go through the front door?'

'No sir, he went down the steps through the servant's entrance.'

Ryan nodded his head, following Kit's line of thought before adding, 'Perhaps they let him out of the front door because Mr and Mrs Rosling had left and the younger one's not in the house tonight.'

'It's possible,' said Kit, but he didn't give any appearance to thinking it likely.

Alfred was the first to see it. While all the others had looked at Kit, his attention had been drawn to the upstairs window of the house.

'There seems to be a light moving around upstairs, look.'

The four men craned their neck upwards to one of the front rooms upstairs, presumably the bedroom.

'My guess is that it's a flashlight,' said Ryan.

'I think you're right,' said Kit.

He looked at the young policeman. A decision would need to be made. Ryan's heart began to pound wildly. If he went to investigate the game would be up for Caroline. But the game was already up wasn't it?

'Let me go,' said Ryan after a moment. 'I'll say I was passing and saw a suspicious light.'

'Good idea,' agreed Kit.

Ryan stepped out of the car, relieved that he was still in control of the situation. If anything, this was an opportunity to speak to Caroline and warn her. As he walked towards the front door, he felt a wave of relief. There was a chance, just a faint chance that this desperate situation could be resolved before it spiralled completely out of control.

Ryan flew up the front steps and was just about to knock on the door when he saw the two police cars arrive. He hesitated.

## The Phantom

From the front police car stepped Jellicoe with a uniformed constable. From the second police car, stepped a grim-faced Bulstrode followed by Wellbeloved.

Caught like a fawn in front of a hunter, fear gripped the young man. He turned to the door and with a heart hanging heavy in his chest he rapped three times shouting, 'Police, open up.'

Chapter 23

For Alfred, the arrival of the police was like the appearance of the US cavalry saving the day for besieged homesteaders in one of those westerns he'd grown up watching at the picture house. He nearly screamed in joy as Kit and Harry Miller exited the car and joined the other policemen on the steps of the Rosling household.

Alfred was not a man to look a gift horse in the rear, and this was truly a gift from the gods. While the police hammered away at the front door of the house, Alfred virtually beat the car door down himself in his haste to get out. Exiting from the other side of the car, he moved, with a rapidity surprising in someone so large, around the corner, to the road leading towards Sloane Square. It was deserted. This was his opportunity to siphon away his distress and he was going to take matters, quite literally, in both hands.

The front door of the Rosling house finally opened. Grantham looked bemused at the sight on the doorstep. A tall, good-looking young man alongside a smaller man that, in any normal situation, Grantham would happily have crossed the street to avoid. They were joined by several other men.

'Yes?' said Grantham for wont of anything better to say.

'Sir, we've reason to believe your house is being burgled,' said Ryan, in a surprisingly loud voice.

# The Phantom

'You don't have to shout young man, I'm not deaf,' replied Grantham with as much dignity as he could muster.

Bulstrode took decisive action and brushed the elderly butler out of the way. His next obstacle was Miss Carlisle. Even Bulstrode stopped momentarily when confronted with the glaring malevolence that was the housekeeper's natural facial repose.

'Yes?' snarled Miss Carlisle. The servants were certainly spare with the questions, thought Bulstrode as he tore his eyes away from the middle-aged medusa and went up the stairs, followed by Ryan and Wellbeloved.

Kit gently tugged Jellicoe and Miller back.

'Harry,' suggested Kit, 'perhaps you should get onto the street in case the thief looks to exit from an upstairs window. If you search this floor, Chief Inspector, I'll head downstairs to check the servant quarters.'

Jellicoe readily agreed to this proposal and he and Kit went in different directions as Miss Carlisle and Grantham looked on in utter confusion. Seeing this, Kit stopped and explained the situation.

'My name is Kit Aston. For reasons I cannot go into, this house has been under surveillance. We believe a thief may have been in an upstairs bedroom looking to take Mrs Rosling's diamond necklace.'

Comprehension dawned slowly on Grantham's features while Miss Carlisle looked on stonily.

'Will you accompany me, please?'

The tone of voice used by Kit was calm and reassuring. It appeared to work on Miss Carlisle as her features softened a little and she nodded, leading the way for Kit to follow. She had been caught off guard by the extraordinary events, but composure restored, she once more became the woman of, if not action then at the very least, narrow self-possession. This would not last long, however.

Kit's motives for wanting to check the servants' quarters were not a little bit self-serving. He wanted to see if Mary was safe. When they arrived in the kitchen, he saw Mary, bewigged blonde, sitting with the cook no doubt having been ordered to remain there by Miss Carlisle. When she saw Kit, she leapt from her seat and exclaimed, 'Kit!'

She immediately ran over to her fiancé and embraced him.

'Miss Tanner,' called out Miss Carlisle in a tone that bordered on apoplexy. Mary, hearing the housekeeper's cry decided to up the ante in the embrace.

'Mary,' laughed Rose as she looked first from Mary and Kit to Miss Carlisle who had turned white in shock.

Mary finally released Kit and looked at Miss Carlisle, trying to avoid any hint of triumphalism. Trying but failing. Rose, meanwhile, was beaming.

'Where's Miss Hadleigh?' asked Kit urgently.

'She went upstairs to see to the handyman fixing the bells.'

'Miss Hadleigh?' asked Miss Carlisle, now thoroughly confused again. Events were rapidly spinning out of control both upstairs and downstairs.

Mary turned to Miss Carlisle and said, 'Long story and there's no time now. Her name is Caroline Hadleigh not Charlotte Hannah. My name is Mary Cavendish, not Mary Tanner. And this is Lord Kit Aston.'

With this, and as a final flourish, Mary removed her blonde wig. Miss Carlisle promptly sat down in the seat recently vacated by Mary and took a long drink of Mary's tea. Rose, by now was moved to clap.

# The Phantom

'Come on, Kit. Where have they gone?'

Kit took Mary's hand and they headed back up the servant's staircase. Kit explaining on the way the events of the evening. By the time they reached main hallway at the top of the stairs they ran into Jellicoe. The Chief Inspector took one look at Kit hand in hand with Mary and smiled, raised his hat and said, 'Miss Mary. It seems we're always destined to meet in unusual circumstances.'

'Indeed, Chief Inspector,' said Mary.

'Any sign of Caroline Hadleigh?' asked Kit.

The shouts from the top of the stairs answered that question.

-

The younger man, Ryan, was the first up the stairs followed by Wellbeloved and Bulstrode. He continued bellowing 'police, open up' although, he was certain that Caroline, unless she was either deaf, or stupid, would have taken the required steps to absent herself from the building. The shouting by Ryan had begun to fray Bulstrode's nerves.

'Shut up, sergeant, you've made your point. I think every burglar from here to Elephant & Castle will be aware we're here,' snarled Bulstrode.

They all moved toward the front bedroom where the torch had been spotted. It was empty. Ryan breathed a sigh of relief. They split up and searched the other upstairs rooms.

Ryan burst into the next bedroom along, he opened the lights and looked around. Taking a chance, he whispered, 'Caroline?' There was no response. 'Caroline it's me, Ben.'

Silence.

The door opened behind him and in walked Bulstrode. The two men looked at one another for a moment. Had

Bulstrode heard him? Ryan's heart began to beat even faster, and he felt the oxygen evacuate his body.

'No sign,' said Ryan, finally.

Bulstrode nodded and then they heard a shout from the other bedroom. It was Wellbeloved. The two men immediately ran out of the bedroom into the corridor. Wellbeloved was in the bedroom at the far end. They saw the other detective standing by an open window.

'She escaped this way. I saw her climbing onto the roof.'

Bulstrode and Ryan both looked out the window, up at the deserted roof, then to the guttering that Caroline had obviously used to climb up. Ryan looked down at the drop and nearly fainted. This was some girl, he thought. If we get through this, I'm either going to jail her or marry her.

Bulstrode was already on the move out of the room. In the corridor he met Kit, Jellicoe, and Mary.

'No sign of her downstairs,' said Jellicoe.

'She went out the window. She's on the roof.'

Mary gasped involuntarily. She wasn't sure if she'd done so out of fear for someone, she felt was almost a friend or out of pride for the bravery of the young woman.

'My man Harry Miller is patrolling at the back.'

'Let's get down there now,' said Jellicoe but Ryan was already halfway down the stairs, followed by Bulstrode.

-

Such was the blissful interlude enjoyed by Alfred as he released copiously against the brick wall the tension that had built up over the previous hour, he failed to notice Harry Miller run past him. Eventually, he became aware of Miller climbing the wall to his side. Even the presence of Miller was not enough to deny the exquisite feeling of relief being enjoyed by Alfred. However, he felt it best to inquire why Miller was breaking into a neighbour's garden.

'What's happening?'

'Lord Aston wants me to check around the back. This is the only way in.'

Alfred took one look at the wall and realised two things immediately. He was probably lacking the circus-supple agility to scale such a barrier; furthermore, the wall was quite high. A fall from such a height could be quite nasty.

'Can you open the gate when you're on the other side?' pleaded Alfred.

Much to Alfred's surprise the gate opened with Miller saying, 'Come on.'

Thankfully the next barrier was a lot smaller and Alfred, in his newly lightened state, found it within his compass to manage, albeit inelegantly. One more fence was encountered and dealt with leaving Alfred feeling decidedly chipper about both this adventure and his own cat-like dexterity.

The moon shone down on the back of the Rosling house, giving the two men a good view of a small figure dressed in black emerging from one of the windows. Miller immediately sprinted forward.

Alfred whispered loudly and rather superfluously, 'Wait for me.' He watched in amazement as Miller, with the grace and sprightliness of a ballet dancer, hopped onto a bin on the back of the house, followed in one swift movement by his grabbing the top of a wall and levering himself up onto the roof of the basement kitchen.

Clearly Miller was on his own at this point, so Alfred found a garden seat and decided to watch the show from this vantage point. And what a show it was turning out to be. Miller's acrobatic skills were extraordinary, for within moments, he was shinning up the guttering that led vertically all the way to the roof, in pursuit of the dark figure that had so recently emerged from the window.

At the picture house, Alfred liked nothing better than accompanying his film viewing with a generous snack. Sadly, this was the only thing missing as the spectacle in front of him unfolded.

Just as Miller had made it onto the roof, a man appeared at the window and shouted at Miller to halt, obviously mistaking him for the thief. Alfred stood up and went to correct the misapprehension but decided against doing so as he saw the highly unattractive features of the man at the window. Instead, he returned to his seat and watched two dark silhouettes clamber over the rooftop. The direction of travel looked to be back towards the road from which he and Miller had come.

Reluctantly, Alfred rose from the seat and retraced his footsteps over the fences, through the neighbour's garden towards the alley. Up ahead he could see the first figure had an athleticism no less than Miller's and was sliding down the roof towards another vertical pipe that led all the way to the ground.

This presented Alfred with a dilemma. If he broke into a trot, something he hadn't done since 1917, he could conceivably reach the alley way before the villain. This would mean he could catch the thief. However, Alfred wasn't a brave man. Nor was he so gifted athletically that the encounter may not end up the worse for him. Discretion formed the better part of valour. Alfred made stately progress to the alley while the two figures descended the pipe.

# The Phantom

He opened the gate just as the first figure landed on the ground, lightly and with perfect balance. The figure was disguised under a black balaclava. Two eyes glanced at Alfred before disappearing into the night.

Moments later Miller hit the ground. A loud groan followed. It was clear in his haste to make up ground, Miller had elected to jump from a greater height than, in other less urgent circumstances, he normally would. The result was a heavy fall. Miller rolled around the ground in agony, clutching his right ankle.

Alfred hurried over to the stricken man.

'Catch her,' ordered Miller through gritted teeth.

But she had vanished, and Alfred was under no illusion as to who would have been the winner in any race between them.

'It's too late,' said Alfred.

Moments later the policemen arrived along with Kit and Mary. Alfred looked up and said, 'I think she's escaped. Mr Miller has hurt his ankle.'

This much was obvious and Kit, along with Mary, immediately made their way forward to Miller. Mary immediately cradled Miller's head in her lap. Alfred looked at Miller, whose face was a picture of agony because of an ankle that was, in all probability broken, and thought: you lucky sod.

## Chapter 24

Kit and Ryan helped Miller back to the Rolls. Alfred agreed to drive Miller to a nearby hospital. The policemen, Kit and Mary returned to the Rosling household. Standing at the door was the younger Rosling. He looked in a foul mood. Beside him was Miss Carlisle with Grantham lurking inside.

'What on earth is the meaning of this?' demanded Rosling.

Jellicoe noticed with some amusement that Bulstrode slowed his stride imperceptibly, leaving Jellicoe to face the first fusillade from the young man. He found this oddly reassuring. It proved to his satisfaction that Bulstrode was either a coward or lacked the seniority and gravitas to deal with the upper classes on a rant.

By this stage Rosling was in full flow demanding to know who was in charge. Jellicoe presented himself.

'Mr Rosling, my name is Chief Inspector Jellicoe. These are my colleagues, Detective Inspector Bulstrode, and sergeants Ryan and Wellbeloved.' Then with added emphasis he said, 'I'm in charge.'

'Well, you better explain to me what in the hell is going on,' responded Rosling, some of the fire dying in the presence of Jellicoe's seriousness.

'Yes, sir. May we step inside?'

224

# The Phantom

As this made eminent sense, even to the indignant young man, the group went inside to the entrance hall. As they did so, Rosling's highly attuned eye for an attractive ankle and more found itself slowly moving upwards to be met by the blue and highly amused eyes of Mary Tanner looking back at him. Only it wasn't Mary Tanner. Gone was the blonde hair, but the maid's uniform remained. Then he noticed Kit.

'Have we met before?' asked Rosling, eyeing Kit closely, desperately searching his memory for where and when.

'Sheldon's, I believe. I think I've seen you in the dining room there. My name is Aston.'

The scepticism in the stare that Rosling gave Kit was positively surgical. However, as his memory had been somewhat dulled by the several bottles of champagne he'd consumed over the course of a convivial evening in town, he was in no position to debate the point. He returned his focus to Jellicoe and tried to ignore the mocking smile of Mary, who he noted with dismay, was holding the hand of Kit.

Jellicoe addressed Rosling. 'Mr Rosling, we came by some information that your aunt might be the target of a robbery. Specifically, a diamond necklace.' He then held his hand up to silence Rosling who was about to interject.

'The first thing we must do is establish if the thief has stolen the necklace.

-

Rosling led the four policemen upstairs to his aunt's room. He marched straight over to a dresser and opened the top drawer. Inside was a metal box. The key was in the box. Rosling looked up at the policemen. Before he could open the box, Jellicoe touched his arm and shook his head. Removing a pen from an inside pocket he hooked it under the lid and raised it up. It was empty.

Rosling stared at the box. With a voice trembling in anger, he turned to the policemen and said, 'The diamonds are gone. And you let the thief escape. You'll regret this.'

Jellicoe had no doubt he would. This was serious. He turned to Kit and Mary. The look on his face was neutral but Kit guessed he was angry. This was a police matter and Kit should have drawn the attention of the Chief Inspector earlier. Kit knew this and immediately felt a profound regret. He'd let Jellicoe down. Now the Chief Inspector would be thrown to the wolves.

Mary glanced up at Kit and saw the troubled look on his face. She too, understood the import of what had happened. A wave of anger and something approaching grief gripped her. The excitement she'd felt at getting involved in this affair had gradually begun to pale as she had grown to like Caroline Hadleigh better. The folly of this was all too apparent. She had let her own feelings and emotions cloud her judgement. She knew Kit would try to make her feel better. He wouldn't blame her. But Mary knew she had only herself to blame.

Rosling glared frantically at the policemen.

'Are you just going to stand there? Why aren't you out catching this criminal.?

Given the circumstances, Jellicoe remained calm and looked Rosling directly in the eye. This seemed to throw the young American who stopped for a moment and looked at the Chief Inspector.

'Mr Rosling, I think we should retire to the drawing room. Detective Inspector Bulstrode and I will question the staff, Miss Cavendish and Lord Aston.'

# The Phantom

Rosling glanced at Mary with something approaching disbelief. Mary looked back at him coolly. However bad she felt about the theft and her role in it, she felt little for Rosling. The loss was not his, but Mrs Rosling's.

'Sergeant Ryan and Wellbeloved will go back to Scotland Yard and set up a search for Caroline Hadleigh or Charlotte Hannah as you know her. Sergeant Ryan questioned her in connection with previous robberies and we will circulate a description to the newspapers tonight.' Turning to Ryan he added, 'I want you with a police artist immediately, sergeant. I want her picture in every newspaper by tomorrow afternoon. Wellbeloved, I want you to get a team down here immediately to look for fingerprints.'

Kit listened to Jellicoe give commands and found himself impressed with what he saw. The clear-headedness and the calm authority would have made him a leader in any circumstances. The aura around Jellicoe seemed to spike the anger of Rosling for the moment and both Bulstrode and Wellbeloved were clearly happy for Jellicoe to take a lead here, knowing that when the blame began to be apportioned, they would be safe.

One thing perturbed Kit, however. Risking a glance at the two other policemen he could see Bulstrode whispering in Wellbeloved's ear and then both looking towards Ryan. Unfortunately, Kit wasn't near enough to hear what was being said. When Jellicoe finished, Kit immediately went over to him.

'Chief Inspector, I recognise I'm probably the last person you want to get advice from now, but may I have a word with you?' Kit indicated with his eyes that they go outside the room.

Jellicoe nodded and they both went outside. Kit put his hands up and said, 'First of all an apology. I should have involved you the second I heard what Mary was doing.' The look on Jellicoe's face confirmed this but the Chief Inspector remained silent, so Kit continued, 'I think that those two men are planning something. I would tell Sergeant Ryan to be on his guard.'

Jellicoe nodded but there was an even more sombre aspect to his face when he said, 'I think, sir, it will be academic. After this fiasco I will be taken off the case and Bulstrode will be given free rein.'

This news made Kit feel even more downhearted. He knew he had let the Chief Inspector down and now, to make matter even worse, this would unleash two unscrupulous detectives on the case.

'Chief Inspector, I feel responsible for what has happened. Please let me speak to Commissioner Macready. I'm sure he'll listen to me.'

Jellicoe gave a slight shake of the head. This mission was his to bear and his alone. Kit knew there was no value in arguing with Jellicoe on this point and respected him even more for his integrity. At this moment, Rosling began to complain again forcing Jellicoe to leave Kit and mollify the young American. Bulstrode stayed out of the line of fire and went in search of the remaining staff to question them.

It was clear Rosling was complaining about the presence of Mary. He appeared to be blaming the police for not keeping the family informed of the work Mary was doing undercover. Mary, hearing this, moved to go over to Rosling but felt her arm being held by Kit. He shook his head and Mary stopped, her brow furrowing, in place of a question.

# The Phantom

'Let the Chief Inspector handle this his way. We've enough explaining to do anyway.' Mary nodded and looked as crestfallen as Kit. She understood that the failure to capture Caroline would play badly for Jellicoe. As yet she was unaware of the consequences for him. Kit decided to refrain from saying anything. It was clear she felt bad enough anyway.

'I'm sorry, Kit. I've really made a hash of things, haven't I?'

'Stop, Mary. It's not over yet. Remember, you've identified the robber. She won't escape far. The police now know who to look for. This wouldn't have been possible without you.'

Mary smiled up at Kit, but her heart wasn't in it. She felt desperately sad on so many levels. Seeing the eyes of Rosling and Jellicoe on her, she took Kit's hand and walked forward to face the wrath of the American. As much as she detested the man, she couldn't really blame him for what he was about to say.

As Kit and Mary walked forward, the door of the drawing room opened and in walked Mr and Mrs Rosling. Everyone in the room turned to them. The elder American's face was puce with anger.

'What in tarnation is going on here? Grantham called the Archbishop's palace. He said there's been a robbery.'

Kit glanced at Jellicoe and his heart sank even further. The Chief Inspector's evening was just about to get worse.

-

Your boss is for it, and no mistake,' said Wellbeloved, by way of conversation. Ryan turned and looked at Wellbeloved but said nothing. He was in no mood to listen to anything from this man but, rather frustratingly, he was somewhat of a captive audience. Wellbeloved was sitting with him in the back

229

of the police car being driven by a constable. They reached Scotland Yard in a manner of minutes.

Sensing that Ryan was already on edge, Wellbeloved decided to press ahead. This was too good an opportunity to pass on. From an early age, Wellbeloved had realised that real power over people came not through physical dominance, although that had its place. No, if you wanted to grind someone into the dust it required a more nuanced approach. It would also be a chance to check out if Bulstrode's suspicions were correct.

'Who'd have thought the girl was the thief? You interviewed her, didn't you?'

'We don't know if she's the thief,' replied Ryan sourly, as they climbed from the car.

'Is she pretty?' asked Wellbeloved. The look on his face suggested that any response would be greeted with a significantly cruder follow up inquiry. Ryan ignored him and fixed his eyes straight ahead. This served only to make Wellbeloved's smile grow wider. 'She won't stay free long and then when we have her back at the nick. I'll set to work on her. Should be fun.'

Ryan clenched his fists. His chest tightened as the rage grew within him. The thought of Caroline being interrogated by this animal was almost unendurable. Fear and frustration created a pressure inside his forehead that made him want to scream.

Inside the building, Wellbeloved, as the senior man ordered Ryan to go and see the police artist immediately so that they could get a description of the Caroline Hadleigh and circulate it to the police officers in town as well as the newspapers. Reading Ryan's mind, he said, 'Make sure you give a good description. You and your boss are in enough hot water. I'm going to make some calls and set up the search.'

Ryan did not attempt to hide his dislike of his fellow officer. However, he had no choice but to do as he was told. He made his way up the stairs to the office of the police artist, hoping he was not there, or busy. Unfortunately, he was there and clearly at a loose end.

'Come in, Ryan,' said Rufus Watts, happy to have some company, 'How can I help you?'

Ryan slumped on the seat and looked at Watts.

'You look like you've lost a shilling and found a sixpence,' said Watts sympathetically. He was a smallish man nearer forty than thirty and dressed very neatly. By London police standards he was somewhat unusual.

He wore his hair slightly longer than was either fashionable for men or, indeed, acceptable for a member of His Majesty's Inspectorate of Constabulary. From time to time when talking, he might brush an imaginary out-of-place lock back behind his ear. This wasn't the only thing that might have been considered a quirk of character for the bachelor Watts.

However, his brilliance as a police artist was recognised by all and a blind eye cast by those around him to the hours he worked, his disregard for rank or authority and his generally artistic manner. Most of the detective-level members of the force had gladly called upon his services at one time or another. It was in no one's interest to get on the wrong side of the little man. In fact, it was a well-established fact that he nourished a quarrel like plants in a garden, watering them daily with sharp words and, surprisingly, his fists.

'Long day,' explained Ryan.

Watts looked at him shrewdly and said, 'Looks like more than a long day to me.'

'With Bulstrode and Wellbeloved?' Ryan responded with a question that was its own answer.

Watts nodded slowly. He understood now. He smiled sympathetically again and said, 'What can I do for you?'

Ryan told him. For the next half hour, Watts magically reconstructed the face of someone who might pass for Caroline Hadleigh or might not. Ryan felt there was just enough of Caroline in the drawing to protect him from any accusation of misleading his colleagues while ensuring it was far from being a perfect match. Just as Watts finished the drawing, the door burst open. Wellbeloved entered, grinning malevolently.

'No need to knock, old chap,' said Watts sardonically. 'Make yourself at home.'

Ryan looked up at Wellbeloved. The sergeant made straight for the drawing and took it from Watts.

'Is this finished?'

But Ryan didn't answer, he was looking at the woman who followed Wellbeloved into the artist's office. Wellbeloved noted the surprise on Ryan's face with amusement.

'Another customer for you, Watts. This is Miss Carlisle. She can help improve the drawing's likeness. After all, it's been a while since Ryan saw the young lady, isn't it?'

# The Phantom

## Chapter 25

'I've heard of blind leading the blind, but this is ridiculous,' commented Mary as she looked at Kit, limping and holding a stick while his other arm was around Harry Miller, helping him down the hospital steps. Alfred manned the other side.

Miller, who had been diagnosed with a broken ankle from his fall, took Mary's jest in good spirit.

'His lordship will have to look after me now,' said Miller.

'Quite right too,' agreed Mary, 'Will do him good.'

They placed Miller gingerly into the back of the car and returned to Kit's apartment. It was around ten in the evening. Having settled the injured Miller down, Alfred drove Kit and Mary to Grosvenor Square where Aunt Agatha was expecting them, having been tipped off by Mary in a phone call a little earlier.

Fish led the couple through to the drawing room to find Agatha waiting. She looked up eagerly.

'How is your man, Christopher?'

'A broken ankle and possibly shin bone. Serious enough, and more than a little painful. The poor fellow's fine otherwise.'

'I'm glad to hear it,' replied Agatha. 'Now tell me what happened.'

So, they told her.

Each took turns to provide the elderly lady with a fairly comprehensive summary of the night's events. Agatha listened intently but said little. Kit looked at his aunt as he and Mary related their story. Her eyes glistened with intelligence, widening from time to time as the details of the rooftop chase were relayed; her skin had the colour and vitality of youth; her hands had a knuckle-white grip of the table as Kit contemplated the likely consequences facing Jellicoe and Ryan. The mention of Ryan's name brought a gasp from Agatha.

'Aunt Agatha is something wrong?' asked Kit when he saw his aunt's reaction.

Agatha glanced at Mary and then at Kit. If anything, and to Kit's wonderment, Agatha's previously alert gaze had transformed into a look that didn't so much suggest guilt as broadcast it. Kit glanced at Mary, who was trying to suppress a grin.

'What's going on?' demanded Kit, not sure whether to laugh or to explode. He decided to keep his options open.

'Well, Christopher,' replied Agatha, regaining some of her *hauteur*, 'I'm not sure I like that tone of voice.'

'I don't care, Aunt Agatha. A good man is about to be pulled from a case and publicly humiliated which might have been avoided if you two and Betty bloody Simpson hadn't decided to play at being detectives.'

Both Mary and Agatha looked at one another. There. It was out now. The cold, naked truth of their folly. Kit was quite right to feel upset. Both knew this, but the knowledge offered little comfort.

'Of course, Christopher, you're quite right,' acknowledged Agatha humbly. She held her hand up as Mary was about to speak. 'I take full responsibility for what has happened. We should have gone straight to the police with what we found. Mary...,'

'Should have known better,' interjected Mary, remorsefully. 'I'm sorry, Kit. Really. I've made a mess of things, haven't I?'

'We all have,' said Kit grimly. 'Now what's this other thing you want to tell me?'

Agatha told him.

When she'd finished, Kit sat back in his chair, head swimming with images of a drunken Betty Simpson attempting to drive. That this was only marginally less astonishing than the fact that Ryan and Caroline Hadleigh were sweethearts was a tribute to just how far this case had spun wildly off its axis.

The two women were sheepishly silent while Kit pondered on what he had heard. Almost to himself he said, 'That does explain some things which were troubling me.'

'Really' said both ladies in unison.

'Yes, Ryan was definitely taken aback when I told him that Caroline Hadleigh was working in the house and could be implicated in the recent robberies.'

'What do you mean implicated, Kit? She's the Phantom. It all fits,' said Mary somewhat exasperatedly. There was absolutely no reason that the feted Phantom couldn't be a woman. She was just about to give Kit a piece of her mind when Kit spoke again.

'Of course, Caroline Hadleigh may be the Phantom. I'm not ruling anything out. I just don't want to rule it in and ignore any other possibilities.'

'Such as?' asked Agatha, equally unhappy at the implication of Kit's words on the *gentler* sex.

Kit shot her a look. Both Mary and Agatha were watching him intently. A part of him wanted to reveal his thoughts but the anger was still too recent.

'You can be as angry as you wish. I'll sleep on this and we can discuss it tomorrow morning. I want to see if this reaches the morning papers, and how it is portrayed. I also want to know what happens to Jellicoe. We're playing a bigger game here. And fundamentally, whatever I may be thinking, I do not have a scintilla of evidence to back it up.'

Mary frowned a little but decided to let it rest. She had hardly covered herself in glory these last few days, and it was not the time to pitch up and make battle. Agatha looked no more pleased than Mary but said nothing. However, she had long since mastered the dark arts that can make a chap feel completely in the wrong even when he is utterly blameless. And an art form it surely is. Mary observed Agatha like an apprentice observes a master.

Such advanced techniques can, in the hands of an amateur of course, resemble mere petulance or worse, a huff. A chap, if he has anything to him, will immediately discern such trifling behaviour for what it is, and disregard it as peremptorily as good manners allow. Beware, though, the expert female practitioner. The manner of Agatha had, historically, suggested little form on this course. Any handicapper would have been taken in and been forgiven for believing this to be a weak nag rather than an uncommon thoroughbred.

All this left Kit surprised by the meek acceptance of his aunt that she had behaved badly: the sorrowful tilt of the head; the mournful glance up, suggestive of, but not quite achieving tears and the silence that spoke volumes, and rather loudly, too.

# The Phantom

Kit felt wretched. He trooped out of the room accompanied by Mary. A swift glance by Mary as she went through the drawing door, unseen by the guilt-ridden Kit, confirmed that the recovery in Agatha's spirit was as swift as it was complete. She was already pouring a generous amount of sherry into two glasses.

When they reached the front door in the hallway, Kit looked down at Mary, with an overwhelming feeling of regret. Had he been too harsh? Would she think him heartless and cruel? Thankfully, one look from Mary established that he had been forgiven and he left the house, feeling once happier and more relieved and utterly oblivious to the way the two women had so artfully manipulated his good nature.

-

It was just nearing midnight when Detective Sergeant Ryan made it back to his flat near Vauxhall station. The air was dagger-cold and the streets empty yet full of life, hidden, lurking around corners and in doorways. Ryan hated the area, but a sergeant's wage was not enough to afford much more. He would move at the first opportunity.

His apartment building would have been nondescript had it not been so noticeably ugly. There were boarded up windows, tiles missing and damaged brick work, the rest of the features were just plain unsightly.

The brightness and beauty of the building captured Ryan's mood perfectly as he walked like a pensioner towards the steps leading up to the entrance. He opened the front door and virtually staggered up the staircase to the second floor where he had a one bed, one room flat.

At the top of the stairs, he paused. He held back and looked through the railings. There was someone outside his flat, sitting on the floor of the corridor. With a shock he realised who it was.

Caroline.

He leapt up the stairs and called out, 'Caroline. What are you doing here?'

'Ben,' cried Caroline leaping up immediately and running into his arms. For the next few minutes Ryan comforted her, or was it himself? He held her tightly and they went inside his flat. It was only when he released her that he realised she was dressed in the clothes of the workman who had earlier passed them outside Rosling's.

Ryan was relieved the flat had been cleaned that day. His one luxury was to have a lady in twice a week. The long hours and a natural male disinclination towards housework, even in such a small space, made the investment more than worthwhile.

They sat down, and Ryan went into the kitchen to make a cup of tea. Wisely he decided against asking the three dozen questions he wanted to ask her. Instead, he gave her time to recover her composure. Whatever she told him, he knew he would believe, because against all the training he was receiving, this is what he wanted to believe. The idea of Caroline as a kleptomaniac was more than he could bear.

They sat for a few moments drinking tea, looking at one another. Finally, Caroline spoke, 'You were outside the Rosling's, Ben. Why were you watching that house?' Her composure had returned, and there was a coolness in her voice that seemed at odds with her earlier reaction upon seeing him.

A voice screamed inside Ben's head, why were you inside it? He gripped the cup so tightly he realised it might break.

# The Phantom

'We were given a tip off that the Phantom would target this house next.'

Caroline looked shocked. She leaned forward, 'Ben, I know you have a lot of questions. I'm sorry, I've not been completely honest with you. But you'll have to trust me. Please, I must know how you knew.'

Ben looked at Caroline. Frustration fought hand to hand with love. He wanted her to tell him everything and more, yet he was the one having to explain.

'It was pure luck, Caroline. The fiancée of Lord Kit Aston somehow connected you to the other houses that were robbed. She followed you and saw that you were now employed in disguise, as a lady's maid to Mrs Rosling. Then she somehow managed to find a job in the house under an assumed name.'

'Mary?' exclaimed Caroline.

'Yes, or Mary Cavendish. She's engaged to Lord Aston. He helped the old man in that chess case last month. He's bright. The old man listens to him. He told us about you and that's why we were outside. And then there was the robbery. Caroline, you must hand over the diamonds. The police are looking for you. They have your description and Miss Carlisle has given a description of you in your disguise as Charlotte.'

Caroline nodded but, oddly, seemed less than perturbed by the latest development. In fact, the more Ryan had related about the night's events, the more at ease she became.

Finally, she looked at Ben and said, 'You must believe me, Ben. I didn't steal any diamonds, not now not ever. But I can't explain more than this.'

'Of course, I believe you, my love, but the evidence is...'

'Misleading,' interjected Caroline. 'Look Ben, I need a place to stay. Can I stay here?'

Ryan thought for a moment. Then he had an idea.

'It's not a good idea, Caroline. It would create too many questions that I could never answer. I have somewhere. You'll have to come with me.'

Caroline looked at him for a moment. He looked back at her. Could she trust him? She made her mind up immediately. She put her hand up to his face and touched his chin.

'I'm sorry, Ben. Sorry for getting you involved.'

'Don't worry. Let's get you to a safe place until we can figure out a solution.'

Ryan helped Caroline on with her coat. His mind was torn, however. If he was helping a criminal escape, his career would be over. This much was certain. He couldn't live with the secret. But he truly believed she was innocent. He believed there was an explanation. However improbable this explanation turned out to be, his faith in her wouldn't waver.

They moved towards the door when Caroline stopped him. She looked up into his eyes, put her arms around his neck and spent the next minute ensuring that Ryan would forever be on her side.

They moved quickly down the stairs, out of the door and into the wet night. Rain had begun falling in sheets. Puddles formed on the pavement, forcing them to run in a weaving fashion towards a taxi rank nearby Ryan's apartment. A sole taxi was waiting. They climbed in and drove off.

Across the road from Ryan's apartment building, in a side street, a car sat in the shadows. Inside, a man lit a cigarette and put it in his mouth. He smiled as he thought of the money he was going to receive for his hour's work. Tidy. Very tidy. He started up his car and drove off in the same direction as the taxi. However, just ahead of him, another car had also pulled off the kerb, evidently following the taxi. As the first car made pursuit, it splashed an old tramp, leaning drunkenly against a lamppost.

'Bloody hell,' shouted the tramp, staring down at his wet clothes.

Moments later the second car roared past the tramp, right through the same puddle providing the poor man with an even more impressive dousing than the first car.

The tramp stared at the car flying off in the pursuit of the first. He regarded his soaked clothes once more.

'You've must be bleedin' kidding me,' he said sorrowfully, before looking back up at the second car receding into the distance.

'Bloody police!'

Jack Murray

Chapter 26

*February 18ᵗʰ, 1920: London*

It was after one o'clock in the morning when the phone rang in Johnny Mac's office. Rusk was alone in the office and answered it. The voice at the other end of the line was instantly recognisable.

'No, it's Rusk, Mr McDonald. Can you wait? I'll find him.'

Rusk rushed outside to the factory floor. Not many men were willing to keep Wag McDonald waiting, and Rusk was certainly not keen to join the hardy minority who had tried and lived to regret this folly. An unwearied patience, and the leader of the 'Elephant Boys' were not, in any way, synonymous.

He found Johnny Mac standing upstairs on a gantry overlooking the floor. He was gazing down at the ant-efficient activity below him. He put a cigarette to his lips. A different brand from the one they were producing, noted Rusk. He didn't blame him. He cared little for this brand either. Rusk hurried towards Johnny Mac and told him who was on the phone.

A minute later, an impressively quick Ulsterman was back down in his office picking up the phone saying, 'Hullo, Wag, it's Johnny. What can I do for you?' He tried not to sound out of breath lest the gangland leader think him nervous. In truth he was a little bit of both.

For the next two minutes Wag McDonald explained exactly what he could do for him. Throughout, what was by McDonald's high standards an exciting and colourful monologue, the Ulsterman said nothing, remained motionless, listening intently, nodding periodically, and widening his eyes in surprise frequently. It was obvious McDonald had quite a story to tell and Rusk, looking on, was desperate to know what it was. Finally, the call finished, and Johnny Mac looked up, grinning eerily at Rusk.

'You're not going to believe what's happened.'

Rusk was all too willing to believe that he would not believe what had happened. This much was clear, even if little else was.

'So,' started the Ulsterman, 'this Phantom, you remember that thief from a few years back, has nicked some diamonds from some 'nob in town. It turns out he is, in fact, she. It's the daughter of the guy they banged up. So far so good. Wag's man in the coppers has told him that she made off tonight with the diamonds underneath the noses of the flat fleet who were waiting outside. You'll love this next bit, one of the coppers turns out to be her boyfriend.'

'What?' exclaimed Rusk in either delight or shock. He didn't know which either.

'No, it's true. And there's more. It turns out the copper is none other than the blue-eyed boy, Sergeant Ben Ryan.'

Rusk looked mystified for a moment. He half smiled but he was really buying time while he searched his memory for why this was important. Johnny Mac's smile faded a little as he realised, not for the first time, just what a moron Rusk was. A thin shaft of light finally penetrated the gloomy darkness of Rusk's mind

'Bloody hell, Ryan.'

'Yes,' said the Ulsterman sourly, still irritated by the slowness of his colleague. 'Guess where he's taken her?' The look on Rusk's face was more than Johnny Mac could withstand and he decided to answer his own question rather than endure the treacle-slow gloop that passed for Rusk's thinking capability. 'He's only gone and taken her to our boy Ryan's house.'

Even Rusk, dear Rusk, could see the implications of this. And he asked the question that was in Johnny Mac's mind and implied within the order the Ulsterman had just received from Wag McDonald.

'Do you think she has the diamonds on her?'

Johnny Mac looked up at Rusk meaningfully, 'I think Wag would like us to find out.'.

-

'I'm sorry it's not much, Caroline,' said Sally, looking around at their tiny living room. She certainly wasn't lying thought Caroline, but she was too grateful, too well brought up and ultimately too nice to say anything untoward.

'Don't be silly. I'm just sorry that I've disturbed you all.'

Sally gave her a hug and said 'Nonsense. Will you be all right sleeping on the sofa? I don't want to wake the kids.' She motioned with her head towards the bedroom.

'Of course, I understand. Are they still sleeping?'

'Yes, would you like to see them?'

Caroline smiled and nodded. The two women crept over to the bedroom door and opened it. They both stood in the doorway looking at the two little figures curled up on the double bed. A little boy and girl, one sleeping silently, the other wheezily.

'They're beautiful. How old are they?' asked Caroline.

'Little Ben is just turned one and Alice is nearly five.'

They moved away from the door and back into the living room. Sally went to a cupboard and removed some bedding for Caroline to use on the sofa. She stole a glance at Caroline as she was sitting. Ben had a keeper here and no mistake. She was beautiful. Her blonde hair bubbled and boiled without any control, her graceful movement was almost cat-like, and her voice was not just from another class but from another planet. Yes, Ben had done well. But then, he always had.

Unlike Joe, Ben had been academic and performed well at school, so much so that he had won scholarships to attend university, only the War came. Much to everyone's surprise he chose the police force after the War. Ben being Ben, there was no mistaking his potential. Yes, Ben had done well all right and Sally was happy for him. Young Ben and Alice needed some cousins. Caroline looked up at Sally and saw she was smiling. Sally explained why.

'We knew Ben was seeing someone but we'd no idea who. He was always a bit careful of saying much, like he was afraid if he did, it would go up in smoke. He really likes you; you know.'

Caroline smiled with relief as much as gratitude. There was a warmth, a sense of family here that she'd missed for so long.

'He's been so good to us, Caroline. Little Ben suffers from asthma,' Sally paused for a moment to compose herself. Her eyes were milk wet. She felt Caroline take her hand. 'He's helped so much, with money and the like. Joe works nights in a factory. I sew a little. It's just about enough but then when

245

little Ben is bad. Well, it costs money for the drugs. A lot of money.'

'Ben never said anything to me. If I'd known I would have helped. I will help, Sally, I promise you. When all of this is sorted, I promise.'

This was too much for Sally and she fell onto Caroline's shoulder, sobbing. As Caroline comforted Sally there was a knock at the door. Sally looked up and said, 'I wonder who that is? Ben didn't say anything about coming, back did he?'

Caroline shook her head and whispered, 'No, he said he'd be back tomorrow at lunchtime. You don't think it's your husband?'

'Can't be. It's too early. He's not usually back until around five.' She looked confused and then worried. She stood up and went over to the window. It was difficult to see who it was, but it was definitely a man. There was another knock. Not too loud, nor too insistent.

Unsure of what to do, Sally walked towards the door and said timidly, 'Yes? Who is it?'

Silence.

The two women looked at each other. Sally's eyes betrayed the panic she felt. Without knowing why, Caroline held her breath. There was another gentle knock at the door. Sally looked from Caroline to the door and back again, unsure of what to do.

Another knock. Less insistent followed by a voice.

'It's me. Let me in.'

Sally looked at Caroline. She did not recognise the voice. But something in Caroline's face suggested she did. Caroline turned to Sally and asked, 'May I?'

'You sure?'

## The Phantom

'I think so,' replied Caroline. Taking that as a 'yes' she walked to the door and opened the latch. A man was standing there. Caroline gasped in shock.

'You?'

## Chapter 27

This was an unusual morning in the Aston household. For the first time in a long time Kit rose first. A few minutes later, also for the first time, he went into Harry Miller's room and opened the curtains. Miller looked up from the bed in speechless-shock. The surreal nature of the morning doubled when he realised that Kit had placed a pot of tea on his bedside table.

'Sir, what are you doing?' asked Miller more in embarrassment than surprise.

'Don't complain,' ordered Kit, 'Or I'll fire the staff.'

Miller smiled and looked at the tea pot. Turning back to Kit he said, 'You forgot to bring the milk, sir.'

'You don't take it black then?'

'No, sir. I also like it with a cup.'

'A cup also?'

'Sorry, sir.'

'You're devilishly demanding, aren't you?'

Kit returned with the milk, a cup and saucer as well as some sugar. He pointed to the sugar and said, 'Just in case. Now, the doctor said you were to rest up for the next few days, so I'm afraid you'll just have to put up with an inferior level of service than you're used to.'

'Very good, sir.'

# The Phantom

'I'm off to my aunt's now. I'll pop by later to see how you are. I've left you the paper. It makes for grim reading, I'm afraid.'

Miller glanced down at the headlines. It was grim for Jellicoe. The headlines told of another jewel robbery. The fact that it was the Phantom was now out in the open. There was no picture of Caroline Hadleigh yet, but one was promised for later editions of the paper.

'There's nothing about the Chief Inspector being taken off the case,' noted Miller, scanning the copy. He opened the paper and looked at the editorial, 'But they do seem to be demanding it.'

'I think they'll get what they want this morning. Jellicoe's head on a proverbial plate. I can't see Commissioner Macready standing up to the press on this.'

'Is there nothing we can do, sir?'

Kit's eyebrow arched, and he looked at Miller, 'There's nothing you can do, Harry, except recuperate.

Miller eyed the lord closely and said, 'There's something on your mind, sir, isn't there?'

Kit didn't answer but grimly shook his head. Something was on his mind, but he couldn't give it form and he certainly could back it up with evidence. Right now, he desperately wanted to give Jellicoe a chance to save his reputation and reveal the truth behind the robberies. But the only solution was fantastical. Kit smiled and looked at his manservant.

'We'll see. All right, I'm off. Alfred's due to collect me now to bring me over to Grosvenor Square.'

The knock at the door had a military air about it. Two sharp knocks followed by silence and expectation of an answer directly.

'That'll be Betty,' said Agatha to Mary. Both were sitting in the drawing room. A few moments later they heard the stately footsteps of Fish clip clopping like an elderly shire horse through a Suffolk village.

As forecast by Agatha, Betty made an appearance a minute later, dressed head to foot in brown tweed. She waltzed through the door and threw her tweed shooting cap, with well-practiced accuracy, over a copy of Canova's Helen of Troy.

'I do wish you wouldn't do that, Betty,' said Agatha, not for the first time. Mary smiled. This scene had played itself out on several occasions during her brief stay. She wondered idly for a moment over how many years Betty had been perfecting her throw.

Although the moment had brought some badly needed levity the air was far from light and frothy. Betty placed her copy of the Telegraph down beside Agatha's Times.

'Makes for disagreeable reading doesn't it?' said Betty, grimly.

'Indeed,' agreed Agatha, equally downcast.

'We need Kit to get his thinking cap on,' announced Betty, with a finality that brooked no arguments. 'He's slowing down. The old Kit would have solved this days ago, and then off to Sheldon's for dinner.'

Mary raised her eyebrows at this and made a mental note to encourage alternative dining arrangements after they were married. The confidence in Kit shown by the two ladies did bring a smile to her face however, and something approaching hope.

# The Phantom

Within a few minutes, there was another knock at the door. This was accompanied by the sound of muttering as Fish made his way back to the front door.

'Must be Kit,' suggested Betty.

Moments later the door opened and into the room walked Spunky Stevens. Mary was standing nearest the door and said with surprise, 'Hello.' Spunky immediately walked over to Mary and kissed her on both cheeks.

'I'm sure Kit won't mind,' said Spunky by way of explanation.

He immediately went over to Agatha and did likewise, 'Looking irresistible as ever Lady Frost.'

Agatha gave every impression of being delighted by this comment by looking sternly at Spunky and declaring him a young fathead.

'That's the spirit,' said Spunky before turning his attention to Betty.

'Aldric, what are you doing here?' asked Betty, more austerely than she felt.

'Auntie Betty, is that any way to talk to your favourite nephew.'

Mary turned to Agatha and mouthed, 'Auntie Betty?'

Agatha looked slightly surprised and said, 'Didn't you know?'

-

The café was beginning to get busy. Chief Inspector Jellicoe and Sergeant Ryan looked at some of the new arrivals. Mostly policemen arriving for duty or on their way home from working the night roster. Jellicoe recognised a few of them. One of them passed him and smiled down and said, chirpily, 'Hello, chief, don't normally see you here.'

Jellicoe looked up and smiled back at the man, 'Hello, Johnson, go easy on the cakes for a change.'

'Will do, sir,' laughed Johnson, as he moved past.

Jellicoe sensed the eyes of the café on him. Most would know or soon know of his humiliation. This would be compounded when the Commissioner made the call and officially removed him from the case.

Ryan looked at Jellicoe with sadness. The morning papers had been merciless. How quickly they turn, he thought. A hero one week, an idiot the next. The anger must have been apparent in his eyes because Jellicoe looked at him with sympathy.

'At least the papers didn't mention you, Ben. I'm glad of that.' He meant it, too.

Ryan nodded but he felt no better. This would have been the worst day of his life had he not spent four hundred equally bad days in France. His fingers drummed on the side of his teacup. He noticed Jellicoe looking at the cup and then him. If he had been a criminal, he could no more have revealed his guilt than by what he was doing at that very moment. The noise in the café was swirling around him, taunting him with laughter and stabbing him with guilt.

Whether the papers had mentioned him or not no longer mattered. His life had been turned upside down a couple of hours ago when Joe had arrived at his flat. The news was as unbelievable as it was horrifying. If Joe hadn't been there, he knew he would have broken down completely in a way he had never done when he was over there.

Over there. It seemed a lifetime ago. Was it really only eighteen months since he'd been climbing over the dead bodies in the mud? Then it was survival. His survival. And by then, anyway, he'd reached a point when it no longer seemed to matter.

This was different. It wasn't just that someone else was involved. It was Caroline. She was gone, and he knew why. And there was the Chief Inspector. The man who had lifted him from the ranks and given him a chance. The man he had betrayed.

The six months working with Jellicoe had been an education professionally but also a rebirth. He returned from France like an unexploded bomb. Anger inhabited him like rats in a warehouse. He detested Bulstrode and Wellbeloved but recognised, also, just how close he had come to being like them. Jellicoe had done more than lift him from the ranks, he had done nothing less than rescue him.

Working with this quiet, diligent, and intelligent man, he rediscovered in himself something he thought he'd lost in France. He learned to care again about the victims of violence, of crime and, yes, even those perpetrating the crime. Finding humanity in those he had to deal with restored the humanity he thought had died in the killing fields of Flanders.

Yet now, a traitor he sat in front of the man he'd betrayed. His loyalty to his job, more importantly, to this man had been tested and found lacking. Why? Was it love? A reason perhaps, but an excuse? Love had trumped duty and allegiance. His reward was to be misled by the one he loved. His punishment was to trust her.

'Is something on your mind, Ben?' asked Jellicoe. Ryan looked at Jellicoe wishing he could hide from the older man's eagle gaze. And here it was. A moment of truth. What was he to do now? Confess his duplicity or hope for a miracle that would rescue his girl? His career was over whatever happened.

He made his decision.

## Chapter 28

Fish set down a fresh pot of tea on the table while Agatha and Betty sought further clarification on why Spunky was not yet married or, indeed, engaged. This was dealt by Spunky with the well-practiced ease of a man with many aunts. Wisely he forswore any attempt to deal rationally with the ladies on the wisdom of sacrificing the exalted happiness only a single chap of means can know for the daily contrition required of man by his partner in wedded bliss.

Although aunts, in his experience were by tradition, nurture and, who knows, even nature, evolutionary machines designed and devoted to the encouragement of connubial associations between young people of an age, indeed, whether they knew them or not; he felt that auntie Betty and her partner in crime, Kit's aunt Agatha, were particularly assiduous. This made his shameless disregard even more maddening to them and entertaining for Mary.

In exasperation, Betty turned to Mary and pronounced, 'You'll have gathered by now, my dear, that Aldric is a hard man to ignore, but you'll find the effort pays dividends.'

'Trifle harsh old girl,' said Spunky.

The arrival of Kit just before eight thirty was like the cavalry coming to the rescue. For the aunts. They could withdraw gracefully, from their siege on the subject of Spunky's bachelorhood and live to fight another day.

One look at Kit as he walked through the doors confirmed to Mary he had slept as badly as she. There was a darkness underneath his eyes that told of a restless night. Hers had been no more peaceful.

'Hello Sp_, Aldric, what are you doing here, old chap?' asked Kit, a little more cheerfully than he was really feeling.

'I saw the headlines in the papers, old boy. They're really letting old Jellicoe have it. Full double-barrelled n'all. Seems frightfully unfair to me. One minute he's helping save the nation from the assassination of the royals, the next he's bally well the cause of all that's wrong in the country today.'

'I know. It's horrible.'

'So, are you saying that this Caroline Hadleigh is the Phantom?' asked Spunky.

'It looks like it,' answered Agatha.

Betty then chipped in and explained to Spunky the events of the last few days. Each subsequent revelation from the two aunts and Mary cracking the case to the subsequent undercover work was greeted with loud acclaim by Spunky. When they had finished, he clapped the table in delight, looked at Mary and said, 'My dear, if you ever get tired of Adonis here and fancy pootling round the foothills of Mount Olympus instead, then I shall gladly be your guide.'

'I will bear that in mind, sir,' said Mary with a grin.

'She's too good for you, Aldric,' commented Betty, 'I suggest you paddle back to the shallow end of the pool where you belong.'

'I say, Auntie Betty, you're really being a bit unfair on a chap today.'

# The Phantom

The look on Betty and Agatha's faces suggested his aunt had provided a kind assessment of what he could offer. Spunky decided to let the matter drop. They were probably right, anyway, he decided. Turning to Kit he asked the question on everyone's mind, 'So come on, Bloodhound. Have you solved this case or what?'

All eyes turned hopefully to Kit. He looked at each person then cast his eyes down and shook his head.

'I'm missing some things. I can't say what they are because I don't know.'

Mary put her hand over Kit's in encouragement. More than anyone, she was desperate that her fiancé would find the connection he was looking for. Her night had been awful. The overpowering guilt made worse by seeing the newspaper reaction to the night's events.

Spunky looked on and said, 'Well, I've no sympathy with all of these people who've been robbed. It's 1920 for goodness sake. We've figured out how to fly, how to sail underwater and how to kill thousands of people in a matter of seconds. Keeping some silly trinkets safely tucked away shouldn't be beyond any sensible person's compass, if you ask me.'

Kit smiled reluctantly at this and said, 'True.'

'I know if I had the kind of money that could buy diamonds, I would have the security that protects them. These people almost deserve it.'

'Trifle harsh, old chap. Do I detect the sound of envy?' smiled Kit.

'You do, sir,' admitted Spunky.

'Your father looks after you very well, young man,' said Betty.

'Your brother is tighter than a monk after lent, Auntie Betty, and you know it,' answered Spunky rising to his feet. 'I spend more time thinking about how I can make ends meet than I do on the safety of our country. I would argue this is probably not good for me or, in all modesty, the nation.'

Kit looked up and laughed, 'Have you any new guaranteed schemes for securing your financial position?'

'Bang out of ideas now, old chap,' replied Spunky before adding, 'perhaps I should open an agency for placing servants. By the sounds of what you've said, this is a goldmine in London. I'll make you a director, Auntie, if you invest.'

'I'd sooner bet on a donkey in the Derby.'

'Thanks for the vote of confidence,' responded Spunky brightly, before going around the ladies and kissing them on their heads. 'On that positive note, I shall head now to the work that pays me, that allows me to serve my country and ensure its security rather than sitting about like the idle rich.'

After Spunky had left, Betty shook her head and simply said, 'That boy.'

Kit stood up from the table and walked over to the window seat. Mary joined him a few moments later. Neither said anything. They looked out of the window and saw Spunky jump into a taxi and drive off.

Kit felt Mary take his hand again and he was glad. Their fingers intertwined, and they looked at one another. Mary smiled up encouragingly towards him. Kit said nothing. He just looked at Mary simply because he could and because he wanted to. The rest of my life, he thought. A warm feeling encased the two of them, sheltering them from the world and the rain that always seemed to fall.

# The Phantom

Mary, too, felt the need to melt into this shared moment. The room was warm and vibrated with a rosy light. The silence between them was like soft music brushing past their ears. The sadness she remembered in Kit's eyes when she'd first met him was back and Mary knew this was guilt. She tightened her grip slightly and gazed so deeply into his eyes that she felt might fall into them. Then she saw it. Was it a change in the darkness of the pupil, a change in his focus? Or was it an almost imperceptible narrowing of the eye? She knew something had changed.

He looked at her face and saw something also. Her head moved slightly. Both eyebrows had raised by the width of a hair. The corner of her eyed crinkled slightly. She knew. He nodded to her and then stood up. Turning to Agatha he said, 'Auntie, can you get Alfred? And I need to get to a phone.'

-

The rain fell gently onto the two policemen's fedoras as they skipped up the steps into Scotland Yard. Neither said much in the short walk from the café to their headquarters, both lost in thought. The sky overhead was a sad grey, and all around the two men, fellow police officers and members of the public rushed past to get shelter.

Upon arrival in the lobby, a policeman behind the counter noticed their arrival and called over, 'Chief Inspector.'

That didn't take long, thought Jellicoe, walking over to the constable.

'There's a message for you, sir.' The constable looked at Jellicoe, his face not difficult to read. He knew. They all knew. His failure was in black and white across all the broadsheet newspapers. 'Sorry, sir,' said the policeman. 'It's a bad business.'

Jellicoe nodded his thanks but did not open the message.

'Before you go,' added the policeman, 'Can you give this to Ryan?' He handed Jellicoe a brown envelope. The name 'Ryan' was scrawled on the outside. Jellicoe took the envelope and walked over to Ryan.

'For you,' said Jellicoe.

Ryan looked at the envelope and felt himself shiver involuntarily. He looked at Jellicoe. Nothing was said. The two men turned and took heavy steps up the flights of stairs to their office.

Bulstrode and Wellbeloved were not around the office which, at least, was a relief. However, Jellicoe had no doubt they would make a triumphant appearance later once he had received confirmation he was off the case.

Jellicoe took off his coat and hung it up. He sat down with a weary bump on the chair and stared at the unopened message. Ryan hadn't bothered to take off his coat. He opened his envelope and stared at the note inside. The Chief Inspector was too preoccupied to see his sergeant almost turn white with shock before turning a burning red. He stuffed the paper in his pocket and sat down.

After a few moments, Jellicoe opened the message. It was short. He looked up at Ryan and said, 'The Commissioner wants me to pop up and see him at my convenience.'

Ryan's mood was already in the unhappy situation that exists between crestfallen and angry, so his appearance didn't change much on hearing this news. The silence was broken by the ringing of the telephone on Jellicoe's desk.

'He's obviously impatient,' commented Jellicoe sourly.

But for once Jellicoe's instincts were wider of the mark than a fourth team schoolboy bowler. When he heard the voice, he sat bolt upright. Colour returned to his face and his eyes grew wide. Ryan saw the transformation and looked at him questioningly. The conversation was not giving much away, consisting as it was of Jellicoe nodding and saying 'yes'.

At last, he put the phone down and said, 'That was Lord Aston. He may have something. He wants to meet us now. I think the Commissioner will have to wait'

'Where?'

But Jellicoe was already on his feet reaching for his coat. The two men went towards the door. However, at that moment, it opened.

'Going somewhere?' asked Bulstrode, grinning vindictively.

'Yes, we were going to get you,' replied Jellicoe evenly. Bulstrode nodded but said nothing. Jellicoe stood at the door, his face inches away from Bulstrode. Ryan tensed himself in case the two men came to blows. Finally, Jellicoe said, 'Shall we?'

Bulstrode stood back to let the two men through. They were walking down the corridor when Ryan asked, 'And where is Sergeant Wellbeloved?'

'Doing what you should be doing, son. Catching criminals.'

-

The room was dark, a shaft of light shone down on the child's face. The closed eyes began to move underneath the lids. The light on his face was not so very bright, diffused as it was by the grey cloud, but all around it was dark, graveyard-silent save for the cooing of pigeons in the corner and the occasional scuttling sound.

A man came out from the shadow and looked down at the child. The little boy lay asleep on the bed. It was the sound of the wheezing. He'd heard it before. Lots of kids had it when

261

he'd been growing up. Many of them didn't last long. For a moment he felt a stab of pity and then, like cake at a children's birthday, it was gone.

He shook his head and looked at the other man. They both turned around as the child began to cough. This was when it would get uncomfortable.

'I don't like this.'

This much was obvious. He shifted uncomfortably from one foot to another. A bead of sweat on his forehead in a room as cold as a morgue. The other man looked back at him with disdain.

'Going soft?'

'I don't care about the nipper, Johnny. It's the rest of it. Wag will go mental. Just see if he doesn't. He just wanted us to take the girl.'

'Never mind Wag,' said Johnny Mac, 'The good Lord has just gifted us something better.'

Out of nowhere a something seemed to attack Rusk. It lasted moments. He looked up. On a beam overhead was a pigeon. Angry now, as well as frightened, Rusk sent forth a volley of abuse that was as surprisingly eloquent as it was probably inexplicable to the pigeon. The coughing grew stronger and then the child woke up.

The boy looked at the two unfamiliar men and the unfamiliar surroundings. Once he realised this was not his home, he began to cry.

Loudly.

Rusk felt like doing the same.

# The Phantom

## Chapter 29

Ryan drove the car with Bulstrode and Jellicoe sitting in the back. Neither was saying much. Bulstrode was oddly ill at ease. Without his partner, he seemed diminished, somehow. From time to time he turned around and looked out of the rear window. Jellicoe's face, meanwhile, was impassive. He seemed happy to stare out the window. Taking his cue from Jellicoe, Ryan said nothing either. His own mind was already spinning quickly at the events of the last few hours.

Perhaps the silence was proving too heavy, but eventually Bulstrode turned to Jellicoe and said, 'This is a fool's errand, and you know it. You're just delaying the inevitable, Jellicoe.'

Jellicoe turned sharply to Bulstrode, 'That's Chief Inspector, to you. I'll thank you to remember that Detective Inspector.'

Ryan coughed in the driver's seat to make it clear he'd heard the exchange.

'You just concentrate on your driving, son,' exploded Bulstrode angrily.

'Yes, sir,' replied Ryan. A minor victory. It didn't feel there would be many more.

A few minutes later they had arrived at their destination. Through the gates they could see Kit's Rolls Royce. He was standing beside the car waiting. Bulstrode was the last to see him.

'Is this it, Chief Inspector? You're relying on some fancy-dan lord to bail you out? I've seen it all now.' His laugh wasn't so much a laugh as a cackle that started as a hacking cough and certainly ended as one. Jellicoe couldn't stop himself from glancing in undisguised repugnance at his fellow officer. This was noted by Bulstrode and only served to make his laugh sound harder, harsher, and generally foul.

The three policemen alighted from the car and were greeted by Kit with a bleak smile, as he realised who had come. Beside Kit was Mary. Jellicoe nodded to her and she smiled back. The smile made his hopes rise briefly but this faded quickly. The situation was a mess. As high as his regard for Lord Aston was, the problems in this case were, to all appearances, insurmountable.

'Gentlemen, this way,' said Kit. 'I have some additional questions to ask here. I hope you don't mind.'

'Certainly not, Lord Aston,' replied Jellicoe. He looked at Kit. There were so many questions in his eyes, but he realised Kit would say nothing until they were inside.

A few minutes later the three policemen were sitting in front of Raven Hadleigh in his cell. At Kit's request Brickhill and Hastings stayed for the meeting.

Bulstrode looked around the cell with something approaching repulsion. He was not a man who subscribed to the view that prison was for rehabilitation. No, in his humble opinion it served three purposes and three purposes only: retribution, incapacitation and deterrence. Deportation was even better, but sadly it had ended fifty years earlier. Hanging was, of course, best. Take away the problem completely. That was your man. The sight that had greeted him when he arrived in Hadleigh's cell was as shocking as it was vexing. What right had a thief like Hadleigh to enjoy such a privileged lifestyle?

Bulstrode wasn't the only man looking a tad displeased. Major Hastings refused to sit and stood to attention like the martinet he'd been these past thirty years. Kit looked at him coolly and smiled. There was anger in the eyes of Hastings, or perhaps it was fear. At this stage Kit was not sure. Over the next few minutes, he would know.

Brickhill looked no more comfortable. He was standing beside Bulstrode. Two peas in a pod thought Kit sourly at the two men. Even Ryan gave the impression of being uncomfortable, unable to fix his gaze on anyone. His mind seemed elsewhere. Kit put this down to the revelations about Caroline Hadleigh. This was understandable, and he sympathised. Love could do this.

Kit looked at Mary. She had a half smile on her face. If she felt nervous, she wasn't showing it. Rather than quiz Kit on what he thought, she had been happy to say little on their trip to the prison. It was clear Kit was still thinking through how he would approach the meeting.

With everyone present, Kit felt it was time to begin. As he was about to speak, there was a knock at the door.

'Who on earth is that?' exclaimed Hastings, betraying the irritation that had been building up in him since the unexpected arrival of Kit.

Two people walked into the room.

'Hello father,' said Caroline Hadleigh, with a smile. Moments later she realised Ben was in the room also. 'Ben,' she cried and ran over to him. She embraced him.

Mary looked at Jellicoe. His features did not change when Caroline embraced his Detective Sergeant. This surprised her. She turned to Kit. But Kit was looking at the man who had accompanied Caroline. His face was almost unreadable. It could have been shock on his face or, perhaps, realisation. She hoped it was the latter.

'Hello, Aston,' said the new arrival, taking a cigarette out of a silver box.

Mary turned to Kit again and saw him smile.

'Hello, Geddes,' said Kit.

Gerald Geddes walked over to Kit and the two men shook hands. While the handshake was not necessarily an indication of warmth in the relationship of the two men, it certainly suggested there was respect.

'May I introduce Gerald Geddes, everyone. Geddes works for the...'

'Foreign Office,' interjected Geddes, thereby confirming in everyone's mind that he was a spy. He was dressed, as ever, in a dark pinstriped suit. The cigarette hung lazily on his lower lip. He glanced at Kit as if he was an entertainer. Kit could see this in his face and smiled inwardly. Maybe that's what he was these days.

Caroline, meanwhile, was looking at Mary in surprise. Mary felt a twinge of regret. More than that, it felt like a gash. The duplicity she had been forced to practice had come at a price. Her peace of mind had been shattered by the thought that she had somehow put Caroline in the frame for the crimes. The look on Caroline's face offered no solace. If she hated Mary, then it was no more than she deserved.

'As I was saying,' said Kit, 'Perhaps it's time we begin again. I think the arrival of Geddes has added a few pieces to this jigsaw puzzle that were missing.' Turning to Geddes, he said, 'If I make any slip ups, you'll fill in, will you?'

'Of course,' said Geddes.

'Where to begin? That is the question. We could begin where I and Mary joined this story, at Lord Wolf's house, when the theft of the diamonds was uncovered inadvertently by a practical joke being played by Lord Wolf. But this is too near the end. Perhaps I should start with the first two robberies at the end of last year. The only thing is, I know little about them except that in each case a young woman had been hired to work in the houses in question as a maid. In each case the maid had been placed by an agency called Holland Placements. There are a few agencies that specialise in placing house staff; this was too much of a coincidence. However, when the police investigated this agency it turned out to be as fictitious as the young lady working for the two houses. It wasn't until Mary,' said Kit turning to his fiancée, 'uncovered the fact that Caroline Hadleigh was working in disguise at the Rosling household that this particular mystery was cleared up.'

Mary looked, once again at Caroline. The dislike in Caroline's face was evident. Mary fought hard to control tears forming in her eyes. She felt angry at herself. It was clear to her that Caroline was not a criminal, but her actions were highly suspicious. She hoped Kit had an answer to the many questions swirling around in her head.

'At this point, the finger was clearly pointing at Caroline. As the daughter of a notorious thief,' said Kit, turning to Raven Hadleigh, who merely bowed slightly, 'she would have had ample opportunity to learn the tricks of the trade from the master. And then there was the calling card left at the scene of each crime. It's entirely conceivable that Caroline could have kept a secret stash of these. And, finally, there's no reason why a woman such as Caroline could not, with all she has possibly learned, commit these crimes.'

Mary was oddly torn by this comment. She agreed wholeheartedly that there was no reason a woman could not be a master thief. She just hoped it wasn't this one.

'Yes, there's no reason at all. Except Caroline Hadleigh was not the thief,' said Kit.

Everyone looked at Caroline. Her emotions were beginning to get the better of her. Ryan looked down and held her tightly.

'No,' continued Kit, 'the Phantom in this case is, was, and always will be, Raven Hadleigh.'

# The Phantom

## Chapter 30

Alfred sat outside the prison in Kit's Rolls. It had been twenty minutes now and he was bored; worse, he was hungry. He cursed the curse that had given him such an enjoyment of food, such a craving for the wicked comfort provided by some bacon and oven-fresh bread. He could feel the saliva forming in his mouth as this delightful picture formed in his mind. With the mental image came an almost visceral sense of the exquisite aroma of the bread and the salt-sharp smell of the bacon.

He hoped they would get a move on inside. His curiosity about what was happening matched the growing hunger pains forming in his stomach. Lord Aston had, sadly, not been very forthcoming on what was on his mind during the journey. Alfred had consoled himself by stealing as many looks as he could at the gorgeous Mary Cavendish. Even with darker hair, she was still something, but he had preferred her with the blonde wig.

The arrival of the other young woman was a pleasant surprise. She was blonde and almost as beautiful as Mary. The thought of the two young women made Alfred feel warm inside on what was, otherwise a rather chilly day. Some men have all the luck, he thought. He didn't begrudge Kit his good fortune. As nobles went, he seemed a good sort. And he'd done his bit, to be fair. Still, though, what must it feel like to have such a beautiful woman in your arms? To have her look into your eyes, lovingly. To do as you commanded, willingly.

As he thought about such unlikely scenarios, he noticed the door open of the main building. A man came running out.

He was heading directly towards Alfred and the car.

-

Young Ben Ryan was asthmatic. He had been born with a condition that narrowed his airways and produced, on occasion, prodigious quantities of mucus. All too often it made breathing difficult, triggered coughing fits that ripped through his body like a hurricane, followed by wheezing and shortness of breath.

This morning he was treating Rusk and Johnny Mac to the full array of his complaints, topped off by a roar of protest that emanated from somewhere in the region of his feet, such was its volume, pitch, and ferocity. Within half an hour of his waking, it was almost possible to feel sorry for the two kidnappers as they struggled to quieten the hell-child.

The latest outpouring of green, gloopy, mucus from young Ben's nose which, by now, seemed more like a tap to Rusk than an organ of the olfactory system, ran like a rivulet over the bridge of the toddler's mouth, onto his lips.

'Bloody hell how can one child have so much snot?' yelled Rusk. This provoked yet more wailing from the disgruntled child. Rusk was sorely tempted to join the ghastly little child's snivelling such was his misery.

'Haven't you a handkerchief for that bloody child?' snarled Johnny Mac.

'I did. I threw it away. You'll never clean that again.' He glanced dejectedly at the sodden green handkerchief lying on the ground. It had been a Christmas present from his mother a few years ago. He still missed her.

'Well use your bloody sleeve, then.'

'Why don't you use your bloody sleeve?' shouted Rusk in response. The situation had veered shockingly out of control. Rusk's mood was, to say the least, frazzled by a lack of sleep, a sense of injustice at the demise of his mum's gift and an increasing scepticism on the wisdom of their unilateral decision to go it alone and kidnap Satan's spawn.

Rusk was not a deep thinker. He accepted that when God had been handing out brains, he'd been in the wrong queue. This was not a problem for Rusk. He had gifts if violence and intimidation can be considered thus. He deployed them on behalf of those more cerebrally endowed than he. The arrangement suited both sides. However, even he could see that going against Charles 'Wag' McDonald was potentially rife with risk.

Once Wag learned that the girl was 'off limits' then he would call everything off. Wag was not a man to take unnecessary risks with the police, even if he did employ more than a few of them. He was certainly not a man to license the kidnapping of children.

This was against the rules.

He was an odd man, thought Rusk, but, on balance, not one you wanted to get on the wrong side of. Right now, he and Johnny Mac were so far on the wrong side of Wag they were virtually in a different country, which is where they would need to abscond to whichever way things went. The thought of this made Rusk feel even more miserable. And then young Ben Ryan applied the *coup de grace* as Rusk wiped his nose with his sleeve: he sneezed messily.

271

-

Raven Hadleigh looked at Kit and smiled slowly. He seemed neither angry nor surprised by Kit's announcement.

'Interesting theory, Lord Aston,' replied Hadleigh, gesturing to his surroundings. 'Perhaps you're unaware of my present situation. This is after all, notwithstanding the obvious home comforts, a prison cell.'

'Yes,' replied Kit also with a smile, 'I had rather noticed.'

'Then are you seriously proposing that I escape from the prison of an evening, make my way to a rich man's home and help myself to some diamond necklaces they've left carelessly hanging around before breaking back into this establishment and continuing with my incarceration?'

'I don't think it's quite like that,' responded Kit. 'Clearly you had some help.'

'Really? From whom? Hastings here?'

'Well, yes. Hastings and Brickhill, in fact. The truth is, you walk out of here of an evening, not break out as you say, and one of these men will drive you to the target location where Caroline, simply, lets you in through the front door.'

Kit looked at Hastings and Brickhill who both had turned puce. Hastings was clearly on the point of exploding when Kit calmly held his hand up.

'The thing that bothered me from the start wasn't the how, it was the why. Why would you return? What was the point of all of this? And then I received part of the answer this morning from my friend and your colleague Spunky Stevens. Did you send him along to me?'

Geddes smiled and said nothing. Kit read that to mean 'yes'.

'Once I realised that it was the...'

# The Phantom

'Foreign Office,' interjected Geddes again with a smile.

'Foreign Office,' agreed Kit, 'then it all made sense, although a few more pieces, as I say, were filled in by your arrival with Miss Hadleigh. I won't inquire about why you've targeted these individuals for theft, but I am rather interested. For another time perhaps. But I suspect the diamonds, in each case, are a cover for an ulterior motive. I'm sure you couldn't possibly say Geddes.'

'Correct,' replied Geddes.

Hadleigh looked at Kit. The smile had never really left his face. But with the smile Kit could also see a sadness in the eyes. There was something else he wanted Kit to say. Kit nodded to Hadleigh and, for a moment, it seemed the room was empty except for the two men.

'We've met before, haven't we?' asked Kit.

Hadleigh nodded but he was no longer smiling. In fact, far from smiling, his face revealed a deeper sadness.

Kit turned to face the rest of the room. He stood up from the table and walked over to Hadleigh's bookcase. He lifted a volume from the shelf. It was Thomas Mann's *Buddenbrooks,* in German.

'When I was last here, I had a feeling we'd met before, but I couldn't quite place where or when. Then I remembered seeing all those books in German in your library. You were there weren't you? During the War. You were working for the,' Kit paused for a moment before saying, 'Foreign Office. I can remember now. You were with my contact when I was given the false papers that inducted me into the German army. You looked a bit different then, of course, the beard, the glasses. Simple enough disguise but it certainly changed your appearance.'

Hadleigh said nothing but there was a sadness in his eyes. He'd met so many young men doing what Kit had done. So many brave young men. He could cry thinking of them. Sometimes, alone in the cell, he did.

'I can only guess at this point, but you either offered your services to the country or they came to you. I suspect the former. In return for using your exceptional talents, Raven, they offered you an amnesty of sorts. I suspect your incarceration will be over soon. I think that just about covers it except for the last, and I suppose, most important item on the agenda.'

'You want the diamonds back.' This was Hadleigh. It wasn't a question.

'Yes, I think they've probably served their purpose now. The Chief Inspector, young Ryan and Mr Bulstrode can receive deserved acclaim for wrapping some of the case up and Miss Hadleigh can return to a normal life without any stain on her character.'

The room seemed to turn, as one, to Raven Hadleigh. The smile returned to his face and he walked over to a small cigar box, sitting on his desk. Opening the box, he extracted from it three small diamond necklaces.

'You'll be wanting these. You know it was always my intention to return them,' explained Hadleigh.

'Damn right, Raven,' said Geddes which brought a ripple of laughter from Kit, Jellicoe, and Mary.

Hadleigh walked over to Jellicoe and was about to hand him the necklaces when Ryan stepped forward and took them. In the shocked silence, Ryan stepped back. He was holding a gun.

'I'm sorry, but I need to take these. Mr Geddes, can you me give your car keys? Major Hastings, I'd like the keys to this cell also. Now, if you please.'

Moments later Ryan walked out of the room, locking the door behind him. The guard at the outer door greeted him as he walked through.

'I think Major Hastings would like some tea brought down to the cell. Can you organise it please?'

'Yes, sir,' said the guard.

## 30

Sally Ryan was living the worst of nightmares. She could barely breathe, she couldn't stop crying and now, she was shaking with fear. Her world was crashing around her. Nothing Joe Ryan could say was of consolation. Curled up on the family sofa, she was wracked her sobs. Joe Ryan felt like he was dying. Their little boy. Gone. He wanted to run out into the street and kick in every door from here to the Elephant and Castle. The rage, the frustration and the fear mixed and washed around his body before crashing like waves against a cliff.

All he could do was try to console the inconsolable. And wait. And hope. It was up to Ben now. He knew what he was asking of Ben would end his career and put his freedom in jeopardy. Equally, he knew Ben wouldn't think twice. He didn't blame Ben for what had happened. How could he? Ben had given so much to them over the last year. Without him, well, it didn't bear thinking about. Little Ben wouldn't have made it this far without the drugs that Ben's money had purchased.

He wasn't sure if Sally would feel the same. This had been such a shock to her. The idea that they had taken Ben because they couldn't take Caroline would eventually rise to the surface. How this would affect her in the future would be an issue whatever happened. All he could do now was wait for Ben to come.

Around mid-morning there was a knock on the door. Then a banging.

'Joe, open up.'

Ryan went to the door and opened it; he couldn't believe what he saw.

-

Alfred recognised the man running towards the car, as the young detective from the other night. He climbed out of the car as it was clear, he was running towards the Rolls. When he reached Alfred, the detective spoke.

'Quick, Lord Aston wants us to deliver a message. I'll show you where. Quickly. We can't wait a second longer.'

Recognising the urgency, crying at the thought of yet more time without eating, Alfred climbed back into the car and started the engine. Within a few seconds the car sped off towards the gates.

'What's happening, sir?' asked Alfred.

'We have to deliver a package to someone near Elephant and Castle.'

With that the detective sat back and stared out the window leaving Alfred in an unappealing state of hunger and curiosity.

-

'I'm off,' announced Johnny Mac at last.

'What?' expostulated Rusk. 'What do you mean you're off? You mean I must stay with this snot machine? Why don't you stay, and I go?'

'Division of labour. You should read Marx.'

'Mark who?'

Johnny Mac shook his head and stood up. He smiled that terrible smile and said, 'Some are born to lead, others to follow. Wipe his bloody nose. I'm sick to death of looking at that stuff. I want to see if there is any sign of lover boy.'

With this advice hanging in the air like an unwelcome farm smell, Johnny Mac stalked out of the room, scattering a few pigeons who were feeding on, what looked like, a dead rat.

Johnny Mac descended several flights of stairs. The sound of the machines grew louder as he neared the factory floor. He went through a door which led to a corridor and his office and picked up the phone. A moment later he asked the operator to put him through to a number. At last, someone picked it up.

'Any sign?' The man on the other end of the line answered. Then Johnny Mac said resignedly, 'Fine. I'll call every half hour.'

He put the phone down and let out a few oaths. He was on edge, that was for sure. This was not something he wanted Rusk to see. The man was already in a big enough funk as it was. The next few hours were going to go slowly. But then, life would become so much easier. He'd get out of London. Maybe go to the continent. Better yet, America. Start over. Start over as a rich man.

This was the plan, anyway.

-

Kit looked at Jellicoe. The Chief Inspector's face was impassive: neither shock nor dismay. Interesting, thought Kit. Also, for another time, perhaps. Bulstrode had exploded with anger and gone straight to the door followed by Brickhill. Both were banging the door for all they were worth.

Kit looked at Hastings.

278

# The Phantom

'Have you a spare set of keys on you?'

'No,' admitted Hastings. 'I hadn't considered the possibility that we would be incarcerated by a member of the police.'

'Nor I,' replied Kit. He then turned to Raven Hadleigh. "I don't suppose we can call upon your talents.'

Hadleigh was clearly angry. The events had been as unwelcome as they were unexpected. It was obvious Hadleigh knew, and even approved of, the romance between his daughter and the young policeman. One look at the numbed astonishment on her face was enough for Hadleigh. He wanted to get hold of Ryan. Preferably by the neck.

He went over to his desk and opened a drawer, pulling from it a small pouch. He extracted what looked like thin metal files. He marched over to the door.

'Out of the way,' ordered the prisoner to the policeman and the guard. He knelt and began to pick the lock. It took eleven seconds.

'I'm slowing down,' muttered Hadleigh. 'Come on.'

Kit looked at Mary. She raised her eyebrows and had a half smile. She walked over to Caroline to console her. Meanwhile Kit headed quickly towards the door alongside Geddes and Hastings. They all ran into the poor guard carrying a tray of tea.

'What in the blazes are you doing?' shouted Brickhill.

'The detective told me to bring in some tea.'

'Blimey,' said Bulstrode, wiping milk off his suit.

The group made their way upstairs to the office of Hastings. Jellicoe turned to the, clearly disgruntled and wet Bulstrode and said, 'Will your man be at the Yard now?'

'Yes,' replied Bulstrode sourly.

Jellicoe dialled a number and waited a moment and asked to be put through to a number at Scotland Yard.

While they waited Kit looked at Jellicoe and said, 'Do you know why he took the diamonds?'

Jellicoe returned Kit's gaze. Everyone who had been in the cell downstairs was now in the office. All eyes were on Jellicoe. Finally, the Chief Inspector said one word before finally being put through.

'Yes.'

-

The estimable sergeant Wellbeloved made it into Scotland Yard mid-morning. It had been a late night. A very late night, in fact. A few hours of sleep and back to the office. He trooped in wearily. One policeman smiled at the unshaven, bleary-eyed sergeant and said, 'Good afternoon, sarge.'

Wellbeloved's two, single syllable word reply was lost in the noise of the reception area of the office. He wanted to be back in his bed. Soon. Blindly he made his way up to the office, ignoring one cheery 'hullo' after another. His only words were to a secretary in an outer office.

'Get me a tea.'

Theresa Malloy, a Dubliner recently arrived in London, looked up at the half-dead policeman. Like Wellbeloved, she also had experienced a late night. Unlike Wellbeloved, it involved a significantly greater intake of alcohol than the teetotal detective had probably imbibed over his two score years. Consequently, she was in a bit of a mood. An already short fuse was considerably shorter on this particular morning.

Sturdily built, she would have made the light heavyweight division comfortably. Standing up to her full six feet, which, unusually, was actually taller than Wellbeloved, the hungover

# The Phantom

Amazonian put her face inches away from his and let rip a volley of abuse.

Wellbeloved recoiled, as much from the alcohol fumes as the violence of her words. And to be fair, they were pretty violent.

'Out of my way, you mad gypo,' snarled Wellbeloved trying to sweep her out of the road with his left arm. This move failed. Theresa was in no mood to be moved. Eventually Wellbeloved had to walk around the angry Irish Valkyrie and into the office shared by Jellicoe and Ryan.

The phone was ringing as he entered. He went towards it immediately and picked it up.

'Hello, Wellbeloved.'

He listened for a few minutes as Chief Inspector Jellicoe summarised what had happened and what he needed to do. When the call finished, he put the phone down and then instantly picked it up again. He gave the operator a number. He waited for almost a minute and then there was an answer.

'It's Lestrade. Lestrade, I said, you idiot. Get me Wag, moron. Now,' shouted the irate detective down the phone.

-

Wag McDonald sat in an office overlooking Waterloo Road. He peered through the drizzle on the windows at the glistening umbrellas of commuters reeling around the street. He was glad to be inside. This was a mother and a father of a cloudburst. He enjoyed watching the pedestrians spinning to avoid being splashed by the passing cars. This light mood was to end in a few moments as his phone rang.

'Yes?' answered McDonald.

He listened for a minute and then replied, 'Look, I never told them to lift the child. I only told them to take the girl. It

281

was Johnny Mac and Rusk. No idea where they'll be holed up. They might have taken him to the factory. He's probably counting on us not knowing.'

When the call finished, McDonald slammed the phone down and shouted, 'Wal, you out there?'

Wal McDonald, his brother, came into the office. The features on his brother seemed almost a blur of rage. In such moments it was best to allow Wag a chance to collect his thoughts. He was the brains of the family. He waited for his brother to speak.

'You're not going to believe this,' started McDonald, 'it seems Johnny-boy has decided to go it alone. The girl was picked up by the police at Ryan's house before Johnny could get her. So, he's gone and kidnapped Ryan's kid. The brother has the diamonds apparently and he's going to meet Johnny to make an exchange. No doubt that's the last we'll see of him.'

'Bloody hell, Wag. What are we going to do?'

McDonald scratched both sides of his temple and swore. Then an idea seemed to hit him.

'Perhaps he's going to follow the original plan. He'll get the shop to contact him directly when the copper arrives. Yes, that makes sense. Call Wellbeloved. Tell him to meet us at the factory.'

'What are we going to do?' asked Wal.

His brother smiled and said, 'We're going to meet the police.'

-

Three police cars arrived at the prison around ten minutes after the phone call between Jellicoe and Wellbeloved. From one of the police cars stepped Wellbeloved. A rapid conference followed.

# The Phantom

'We've had a tip off. It's Johnny Mac. We have an address, too,' announced Wellbeloved.

Kit climbed into one of the cars with Jellicoe. Bulstrode joined Wellbeloved in the second car and the third car took Caroline and Mary away, to the obvious chagrin of both ladies who wanted to join the others.

Mary and Caroline went reluctantly to the police car. The anger felt by Caroline towards Mary had been suspended briefly by the sudden departure of Ryan. Now, alone in the police car it returned full bore.

'Don't speak. I can't bear to hear you,' snapped Caroline as she saw Mary about to say something.

'Not even sorry?'

Caroline glared at Mary. She could see the distress on Mary's face. There was no doubting the remorse. Mary had befriended her, misled her, and then would have happily seen her imprisoned. Or not. Caroline accepted that she too, had been part of a deception. She was also an accessory to a robbery, albeit one tacitly sanctioned by the state. She had done what she'd done for her father. For this, no apology would ever be uttered by her.

The two ladies rode in silence, each lost in their own thoughts. Occasionally Caroline would glance at Mary. The rain streaming down the window, perfectly reflected the tears she could see on Mary's cheek. Caroline felt an emptiness. Worse, a sense of loneliness. This was selfish she knew, but her world had been torn apart.

Again.

Ben's actions had been explained by Jellicoe in the office. The thought of the child caused her eyes to sting and then the tears became sobs. The poor child. Ben had been trying to protect her and now it had endangered the life of this little boy. She didn't resist when Mary's arms enfolded her. Her face against Mary's shoulder, all she could think to say was, 'It's all my fault. It's all my fault.'

'Don't ask,' was all Ryan could say to his brother as they both ran forward to the Rolls. 'I have the diamonds. We have to get to a shop called Bennett's on Lambeth Road and get instructions there.'

Ryan sat forward in the Rolls and directed Alfred as they drove along Walworth Road. Less than a few minutes later, Joe Ryan spotted the shop.

'Over there,' he said pointing to a shop further up.

'Pull over here, Alfred, please,' said Ben Ryan, leaping out of the car. He ran into the shop and demanded to see the manager. It was fairly clear to the young assistant that Ryan was with the police. The manager came immediately.

'I was told to ask for Donald Bennett.'

'By whom?' asked the shopkeeper.

'Mac. That's all I know. I was told you'd know what to do.'

The shopkeeper nodded. This was not how he wanted his day to go. Upsetting the coppers was never a good idea but then upsetting the 'Elephant Boys' was even worse. Bennett walked to the front of the shop and pulled a yellow blind halfway down the window.

Bennett turned back to Ryan. It was clear the policeman was in a highly agitated state. This was even more worrying.

'Look, I know nothing all right? I was told to pull the blind down if someone came asking for Mac. You'll have to wait.' Ryan nodded, and they stood there looking at one another. 'I don't know how long it'll be.'

# The Phantom

'I'll be outside in the car,' said Ryan and walked out.

With something approaching amazement, Bennett watched Ryan climb into Kit's Rolls Royce.

'Bloody hell,' or something quite like this, said Bennett out loud. 'D'you see what we're spending our taxes on, Hilda?'

-

In the lead police car, Kit glanced at the Chief Inspector who was deep in thought, looking out of the misty window, as it exited through the gates of the prison. Kit's knowledge of London, south of the river was, to say the least, hazy. He hoped the journey would be quick because it sounded as if time was of the essence. But another thought was swirling around his mind. He wondered if the same thought was also with Jellicoe.

'Remarkable we should get such a tip off, don't you think?'

'I was just thinking that,' volunteered Jellicoe. 'Remarkable indeed.' He turned to face Kit and it was clear they were thinking the same thing.

Finally, Kit asked the other question that was on his mind.

'Who is this Johnny Mac?'

Jellicoe looked troubled as Kit asked this.

'He's a hoodlum from Ulster. He's associated with the 'Elephant Boys', a gang based in the Elephant and Castle area of London. They're involved with illegal bookmaking at the racecourses in the south of the country and other things no doubt. They're run by the McDonald family.'

'I see. Do their interests extend to kidnapping children?' asked Kit.

'There's always a first time, I suppose,' said Jellicoe, however his tone suggested he thought otherwise.

'Johnny Mac is just a nickname, I take it,' suggested Kit.

'Yes. His real name is John...'

-

Three men approached the Rolls Royce as it sat on Waterloo Road. A rap on the window and then the rear passenger door opened as well as the passenger door at the front. Two rough looking men and one dressed in a suit climbed in to join the Ryan brothers and Alfred. Ben Ryan quickly reached inside his pocket for his gun.

'Don't,' warned the man in the suit reaching towards Ryan's arm and putting it in a vice-like grip. 'My name is Wag McDonald. I presume you know me.'

The young policeman moved his arm away from his pocket and nodded, 'Yes. What's the game here?'

'Look, this isn't anything to do with us. Wal and me, we run some bookies, fine. You know, we know, punters are safe, everyone's happy. We don't kidnap kids, understand?'

'Fine, I understand,' said Ryan, 'But someone has.'

'Yeah right. We think we know who it is and where he's taken the kid. Who's this by the way?' asked McDonald, nodding towards Joe Ryan.

'My brother, Joe. The little boy's father.'

Joe Ryan spoke up, 'We have to hurry. My boy needs medicine. He has asthma.'

McDonald nodded, recognising the urgency. He gave Alfred an address and the car moved off along the road in the direction of Southwark.

'Nice car you have here,' said McDonald, looking around the inside of the Rolls. 'Who says crime doesn't pay?'

Ryan ignored McDonald's comment and asked, 'So who has the boy?'

# The Phantom

McDonald looked at Ryan and replied, 'Have you heard of Johnny Mac?'

'The name's familiar but don't know him,' responded Ryan. 'What's his real name?'

'McGuffin. John McGuffin,' said McDonald, noticing Alfred looking at him in the mirror.

## 32

Johnny Mac stared at the telephone. There'd still been no contact. This was not good. In fact, this was a problem. His senses were tingling and the tingle they gave was bugger, bugger, bugger. Rationally, there was no reason to suppose that the girl had the diamonds, although it sure as hell looked that way. In addition, it was possible that she was still out of contact with lover-boy. All of this was possible, but it did little for the big Ulsterman's peace of mind. He wanted the diamonds, he wanted rid of the little tyke and he wanted all of this to happen immediately.

None of this was helped by the increasingly unstable Rusk. A few hours spent with the admittedly difficult child seemed to have reduced the hard man to a shadow of his former self. Gone was the hoodlum who could intimidate factory workers, women, and old men. In his place was an erratic, vacillating cretin who could also break arms. Not a dream combination for a babysitter, reflected Johnny Mac.

In truth he was spending more time down here to take refuge from the continuous whine of the child. Then he had a brainstorm.

Food.

Children liked food, he seemed to remember. Well, if he was anything to go by anyway. His experience of children since that unhappy time had been deliberately kept to a minimum, both out of personal choice as well as through the desire of the many parents who used to rush their children indoors when he was around.

He found some milk used for making tea and rich tea biscuits. This was bound to be a success. What child would refuse milk and biscuits? To Rusk, he would appear as nothing less than Santa Claus.

Mounting the stairs three at a time, courtesy of a six-foot stride, he arrived at the top floor as quickly as carrying a glass of milk and a plate of biscuits would permit. Inside the room, the birds flew away as soon as he entered.

He called out into the gloom, 'Rusk?'

No answer.

'Rusk, where the hell are you?' shouted Johnny Mac walking forward. The sofa was empty. There was no sign of Rusk or the boy. To his right he heard cooing. 'Damn birds.'

Then he heard a laughter then a child's coughing. He set the glass and plate down and walked towards the sound of it. It was coming from the other end of the long room. His view was obscured by wooden support pillars.

And then he saw it. Or him to be precise. The little boy had either crawled or walked towards the open window at the other side of the room. There was no sign of Rusk. The child was standing on a wooden chair looking out of the window. No, correction. The devil child was trying to climb out the window. Johnny Mac's heart stopped for a moment before he shouted, 'Stop!'

At one year of age, young Ben's vocabulary was still some way short of Shakespeare's. An Ulsterman shouting at him to stop climbing immediately made as much sense as the pigeons cooing nearby. Moments later, after having successfully opened the window, baby Ben found himself being lifted bodily from this fun activity and carried back into the other room.

Young Ben Ryan wasn't going to take this kind of treatment without protest. He remonstrated in the only way he could: a combination of tears, shouting and effective kicking. Tempting as it was to throw the little monster out the window, Johnny Mac kept his mind focused on the prize. However, the appeal of the prize in question was beginning to dim with every howl from the hateful child. In addition, and more worryingly, he had a strong feeling that his getting hold of the diamonds was becoming more and more unlikely.

Now a new problem had presented itself: where was Rusk? It was criminally stupid to leave the child on its own, even if he did need to answer the call of nature. Johnny Mac planted the crying child back on the seat and showed him the milk and biscuits. This heralded hurricane-force howling from the toddler.

Johnny Mac was officially at his wit's end, which in truth wasn't the longest of journeys. The end of his tether, a similarly limited voyage, had also been reached and he shouted back at the child in language more traditionally associated with working men's clubs in Belfast than childcare.

Incredibly the child stopped crying immediately. Both child and adult were shocked by the intensity of Johnny Mac's incandescent impotence. Using the window of silence, Johnny Mac shoved the glass of milk towards the child's mouth in the hope that it would drink. He tipped the glass towards Ben's mouth and, at last, the child began to drink the milk greedily.

# The Phantom

'There,' said the Ulsterman, 'what was all that crying about?'

Silence.

He, Johnny Mac, had mastered the art of parenting. Feed the child. Show it who is boss. It really was that simple.

Or so he thought.

And then two things happened that undermined his recently obtained sense of achievement. Far from solving the problem of baby Ben's misery, the milk only served to hasten a further fit of coughing. Suddenly, the baby looked as if its head was going to explode such was the intensity of the red and, of more concern, the seeming asphyxiation. The child was unable to breathe, and panic had set in, for Johnny Mac as well as baby.

'Oh, for the love of...' screamed Johnny Mac, lifting the child up in the air and patting its back. As he did this the coughing seemed to ease and he held the child up in front of him to get a better look at his handy work. This coincided with Ben choosing this moment to expel the contents of his stomach with the force of a bullet into the poor giant's face.

Momentarily blinded, Johnny Mac staggered towards a small hatch which opened into a chute leading down to the factory floor. Still holding the child, he wiped his face with his right bicep. Eyesight restored he heard a noise from the corridor. He held his breath. So did Ben. Then the door to the room flew open. Johnny Mac was confronted by a sight that was certainly not Rusk, nor any more welcome.

-

The prison was relatively close to the factory. No more than a couple of miles. Traffic was light, and they made good time. As they drove down the road leading to the factory, Kit looked around him at the desolate buildings either side of the road.

'Nice area,' he commented.

A few toughs looked at the police car speeding past and made obscene gestures.

'Nice people,' replied Jellicoe.

Kit smiled and then he saw it up ahead.

'I think we've arrived.'

'How do you know?' asked Jellicoe.

'I can see my Rolls,' pointed out Kit.

Not quite the answer Jellicoe was used to in crime cases but at least it meant they were closer to their quarry. The police cars pulled over and the men streamed from the two cars through the factory gates, much to the confusion of the workers sitting outside taking a fag break. One or two looked at the sight of the police nervously before realising that they were not of interest. One of the policemen came limping towards them. As detectives went, he looked a bit better dressed. His voice, when he spoke to them, was certainly not typical of a rozzer.

'Hello, gentlemen. Would any of you be so kind as to take me to Johnny?' The man held out a few five-pound notes. The three men leapt to their feet in moment.

-

The arrival at the factory had presented Alfred with a dilemma. He wasn't sure if he was enjoying the experience of chasing down a notorious criminal. He unquestionably wasn't enjoying chauffeuring, what sounded like, London gang members in pursuit of said criminal.

At the same time, he was excited. Nervous, yes, but excited also. Perhaps he could use this in his art. When the crunch came at the factory gates, taking his life and future in his hands, he followed the passengers into the factory. They split up into groups. The Ryan brothers went to the offices at the side of the factory floor. The gang members chose instead, to head upstairs. And here was the dilemma. To go with the brothers or with the hoodlums?

The brothers both looked well able to handle themselves, but Alfred's decision was almost instantaneous. He followed the gang members at a safe distance. By the time he arrived, they would hopefully have matters in hand. More practically, Alfred was not able to keep up with them.

Wag McDonald led his men through a door at the back wall of the factory floor. When Alfred went through the same door, he realised it was a stairwell leading up several flights. He gazed upward to the sky light. This gave him pause to think. The stairs were wooden and appeared to be far from safe. It looked an awfully long way up for someone not in the peak of condition, which Alfred would have been the first to concede he was not.

The other men were already two flights up when Alfred, with no little amount of internal grumbling, began to follow them up at a more leisurely clip. He was two flights up when he heard the shouting. He looked down, which was mistake. For it was at this moment he realised he suffered from vertigo. Looking up, it dawned on him that there was another couple of flights to go. A glance back down decided him. Staying close to the wall, he started his descent.

It was with something approaching ecstasy that Alfred reached *terra firma* once more. He pushed the door he had originally entered through and realised he may have jumped out of the frying pan into a stampede.

'His office is over here,' said Joe Ryan sprinting through the factory.

Ben Ryan, weighed down by his heavy overcoat, struggled to keep up. Up ahead he saw Joe burst through a door. He was with him moments later, inside an empty office. Fear gripped Joe Ryan. Then a thought struck him.

'Upstairs. I haven't been up there but there's a big space on the top floor of the building that's not used.'

Both men rushed out of the office. They found Jellicoe and Bulstrode accompanied by several constables arriving in the corridor outside the office.

'We think he's on the top floor,' said Ryan to Jellicoe.

Jellicoe nodded and said, 'Which way?'

Ben Ryan turned to his brother.

'There are two stairwells,' said Joe Ryan pointing to a door at the end of the corridor, 'this one and one on the back wall of the factory floor.'

Jellicoe turned to Bulstrode, 'Go with Ryan here to the other stairwell. Ben you come with me.' The two men and a constable immediately ran to the end of the corridor. Ryan, meanwhile, led Bulstrode and another constable back out to the factory floor.

Joe Ryan rushed past confused factory workers towards the back wall near to the packing section of the factory where once he had stood with Abbott. The sound of the machines was, as ever, close to deafening and he had to shout to make himself heard.

'This way,' said Ryan pointing to a door at the end of the factory floor. As they sprinted towards the door, it burst open.

# The Phantom

The portly chauffeur appeared. He looked out of breath and then his red face seemed to turn white in the blink of an eye.

Then Ryan saw why. He sprinted forward. Wellbeloved and Bulstrode followed. At a discreet distance.

-

Wag McDonald burst through the door followed by his two men, Dan 'Haymaker' Harris, a former middleweight boxer whose ranking had never reached the dizzy heights of the top ten, and Chris 'Crazy Bastard' Christie a man who had spent his life fighting anyone who laughed at his name, which he was oddly proud of. How often in his life had the words, 'Chris Christie, what kind of a stupid, f___' resulted in a swinging left hook that usually started from somewhere around Alaska?

Johnny Mac looked in shock at the appearance of McDonald. Meanwhile, McDonald was equally shocked at Johnny Mac's appearance. His face was dripping with what looked like an unpleasant cocktail of white glue and something green which McDonald really didn't want to know more about. Then McDonald glanced down at Johnny Mac's arms and saw the toddler.

Perhaps the effort expended in forcing the contents of his stomach so prodigiously over the Ulsterman had exhausted the poor child or it was just simple curiosity. But for the first time that morning, seemingly, he had stopped crying and was dividing his attention between Johnny Mac and the new arrivals.

Time was on the point of standing still when young Ben did something completely unexpected. He began to laugh. Wag McDonald, who had been about to request the child be handed over looked at the youngster in utter confusion.

This was nothing compared to Johnny Mac's reaction. He glared at the child which only provoked further howls of mirth. Perhaps it was an appreciation of his handy work on the features of the big Ulsterman or the excavation of his stomach, but something had clearly done wonders for the mood of young Ben.

Johnny Mac walked backwards towards the hatch. His face and eyes, at least the parts that were visible under the dripping contents that formerly occupied the child's stomach, displayed signs of mania.

'Give me the child, Johnny. You don't want to do this,' said McDonald fearfully, when he had at last, found his voice.

Harris and Christie fanned out either side of McDonald. Each tensed their muscles, ready to spring forward if Johnny Mac did anything.

And he did.

All the while Johnny Mac had, either through instinct or, well, instinct, been manoeuvring himself closer to the hatch that led to the laundry. Now, standing directly in front of it, he reached a decision.

'Catch,' he shouted, and hurled the child through the air, in the direction of McDonald. Years spent playing goalkeeper on the streets of Lambeth meant McDonald's reaction was as quick as it was agile. He leapt forward and caught the delighted youngster, who was enjoying this new game immensely, in mid-air, a foot from the ground and serious injury.

Harris and Christie rushed Johnny Mac, but he disappeared backwards and down the chute.

Harris looked in. It was an uninviting black. He turned to the other two men and said quite accurately, 'He's disappeared.'

# The Phantom

-

The conversation with the three men accompanying Kit was convivial. None of the men particularly liked the Ulsterman and the prospect of a fiver each turned vague uneasiness in the big man's presence into active antipathy. They walked at good pace through the factory floor, but they seemed to understand intuitively that walking too fast would not be possible for the gentlemen with a pronounced limp and a stiff wooden walking cane.

'Do you see the door over there, sir?' said one of the men to Kit.

'Yes.'

'We've seen Johnny go up there a few times this morning and Rusk also.'

'Rusk.'

'Johnny's right-hand man.'

'They're both there now you think?'

Another man piped up, 'Not Rusk. He left twenty minutes ago out the factory gates. Didn't see him return.'

Kit nodded and put held out three crisp, five-pound notes to the men who grabbed them hastily.

'Thank you, gentlemen

As he said this there was a strange sound emanating from a nearby hatch. And then a crash. Kit looked at the three men who, almost as one, shrugged, clearly mystified by the sound. The three men approached the hatch. Someone was inside trying to get out. The banging increased in intensity until finally the door burst off its hinge.

Outstepped one of the tallest and meanest man Kit had ever seen. To his side, Kit was aware of his three companions beating a rapid retreat. The man, meanwhile, still unaware of

Kit's presence, patted himself down and tried to stretch the pain in shoulders and back away. The tumble down the chute had been at the cost of several bruises and, what felt like, a cracked rib.

Kit sensed immediately he was looking at Johnny Mac. There was no sign of the child. Finally, the hulking hoodlum looked up and perceived a tall, well dressed gentleman looking at him. The man smiled and spoke casually.

'I presume I'm addressing Johnny Mac. May I ask what you've done with the child?' Johnny Mac watched as the man calmly removing his gloves, placing them in his pockets, before looking him directly in the eye.

The man, unusually, did not seem afraid. In fact, there was a hint of malice in the eye if Johnny Mac read him correctly. There seemed little point in trying to intimidate him. In fact, there was probably not much time to do so, anyway. Johnny Mac recognised he needed to make a swift exit. These thoughts flew through his mind in a split second. His reaction to them was immediate.

Years of boxing at school and then university, as well as a painful lesson handed out by the great lightweight boxer, Jem Driscoll meant that Kit easily sidestepped the first clubbing right hand, aimed by Johnny Mac at his temple. The punch had upset the balance of the Ulsterman which Kit took full advantage of by smacking him with his cane a stinging slash across his cheek.

The goliath let out a yelp of pain. An already bad morning had just become worse. His plan had failed; there would be no set-for-life diamonds to enrich him; the hell-child had thrown up over him; he had endured a bruising fall down a laundry chute and now, a poncey-looking posh bloke was handing out what he would, no doubt call, a thrashing.

Johnny Mac snapped. Roaring in rage, he charged at Kit only to be met with a stiff left jab made with the heel of Kit's fist. However, his momentum carried the big man forward and he crashed into Kit. Both men fell to the ground.

The size and weight of Johnny Mac came to his advantage and he managed to roll Kit onto his back. Now he had the upper hand. He raised his fist to deliver a hammer set of blows when suddenly, an arm appeared around the giant's neck which yanked him backwards.

The man responsible looked very like Sergeant Ryan, and he looked none too pleased with Johnny Mac.

'Where's my son?' yelled Joe Ryan at Johnny Mac.

The Ulsterman leapt to his feet, grinning madly, and stepped towards Ryan. In the background, Kit could see Bulstrode regarding the scene with some concern but not taking any action.

He didn't need to.

Ryan tore into Johnny Mac with a ferocity and a hatred that had been building for days and reached a peak when it was apparent, he had kidnapped the boy. The fight, if it can be so described, was mercifully short but just long enough for Johnny Mac to experience a severe rearrangement of his features, a possible broken jaw, and a pain in his groin that would discourage conjugal relations with his cell mates for quite a long time.

Kit and the two policemen had to drag Ryan off the colossus before there were more serious consequences to the violent retribution being meted out. Ryan was in tears, mad with rage, crying with worry.

299

'Joe,' shouted Ben, 'Look.'

Walking towards the group and the stricken figure of Johnny Mac was the leader of the 'Elephant Boys' holding a gurgling toddler in his arms. He handed the child over. Ryan buried his boy in an embrace.

Relief flooded through Kit. He looked at McDonald and nodded. Then Jellicoe arrived on the scene. He glanced at McDonald and said, 'Well done.'

McDonald acknowledged Jellicoe but said nothing. Then he put on his trilby and turned to his men and said, 'Time to go.' He started to walk away then stopped. Moments later he turned around and came back to Jellicoe.

'I don't suppose there's any chance of a lift?'

# The Phantom

As the police car approached Caroline's house on Eaton Square, it was apparent there was a big crowd of newsmen, photographers and passers-by standing outside. Mary saw immediately that it would be impossible for Caroline to return there.

'Keep driving,' ordered Mary and then gave an address in Grosvenor Square where they should go.

A few minutes later, Mary helped Caroline up the steps of Aunt Agatha's house. She knocked on the door which was soon answered eventually by Fish. They walked through to the drawing room. Agatha and Betty were there drinking tea.

'Good lord,' said the ladies in unison.

'Meet Caroline Hadleigh,' said Mary and sat her down on the sofa. "Fish, more tea please.'

'What happened?' asked Agatha, unable to contain her curiosity before her innate good manners took over and she remembered to greet Caroline more warmly.

Mary took the next few minutes to explain the events at the prison.

'And the child?'

'I don't know, we're waiting for news.'

The two ladies looked at Caroline, still distraught by the possibility of any harm coming to the child.

'You mustn't blame yourself, my dear. These are wicked men. You've done nothing wrong.'

This last statement was a little disingenuous. After all, Caroline had been a co-conspirator in several robberies. However, it seemed churlish to point this out although it was clear to Mary by the look on Agatha's face the thought had crossed her mind.

The tea arrived and with it came the miraculous cure that this astonishing drink has delivered for Englishmen and Englishwomen over countless generations. Caroline finally regained her composure but with it came confusion. She looked at Mary, now unsure as to whether she was a saviour or her enemy. Mary could see the conflict in her eyes.

'I should introduce these ladies more formally, Caroline. They, after all, helped crack this case even if it did cause you some discomfort.'

Caroline looked askance at the two elderly ladies. They both seemed harmless enough although one of them certainly looked like she had a low tolerance for fools.

'May I introduce Lady Frost. She is the aunt of my fiancé, Lord Aston, who you met earlier. And this,' said Mary, indicating Betty, 'is Lady Simpson. Both ladies have followed the career of your father with, I must say, something close to fascination.'

'He's a great man,' said Betty excitedly, thereby proving that describing her as a fan would have been more accurate. 'And now that I know he was also doing his bit for us during the War, well, I must say, he has gone even higher in my estimation.'

The process of thawing towards this group of ladies was now well under way for Caroline. It was clear, despite everything, they had her interests at heart. With such knowledge comes an obligation. Continuing to be 'put out' was no longer either sensible, rational, or right. But the words to frame such thoughts would not come. Tears welled in her eyes. Once more she felt Mary's arm around her shoulders.

Less than an hour later there was a knock at the door. From inside the room, they heard Kit's voice as he entered the house. The four women looked at one another. All shared the same sense of dread and hope. Each held their breath. The only noise in the drawing room was the sound of a carriage clock on the mantelpiece. Even Agatha found herself experiencing a level of apprehension that she had rarely felt before. The doors to the drawing room finally opened. In walked Kit followed by Sergeant Ryan.

'Ben,' exclaimed Caroline rising from the sofa and running towards the detective.

Mary looked up at Kit, her eyes brimming. Kit smiled to her and nodded. All at once the fear dissolved and the guilt was swept magically away from Mary to be replaced by relief. She, too, leapt up from the seat.

'We found the child. It's going to be all right,' said Kit. Moments after saying this Kit, once more had to deal with an adult running at him full tilt. This time it was in the smaller and more attractive form of his fiancée. Mary jumped into his open arms and buried her head on his shoulder.

Agatha looked at the smiling Betty with reproach, 'The lack of control from young women nowadays is most unseemly. You shouldn't be encouraging it, my dear. You wouldn't have caught me doing this, I can tell you.'

'Oh, do give over, Agatha.'

Jack Murray

# The Phantom

## Coda – One Year Later...

*February 14ᵗʰ, 1921: St Bartholomew's Church, Little Gloston*

Kit's face broke into a smile as he looked at his friends Charles 'Chubby' Chadderton, Dr Richard Bright and Aldric 'Spunky' Stevens. They were sat together providing Kit with some badly needed moral support. The moral support was in the form of a brandy they were swigging from a hip flask, magically produced by Spunky.

'I knew this would come in handy, bloodhound,' commented Spunky.

'Good thinking, old boy. Just what the doctor ordered,' added Bright, taking his turn to have a nip.

'I meant to ask you, Spunky, that affair with the Phantom, last year. I've been reading a few reports about a series of robberies on the Riviera. Same sort of thing, jewels stolen off suspiciously rich big wigs from the continent. If I didn't know better, I would've said they were committed by a mutual friend of ours.'

Spunky grinned and put his monocle in his one good eye.

'Would you now? Well, obviously I'm not able to confirm or deny anything. As you know, I stay well away from the factory floor.' This brought an eruption of laughter from the men. Spunky held his hand up as he wished to add something else.

'All I will say is that "C" also drew my attention to said dastardly crimes inflicted on our dear continental cousins and I can report he was virtually dancing a jig of delight.'

This brought more uproarious laughter from the three friends.

'I must say, I'm sorry I missed that show,' said Chubby.

'Me too,' added Bright. "What happened to the little boy?'

Kit smiled and said, 'Well, as a top-notch medical practitioner, you will be delighted to hear that he has spent the last year being taken care of by his family in warmer climes. If not exactly cured then at least, he's enjoying much better health.'

'Where did the money come from?' asked Bright.

'A number of offers were made, shall we say, but one in particular stood out. The father and mother are now gainfully employed at a house in the south of France. A toast to my aunt Agatha for that. The heroic actions by Sergeant Ryan inevitably cast a shadow over his career with the police but thankfully, common sense prevailed. He is now working with a small, multi-national police task force which liaises on pan European crimes. Funnily enough he's also based in the south of France. This means he's near his brother and nephew.'

'And what of that rather scrumptious daughter of Hadleigh's?' asked Chubby.

'Too late, old chap,' said Kit, 'She and Ryan married. I presume she's with him in the south of France. By the sounds of it, means she's not too far away from her father either. Hopefully they can keep him out of trouble.' Kit glanced archly at Spunky.

# The Phantom

Spunky held his hands up and indicated nothing short of torture would obtain the truth from his lips. At this point there was a knock at the door and Harry Miller popped his head around the door, in a pitch of excitement.

'Sir, the car has just pulled up. Mary will be here in a minute.'

The four men leapt to their feet. The door opened, and they walked into the brimming church. Soft organ music piped around the church. At the altar, Kit could see Reverend Simmons, whose face broke into a wide grin when he spied Kit. As they trooped into the church, Spunky tugged Kit's arm.

'By the way, Kit old boy, I meant to say before now, it would be really useful if you could divert your honeymoon towards Egypt. Winston's up to high doh about what could happen at the Cairo conference with our friends from ORCA.'

'It depends on Mary, old boy. I can't do anything without her say so.'

'I've already asked, bloodhound,' laughed Spunky. 'I hope you know how to ride a camel.'

The End

**Please consider leaving a review so that others may find it and, hopefully, enjoy also**

Jack Murray

# The Phantom

## Research Notes

I have made every effort to ensure historical authenticity within the context of a piece of fiction. Similarly, every effort has been made to ensure that the book has been edited and carefully proofread. Given that the US Constitution contained around 65 punctuation errors until 1847, I hope you will forgive any errors of grammar, spelling and continuity. Regarding spelling, please note I have followed the convention of using English, as opposed to US, spellings. This means, in practice, the use of 's' rather than a 'z', for example in words such as 'realised'.

This is a work of fiction. However, it references real-life individuals. Gore Vidal, in his introduction to Lincoln, writes that placing history in fiction or fiction in history has been unfashionable since Tolstoy and that the result can be accused of being neither. He defends the practice, pointing out that writers from Aeschylus to Shakespeare to Tolstoy have done so with not inconsiderable success and merit.

I have mentioned several key real-life individuals and events in this novel. My intention, in the following section, is to explain a little more about their connection to this period and this story.

For further reading on London gangs, I would recommend Brian McDonald who has written several books including 'Elephant Boys', 'Gangs of London' and 'Alice Diamond and the forty Elephants'. There have been many biographies of

Alfred Hitchcock. I can recommend Patrick McGilligan's, 'Alfred Hitchcock: A Life in Darkness and Light'.

## The Conference of London 1920

The Conference of London took place, around a year after the Paris Peace Conference. Britain, France, and Italy met to discuss the partitioning of the Ottoman Empire. The negotiation formed the basis of the Treaty of Sèvres. Under the leadership of British prime minister David Lloyd George, Prime Minister of France Alexandre Millerand, and Prime Minister of Italy Francesco Saverio Nitti, the allied powers finalised this treaty at the San Remo conference.

### Arthur Balfour (1848 – 1930)

The 1st Earl of Balfour was Prime Minister of Britain between 1902 and 1905. He was very much an elder statesman at the Paris Peace Conference, supporting Lloyd George as his Foreign Secretary. Famously brilliant in debate, he lacked interest in the detail of management, preferring abstract thought to concrete action. However, his famous letter, which came to be known as the "Balfour Declaration" was a pivotal moment in the formation of Israel.

### Alfred Hitchcock (1899 – 1980)

Alfred Hitchcock was born and educated in London. After studying art at the University of London before doing various jobs. In 1920, Hitchcock entered the film industry with a full-time position at the Famous Players-Lasky Company designing title cards for silent films. Within a few years, he was working

# The Phantom

as an assistant director. He began to direct his own films from the mid-twenties and had notable success from the thirties with films such as *The Man Who Knew Too Much* (1934) and *39 Steps* (1939). He went to Hollywood in 1939. One of his most popular films was about a retired cat Burglar, John "The Cat" Robie, starring Cary Grant with Grace Kelly, one of her last films before her marriage to Prince Rainer.

## John MacGuffin (Johnny Mac)

John McGuffin is, of course, entirely fictional. The surname MacGuffin or McGuffin was used, famously, by Hitchcock to describe a plot device. In 1944, Time Magazine reported Hitchcock saying, "The McGuffin is the thing the hero chases, the thing the picture is all about ... it is very necessary." There are various theories on its origin. This is mine and mine alone.

## Charles 'Wag" McDonald (1885 – 1943)

McDonald was a leader of a south London criminal gang known as the 'Elephant Boys' who were based in the Elephant and Castle area of London. He was assisted by his brother Wal and they formed an effective partnership with Billy Kimber (who features in the TV series 'Peaky Blinders). McDonald led an interesting life. He fought in the Boer War before to returning to England to take over the leadership of the Elephant Boys. He then volunteered for active service during the Great War. When he came back from France, he took over leadership of the gang once more before escaping to the US in 1921. He worked in Hollywood for several years getting to know many of the stars. His life and the life of gangs in the area have been captured in several books by his descendant, Brian McDonald.

# The Phantom

## About the Author

Jack Murray lives just outside London with his family. Born in Ireland he has spent most of his adult life in the England. His first novel, 'The Affair of the Christmas Card Killer' has been a global success. Four further Kit Aston novels have followed: 'The Chess Board Murders', 'The French Diplomat Affair' and 'The Phantom' and 'The Frisco Falcon'. 'The Medium Murders' is the sixth in the Kit Aston series.

Jack has also published a spin-off series from the Kit Aston mysteries featuring a popular character from the series, Aunt Agatha. These mysteries are set in the late Victorian era when Agatha was a young woman.

Another new series is released in June 2021 featuring the grandson of Chief Inspector Jellicoe. The DI Nick Jellicoe series is set in the late fifties / early sixties – perfect for fans of the Adam Dalgliesh or George Gently books.

In 2022, a new series will be published by Lume Books set in the period leading up to and during World War II. The series will include some of the minor characters from the Kit Aston series.

# Jack Murray

## Acknowledgements

It is not possible to write a book on your own. There is a contribution from so many people either directly or indirectly over many years. Listing them all would be an impossible task.

Special mention therefore should be made to my wife and family who have been patient and put up with my occasional grumpiness when working on this project.

My brother and John Convery have also helped in proofing and made supportive comments that helped me tremendously. In addition, Kathleen Lance has been invaluable in helping correct some of the grammatical errors that were present in earlier editions of the book as did BJ Thomas. Many thanks!

My late father and mother both loved books. They encouraged a love of reading in me also. In particular, they liked detective books, so I must tip my hat to the two greatest writers of this genre, Sir Arthur, and Dame Agatha.

Following writing, comes the business of marketing. My thanks to Mark Hodgson and Sophia Kyriacou for their advice on this important area.

Finally, my thanks to the teachers who taught and nurtured a love of writing.